LATE LOVE

Scarlett Hopper

Scarlett Hopper

Late Love
Scarlett Hopper
Copyright © 2020 by Scarlett Hopper
Cover Design © 2020 by Sarah Hansen, Okay Creations

This is a work of fiction. Names, characters, places, and incidents are the product of the author's imagination or are used fictitiously. Any resemblance to actual events, locales, or persons, living or dead, is purely coincidental.

Formatted by Brenda Wright, Formatting Done Wright

Edited by Nicole Mentges Nam Editorial

Porcelain by Moby
In My Arms by Kylie Minogue
Sea of Love by Cat Power
Bare Bones by Rainbow Kitten Surprise
ILYSB by LANY
Home by Edward Sharpe & The Magnetic Zeros
Here Comes the Rain Again by Eurythmics
Pull Me Down by Mikky Ekko
Toledo by Elvis Costello
Believer by Imagine Dragons
I Need My Girl by The National
Fancy by Iggy Azalea
Farther Figure by George Michael
Million Reasons by Lady Gaga
Lover, You Should've Come Over by Jeff Buckley
Hands Clean by Alanis Morrissette
After The Storm by Mumford & Sons
Tears Dry On Their Own by Amy Winehouse
Somewhere Only We Know by Lily Allen
Fade by Egyptian

Scarlett Hopper

For my B,

My soulm8 till the end.

Scarlett Hopper

Prologue

Early July 2018

I count out the wad of bills, each of them eventually leading up to two hundred pounds. The man in front of me looks at the cash, probably annoyed I'm making sure it's all there. His scent of stale tobacco and beer fills the small flat, but I say nothing. In fact, I'd love it if the scent lingered long after he was gone, long after I'm gone too.

But I doubt I'll be so lucky.

"You sure you're okay with parting with all this for two hundred quid? I mean, it must have cost you at least nine hundred."

It was nearly two thousand, but I don't tell him that.

His deep voice yanks me away from my counting, and I pocket the cash into my skintight black jeans, hoping he paid in full. To be honest, I don't really care if he didn't. This transaction is a symbolic act more than anything; I won't even keep the money. Bobby the homeless man on the corner could use it more than me. Hell, maybe the two of us could grab a pint before my departure.

"Lass?"

I'm pulled out of my tangled thoughts, my attention redirected to the big burly Kevin. Wait, is that his name? Maybe it's Cullum. Who knows at this point? It honestly doesn't matter. After today I won't see him or anyone in this town again. I guess I should feel sad. Edinburgh isn't a bad place, and I've even come to love it over the past six months I've lived here. Too bad it took one night to taint the entire thing.

"Sorry," I quickly reply, trying to sound attentive. "No, it's honestly no problem. I'm moving soon anyway and can't keep it."

He nods, his long salt-and-pepper beard moving up and down with his face. "Well, I guess it's my luck then to stumble upon your ad. Whereabouts are you moving to?"

"London," I reply, hoping we can move this all along so I can continue to pack. Kevin or whatever his name is genuinely seems curious, his attention not causing me discomfort, but if it did, I'd have no issue pulling out the pepper spray I keep nearby.

"I can hear that classy accent of yours. You're definitely a London girl, although I have to say you don't look too posh." He chuckles to himself, as if it's some big revelation that my tattoos, combat boots, and jeans aren't exactly blue-blooded.

I squint at him, not sure how to respond.

"Now I see why I'm getting such a deal." I know what he's implying, that I come from money so I don't need money, but that's not the full case. Sure, my parents have money, but I've been independent from them for years.

"Well, it's been a pleasure," I lie, "but packing calls."

He quickly grabs the TV and I pick up the stereo, then walk him to his car so I can continue to get my things together. He carefully places all Beck's shit in the backseat.

"You have a good day, lass," he says, rounding the car and pulling open the creaky driver's-side door. The car jolts as he jumps into the driver's seat, a shit-eating grin on his face.

I give a half-hearted wave before retreating into the flat.

I look at the empty TV stand, the space where the stereo went next to it, also bare.

He is going to lose his shit.

A smirk double the size of Kevin's overtakes my face.

I don't have to wait long for the reaction, because an hour later I'm sitting in our living room, boots propped up against *his* coffee table, my Betsy Johnson suitcase at my side, when he comes home. I've made sure to have my makeup done, bleached hair straight, just resting upon my shoulders.

My eyes are locked on the front door when he enters, his hair disheveled and some slight stubble growing on his chin. It's unfortunate he's so pretty and has a fit body to match, because his personality is probably the worst fucking thing in the world. His eyes are laced with deception and his lips tainted with venom. Every kiss, every promise he's made me over the past year has been a lie. While I changed my entire life for him, moved countries and left my friends and family, he's been fucking some whore down the road.

"Lottie," he says, taken aback when he sees me, probably because he assumed I'd be at work. It doesn't take a rocket scientist to figure out that his ruffled collar and ruffled hair are the result of his latest girl.

Since I found out about his little rendezvous over two weeks ago, I've been avoiding him like the plague, taking more shifts at work and planning my escape back home. Sure, I might have had a slight slip-up and slept with him the other night after an entire bottle of whiskey, but what can I say, I was so blind drunk it could have been anyone. Seeing his smug face the next morning was the stark wake-up I needed to get my ass into gear. I knew instantly I had to get out this week.

I smile at him, and it's completely calculated and probably slightly deranged, but that's the point.

"Lottie?" He squints at me before finally looking around the room. When he spots the missing TV, I can see the wheels churning in his mind. Beck knows how I am—hell, we've been together over two years. That's why I'm so shocked he didn't expect me to retaliate earlier. I live by extreme emotions and I'm highly loyal, to the point of blindness clearly, but this past week has also taught me I'm highly reactive too. Hence all his sold electronics.

"Lottie, what the fuck did you do?" he yells, spit flying out of his mouth.

I unhook my legs, the studs on my boots clicking together. Standing tall, I look him directly in the eye.

"Well, Beck, I sold them."

His face distorts, crimson overtaking it in patches. "What do you mean you sold them?"

"Let's just call them payment for emotional damages." I lift my suitcase handle up, beginning my retreat from the living room, from this *life*.

Beck pulls at the strands of his hair, looking around as if everything might somehow reappear.

"You crazy fucking bitch!" he screams in my face as I walk by him. I stay neutral, not responding to his reaction, which only furthers his anger.

"What, you're pissed I cheated on you? And so you fucking sell my shit. Wow, so fucking mature, Lottie."

"Goodbye, Beck," I tell him, not giving in to the plethora of swear words I want to hurl at him. I already did that when I found out. You see, I've never been one to contain my anger well; my dad always called me a firecracker for a reason. But today feels different. Selling the stuff we got together when we moved here, the stuff I didn't want to waste thousands of pounds on but he insisted on having, the stuff that because I loved him, I gave in about... Selling all that shit was liberating, if I'm being honest.

"You better get it back, Lottie. I fucking mean it!"

He reaches out to grab me, but I shake his hand off. Beck is a lot of things, an arsehole being the first, but I know he wouldn't get violent with me. I just don't want him near me because his touch repulses me.

I walk out of the flat, feeling overly pleased with myself as I hear Beck screaming in the flat about his precious belongings. Sure, some could say this is cold, illegal even, but I consider it compensation for how epically he's fucked up my life over the past six months, and for the two extra years of my time he wasted.

"Fuck you, Beck!" I yell out merrily, voice filled with cheer as I spot the cab out front, ready to take me back home to London.

I guess it's true what they say: revenge is a dish best served cold.

One

I pace around my Notting Hill flat, looking for anything to keep me occupied until it's time for me to pick up Emilia at her place. The blank cream walls practically scream for some color, but since I've been back, the only thing I've been able to do is trash the floors with my mess of clothes. I guess most people would tidy up, considering it looks like a small grenade exploded in my bedroom, but I can't be fucked. Why clean all that mess up if I'm just going to destroy it again tomorrow? I guess that's probably the wrong way to look at things, but oh well.

I laugh thinking about what Stana, my cousin, would think of the way I've left the place in less than a month since I've been back. I've had this apartment for three years, and not once was it as clean and sparkling as it was when she moved in at the beginning of the year. But then again, I wasn't here to mess it up.

How so much has changed in seven months.

Relationships ended, some started, new friendships, some old.

It's been a roller coaster, that's for damn sure. When I left this very apartment and moved with my then-boyfriend, Beck, to Edinburgh, I never thought I'd end up right back here in less than a year. I also never expected the lad I thought was my future to have been cheating on me for the last year of our relationship.

But I guess that's life, isn't it? I also never thought I'd convince Stana to leave her life back in LA and move to London, but here I am, wrong again. The girl packed up in January and came to London, then took care of my flat for me while I was away—that is, until six weeks ago forces back in LA pulled her in again, leading her back there.

But tonight, she's finally coming home. Emilia, Stana's first friend in London and the sister of Stana's boyfriend, Alistair, is helping me pick up Stana in less than an hour. To say I'm excited is the world's biggest understatement. Plus, we may or may not have some surprises for Stana up our sleeves.

It's been months since I've seen the girl, and well, I've managed to understand why she's so desperate to get back here. The friends Stana made while I was in Edinburgh have so graciously welcomed me into the fold after everything in my life went south.

So, despite the horrific year filled with the world's shittiest boyfriend and a traumatic life upheaval, *twice*, I have to say things could be worse. It's better I know Beck is a lying, cheating tosser with good hair now rather than two years down the line. I'm only just twenty-five, and I've still got my entire life ahead of me to figure this shit out.

My mobile chimes and I realize that all my overthinking and reminiscing has in fact made me late to pick up Em from her place in Shoreditch.

Fuck!

I grab the black Valentino Rockstud purse my parents gave me for my birthday last year—I've never been one to own designer, but I've got to say, it's fucking nice—and then I snatch up my hot-pink combat boots and hastily jam my feet into them. My fishnets get caught, almost tearing in the process, but thankfully we escape unscathed.

I don't have time to do a double take in the mirror, just hoping my shoulder-length bleach-blonde hair isn't sticking up in all different directions.

I spot the vintage Mercedes keys sitting on the side table, and my insides dance at the thought of driving this beauty. My parents have been living in France for the past three years, so they don't exactly have a lot of use for the old car. I could possibly risk certain death if they find out I've driven it to collect Stana, but it's a price I'm willing to pay.

I pull open the door to my flat and walk through the old building's hallway, a slight smell of damp clinging to the air, yet as soon as the main door is opened, all is washed away. The dimly lit streets of Notting Hill greet me, the scent of brisk night air invading my nose.

My shoes ring out with each step on the paved sidewalk, tall black streetlamps illuminating my way and the grand white Victorian terraces surrounding me. All of it reminds me how much I've missed West London. I take a moment to myself, breathing in the familiarity and accepting the small moment of serenity before moving on. It's time to bring Stana home.

I'm going to get our girl.

After a quick trip to the airport, Em and I force a confused Stana into Saint Street, the bar her boyfriend owns. To say the two of them need some alone time would be an understatement, and I know Stana—she wouldn't have shown up without a push from Em and me. So that's how I've ended up at the underground bar, music playing as happy patrons share drinks and laughter.

"I gotta say, we make a great team." I grin at Em, thankful that our plan worked. After Stana's abrupt exit from London last month, things between her and her boyfriend, Ali, were a bit up in the air. But from the look of the two of them slipping out of Saint Street, it is clear we've done a pretty good job.

I sip my mineral water, my poor stomach still upset from last night's dinner. As much as I'd love to down a pint and call it a night, I just can't. My back is sore as I lean into the wooden chair, wishing we'd secured one of the red velvet booths in the corner. Those have always been my favorite.

The décor at this place is one of the main factors that drew me to it years ago. Velvet booths line the walls with brown wooden tables in front, while small tables and chairs surround a stage the lads play at most Wednesday nights. But my absolute favorite thing has to be the bar. It's big, it's shiny, and it's gold. Mirrored glass and top-shelf liquor. It's like being transported back in time.

"We should be professional matchmakers," she replies, cutting into my thoughts as her eyes scan the crowd and stop at the exit. I look up, then smile as Ali and Stana slip out together.

"Have you seen Reeve tonight?" I ask Emilia, giving the room a once-over to see if I can spot him.

"Seen him, yes. Spoken to him, that is a big fat no. I just need time; I'll get over it. I mean, I'm not the first girl to be told a guy isn't interested in them. I'll live." Em looks away from me, her body language indifferent, but I don't think she knows her acting skills aren't exactly award winning. Anyone with a brain can see she's waiting on a guy who might never come around. My heart breaks for her because even though I haven't known her long, it doesn't take much to see how great she is.

Not wanting her to feel bad, I nod, pretending I buy her story. Lord knows I don't want to get into the nitty-gritty of my own failed relationships, so why should I push her into it?

"Ladies, what did you think of the show?"

Em turns around, flashing her teeth at the sound of the voice. I recognize him instantly, as I've seen him on Em's Instagram from time to time. Big, tall, blond, he's basically an Adonis. And he is so off limits for me. Don't shit where you eat and all that jazz.

"Great as always, Owen," Em replies before he looks my way. His gaze is penetrating, as if he's opening me up in one sitting. So, of course, I shut that shit down.

"You seem great, but I'm not interested," I quickly tell him, knowing I might be in for a rude comment or two before he fucks off. But lo and behold, he does something I didn't expect.

He laughs.

"Quick and to the point, I like that. How about friendship? Interested in that?" His lips tilt upward, his eyes crinkling at the corners, and damn me to hell if it doesn't make me crack a smile. Gotta give the man credit.

"One can never have too many friends," he insists, raising those dark blond eyebrows.

I rake my gaze over him. "Sure, Owen. We can be friends."

His grin only gets bigger, flashing those pearly whites at me. I'm sure it woos all the ladies, this gal not being one of them.

"We can be friends, but there is a condition," he points out.

I raise my eyebrows. "Oh yeah? And what's that?"

"It's an important question, Lottie. I don't know if you're ready for it."

I roll my eyes. "I'm sure I am."

"Okay." He takes a big breath, his smile now washed away with seriousness. "What is your favorite TV show?"

My face twists up. "What?" I laugh at his ridiculousness. "I don't really watch much TV."

His face breaks, incredulity sweeping over it. "It's 2018—everyone watches TV!"

I lift my shoulder in a "what can I say?" movement.

"I don't know if we can be friends then."

"I guess you could give me a TV education." I'm completely kidding, but from the expression he's wearing, he isn't.

"Done. My place this weekend, six p.m."

Before I can tell him no, Em's voice cuts in.

"As happy as I am that Stana's home and that we're all here tonight, I'm truly knackered, so I'm going to head off. Can you tell Stana and Ali that I'm sorry to miss them? That is, if they even come back." She tries to force a smile, but I see through it.

I turn to Owen. "Give us a second." I gently grab her arm and lead her away from prying ears and eyes.

"You're not leaving because of Reeve, right?" I ask, but I already know the answer.

Em shakes her head. "I'm over that. I just need to get home; I'll call you tomorrow."

I nod, quickly giving her a hug and mentally reminding myself to check up on her in the morning. I watch her petite figure retreat out the door, leaving me in the middle of the bar with people I don't actually know.

I make my way back to the table, noticing Owen has gotten me a refill of my water.

"So, *friend*, want to hang out this weekend?"

"You know what you remind me of?" I ask, knowing he will take this one of two ways.

He grins. "What?"

"A little puppy with a bone. Can I call you 'puppy'?" I tease.

His brows draw together. "Uh, I'd really rather you didn't."

He's definitely not mad about it, so I test the waters. "Okay, puppy."

He bursts out laughing. "Trust me, I'm not a puppy. I'm more like a big Great Dane or a Rottweiler."

Now it's my turn to laugh. Maybe most people who see this blond Adonis think that, but something about him reminds me of a baby golden lab instead.

"Anyway, I can't this weekend. I'm working all weekend."

"What do you do?"

I take a sip of water, eyeing him. "I'm a pharmacist."

"Wow, can't say I know many of them. How did you get into that?"

"I always liked science in school, then just decided to pursue it at uni and here I am. I love it, which is great, and I'm not totally shit, so that helps too."

He nods, seemingly impressed.

"And you?"

He brings his pint up to his lips, then takes a sip before wiping away the foam. My fingers have that itch to wipe it away for him, and I know I could be in trouble with this one. I also know I'm still nursing a broken heart and it was only six months ago he was trying to date my cousin, so best to stay away.

"Graphic designer," he replies, reminding me that I asked him a question.

"I could see that," I tell him, easing up on the tight clutch I have on my water.

He laughs. "How so?"

My lips turn up as I lean back in my chair. "You're in a band, so you must be creative, and you've got good style." I motion to his denim jacket, white T-shirt that's stretched across his chest, and dark jeans. He's a modern James Dean, but there's a playful aspect to him that I'm beginning to understand. A charm.

"Should I get you another drink while you check me out? Wouldn't want you to be too thirsty." His words get to me, my face betraying me by breaking into a smile. A small laugh pops out of me, to his entertainment.

"What, it's not like you think you're bad to look at. No shame in taking pride in yourself."

He seems to appreciate that, a smile dancing upon his lips.

"Anyway," I interject, "as I was saying, you clearly have some artistic aspect to yourself, so I get how you're a creative, Mr....?"

He chuckles. "Bower, Owen Bower."

I wrap my hand around the cold body of my drink, quickly looking at him, then to the floor. *Owen Bower.* I mentally say his name.

"Any hidden talents with you, Ms....?" He pauses. "What is your last name?"

"Knight," I toss in. "Stana's dad is my mum's brother, so we don't share the last name of Prescott."

"Lottie Knight." He says my name thoughtfully, tasting it on his lips, and I internally kick myself for having any sort of reaction.

"It's Charlotte Knight, actually, but I've never really been a Charlotte."

Now it's his time to look me over, his gaze starting at my black biker boots, then traveling past the fishnets and ending on my glittery silver dress. As Emilia once told me, I'm a punk-rock Barbie.

"Unlike you and everyone else in this bar, I have an artistic side that stops at fashion, and some people would call even that questionable."

"Well, I'd have to say those people are bloody mental. I like the way you dress," he replies, his vision locked on mine. A little too keen, if you know what I mean.

"You don't want any part of this, Owen," I tell him, attempting to keep my voice light. "I'd swallow you whole and spit you out in pieces."

Unfortunately, my words do the opposite of what I intended, his interest only piquing.

"And on that note…" I stand, grabbing my bag. "I gotta get going."

His face falls slightly but he recovers, a carefree smile slipping into place.

"The night's only just getting started," he says, standing with me.

"Not for this lass. I've got work in the morning, plus a vintage car that needs to get back to its garage."

His brows come together, looking as if he will say more, but I don't give him the chance. This interaction with him is already more familiar than I'm ready for.

With a quick wink, I grab my purse and slip across the congested floor of Saint Street.

I risk glancing back at him once more before walking up the stairs to the exit. To my surprise, he's still watching my retreat, his mouth tilted up at the side.

Hating the way my body reacts to that, I scurry up the stairs, but not before a small smile sneaks its way onto my lips.

After that night at Saint Street, my week continues on and every day I manage to get back into my routine a little more than the day before. Like today, I've been on my feet for the past eight hours filling scripts for customers, and of course it has to end with a rude one.

"I need two refills on this medication. Why are you being so difficult?" the woman, who initially looked sweet, yells at me. Sweet my ass. This woman is a right bitch and I don't care how old she is.

"As I told you before, Ms. Bonneville, I can't give you two refills at once. There are specific instructions on your script that say no more than one every thirty days." I try to keep a firm, even voice. If I'm too soft, people will think enough nagging could eventually cause me to give in, but if I'm too firm, they'll accuse me of being rude. And man, I really want to be rude.

"What do you know? You're not my doctor. You're not even *a* doctor. I want to speak to your superior." Her face twists up in a snarl as she tries to peer over the counter, probably looking for Joan. Too bad for Ms. Bonneville, because I'm the only one here today. Tuesday afternoons are notoriously slow for us. Well, honestly, most days are pretty slow. With big pharmacies opening all over the place, it's hard for the little guy.

I resist dragging my hand over my face, instead plastering on a smile and looking her in the eye. "I'm sorry, Ms. Bonneville, but I'm the only pharmacist here today. Now, I can happily fill this prescription for a one month's supply, or you can come back tomorrow when Joan is in and speak with her. But I must tell you, she will say what I've already told you. Unless your doctor calls us, we can't give you double dosages. I'm sorry."

Just when I think she'll relent and let me help her, she narrows her gaze at me before spinning on her heels and hobbling out of the store. But not before I hear her mumble "bitch" and "kid" in the same mouthful.

A small laugh bubbles out of me as she reaches the door, her head lightning quick as she turns to glare at me one final time. Despite my professionalism gnawing at my insides and telling me to stop, I lift my hand and wave at her.

Huffing, she leaves the store, and I attempt to hide the shit twinkle in my eye.

Definitely worth it.

Good thing Joan isn't here; otherwise, I might get reprimanded.

Another thirty minutes later and I'm finally able to get the fuck out of here, my stomach grumbling for a snack and my feet a comfy chair.

The keys to the front of the store jingle in my hand as I turn them in the lock, making sure we're secure for the night. I resist the urge to smell my fingers, knowing that pesky lingering metallic scent will still be there.

With all in order, I begin the walk home just before seven p.m. My feet ring out against the cobbled pavement as I walk through Notting Hill, the pastel houses a stark reminder that I'm finally home.

I know by tomorrow the streets will be filled with market stalls and merchants ready to sell everything ranging from crepes to antiques. You might occasionally find Emilia there; that's how she met Stana.

As I pass the array of shops closed up for the night, the small crowd of people in front of the movie cinema gives me pause.

It feels like years since I've been, and for some reason, despite my aching feet and hollowed stomach, I can't help but drift over. My hands reach for my wallet to pay for a ticket. I pick the only seven o'clock showing, some Marvel movie about an ant. I'm not sure it's going to be my cup of tea, especially considering I've seen none of the other films and have no idea how an ant can be a superhero. But, well, here we are.

I pay, then shove my debit card back into my wallet and practically sprint to the snack bar. With a large popcorn and Maltesers in sight, I'm a happy gal. I might not love movies, but the snacks always make it worth it. Throw in a large Coke for good measure.

I can practically taste the goodness on the tip of my tongue. Ugh, my mouth waters at the impending deliciousness coming my way. After the lad in front of me pays I quickly read off my order, my acrylic nails tapping against the murky glass cabinet below my hands. First the stinky keys, now this; I need a sink and soap ASAP. I pull my hands away when the young boy comes back, my glorious treats in hand.

I don't care what anyone says—you can't go to the cinema and not get food. I mean, why would you go then? And don't say it's to see the movie.

"Thanks," I tell the boy, whose face tells me he's about as thrilled to be working here as a squashed animal on the side of the road.

Hands full, I attempt to sneak a bit of popcorn, sticking my tongue out to grab the top piece. After a skillful move on my part, it's a success.

"Lottie?"

My name being called catches my off guard until I see Owen standing by the snacks, quickly thanking the same boy who served me before walking over, treats in hand. I mentally take in his large popcorn, Starbursts, and drink. Good lad.

"Puppy," I greet him, my lips turning up at the sides. Despite knowing I need to stay away, I can't help but gravitate toward Owen. And I know that's a bad sign on my end. Not that I'm comparing him to the likes of Beck—I just know I'm nowhere near ready for a relationship or even something casual, especially with a friend of a friend.

"I thought you weren't a movie person," he says, his pearly whites on display.

"Let's just say it's been a day and I needed to turn my mind off."

"With *Ant Man*?" His eyebrows draw together.

I lift a shoulder. "I've got no idea, but snacks and a comfy chair were too much to pass up. You?"

"I'm actually here for the movie. I'm a bit of a Marvel fan."

I nod, hoping it looks as if I know what he's talking about. But in reality I'm totally lost.

"Marvel?" he says again, clearly sensing my confusion.

A laugh slips out of me. "Sorry, I wasn't kidding when I said I didn't know movies. I've got no clue what a Marvel is."

He bites his lips as if he's trying not to laugh at me. It's not condescending, but rather adorable. I can't help myself, letting my gaze roam over his body. Dangerous. Being around him could be dangerous. He's literally a walking Abercrombie ad with, from what I've heard, a heart of gold. A guy like him can do serious damage.

"Well, we better get in there before it starts," he remarks, cutting through my blatant perusal of him. I'd hide my head in the popcorn bucket if I thought it wouldn't spill everywhere.

I trail behind him, thanking him as he holds the door for me.

"I'm over here." I motion with my head. The cinema is surprisingly empty so Owen follows me.

"I doubt they'll care if I switch," he says from next to me. "Do you mind?"

"By all means," I respond, signaling for him to take a seat next to me. I open my Maltesers, then tip them into my popcorn bucket before taking a huge handful and shoving them into my gob.

Owen starts munching himself, both of us settling into a comfortable silence before the adverts commence. I begin to zone out when the movie starts, not really caring for the plot. Owen, on the other hand, seems enthralled, listening to every word, eating it right up.

In some ways he reminds me of a small child at Christmas, his innocent enthusiasm for things like this. I've met this man a handful of times and I don't even know him yet, but the desire to is there.

I spend the better part of two hours inhaling my food and then some of Owen's when he taps out. I try to pay attention but it's a lost cause when the characters start shrinking, my mind having no clue what is going on.

Owen makes us stay past the credits, practically on the edge of his seat waiting for little clips of the film at the end. Again, I've got no idea what's going on, but I don't mind—it was two hours relaxing and vegging out.

"So, what did you think?" he asks as we exit the theater.

"It was good." I try to lace my words with extra enthusiasm, but I think he sees through it.

"They're not for everyone." He shrugs. "I did love it, though."

"I'm glad, puppy." I feel a yawn building, quickly catching it with the back of my hand. "I'm knackered. Thanks for the company, but I should get going."

"Let's go," he says, beginning to walk in the direction of my place. Usually this would be a red flag that he knows where I live, but he's close with Stana so I know he's not a creep. If anything, he's the complete opposite. A good lad raised by his mum.

"I can get home myself, you know," I tell him.

"Oh, I have no doubt," he replies, voice full of cheer. "But it's late, and what kind of guy would I be if I let you go home alone?"

"I don't even know you," I quip back.

He lifts a shoulder. "Don't you?"

"Whatever." I laugh, knowing I'd probably be more comfortable with him than a lot of the other lads I know. Before I can stop myself, I playfully nudge his side, then instantly regret it until that smile of his comes into view. I can't help but reciprocate.

My stomach does a small somersault, and I know I've just crossed some invisible barrier I created for myself.

I decide to ignore it, though, as we walk together in a comfortable silence for about five minutes until my flat comes into view.

I slow down, motioning with my head toward my place. "Well, this is me," I say, my voice suddenly breathy. Owen stops next to me, turning so we're facing one another.

We stand close, the tips of our shoes almost touching. Far closer than anyone who's just met would. It's intimate, as though somehow we've known each other a lifetime. The thought is corny, ridiculous, and something I'd never say. Hell, I wish I had alcohol to blame it on, but alas, Coke is all that's in my system. Well, that and the fire brewing from his presence.

The warm summer air has a slight wind, brushing tendrils of my hair around. That seems to be the only thing moving.

Owen's stare digs into my soul, sparking a fire that I thought had been put out months ago. Scratch that—this is a fire I never knew existed. I'm not one to lie about how many people I've dated; there have been plenty. But in all that time, I've never experienced a pull as intense and quick as the one I feel when I'm with him.

I know, I just *know* this wouldn't be nothing. This wouldn't be your average "one night and never speak again." It would be more. And more is dangerous.

So instead of letting either of us take that step, breaking the invisible barrier between us and crossing into more, I move back.

I notice the surprise on his face, Owen probably having pinpointed me as game for a good time. He wouldn't be wrong, and perhaps if he were anyone else, anyone *less*, maybe I would forget about returning my car and hail a cab with him right now. But that isn't the case.

"I'll see you around." Despite wanting to say "come inside," I hold off. Because I can already see that, despite the bravado he puts on in front of everyone, in front of women, he wants it. I can see it in his eyes. He wants the one thing that people spend their whole lives searching for, the one thing that manages to elude so many.

Love.

Owen Bower can deny it all he wants, but it's clear. He wants to be loved.

And that's something I can't give him, can't give anyone right now.

So, for that reason solely, I turn and walk inside. Alone.

Two

The weeks post my return to London continue to slip by. It's coming up on six weeks since my return, Stana herself having been home for nearly a month.

Today she's moving in with Ali, and the entire cavalry has come to help. Well, everyone except Emilia. I've yet to see Owen again solo since our movie, but that doesn't mean he hasn't been on my mind.

"So, tell me again why Em isn't here?" I call out to Stana as I attempt to organize her spice rack. Some would say this is a pointless exercise, but some would be wrong. Who knows, you could mix up curry powder and cinnamon, then what are you gonna do, have curry-flavored porridge? Exactly, my time is put to good use.

I lift up a dark brown powder before dumping it into one of the labeled bottles I picked up along the way.

"Her new flatmate is moving in today. She wanted to help but apparently the girl didn't have keys yet, so Em decided to stay and help her out."

I nod, my attention still stuck on if I've just put the curry powder in the cinnamon box. Fuck. I sniff it, hoping to differentiate between the two.

Curry powder! Fuck yes, I'm a spice genius.

"I give up," Owen says, walking out of Stana's bedroom. He's been helping build their new bed, but from the look on his face, it isn't going too well.

"It's practically all in German. How is a bloke supposed to read all that?" He huffs, his usually tan face slightly flushed.

"It's Swedish," I call from the kitchen, trying to swap the mixed-up labels.

Owen's attention turns toward me.

"Uh, you've got something." He motions to my nose. I attempt to see what he's pointing out, but no one can actually see their nose.

I look at him expectantly, waiting for a clue as to what he's saying.

Grinning, he walks over, and his thumb brushes across my nose, dark orange powder coating the back of it.

"Thanks," I tell him, feeling my ears heat at the action. *Dumb, absolutely ridiculous, Lottie.*

I internally chastise myself for having a reaction to something so small. I pray he doesn't notice because the last thing I need right now is getting tangled up in a friendship-to-romance gone wrong. It may have worked for Stana, but I'm not on that path.

"I'm gonna check on Ali," Stana says to us before clearing the room.

"You know, they're showing the first three Star Wars films this weekend at the theater near my house. Any interest?"

Owen's question catches me off guard. In the few weeks I've known him, we've had fun banter back and forth, strictly friendly, but aside from our movie run-in, there have been no solo hangouts.

"I may not have seen those films before, but I'm guessing that will take at least six hours of my afternoon?"

His shoulders shake. "It may or may not be longer than that."

I rub my hands together in an attempt to remove the excess powders on them. I'll probably have an allergy attack on my way home tonight from all the shit flying up my nose in this kitchen.

"I think six hours of my life might be too much of a commitment," I reply. "But I reckon I could give you two."

"I'll take what I can get."

I smile and continue to place everything in order, sporadically having to redo Owen's work, yet I can't bring myself to care. A sense of comfortability overtakes our interactions as the hours slip by, neither of us seeming to mind.

I leave Stana's a few hours later, a small smile on my face that doesn't want to leave. Despite the fact my stomach started feeling uneasy toward the end of the day, I can't seem to stop smiling. It should worry me the comfort I find from spending time with Owen, the ease of our conversation. I've only been single again for less than two months, but if I'm honest with myself, my relationship with Beck began to break down months before that.

I'm not one to stick my head in the sand and go off with the fairies, but I changed my entire life for a man and the thought that he could be unfaithful was just too horrible to imagine. So instead I spent six months in Edinburgh feeling utterly lonely and attempting to salvage something that belonged straight in the bin.

It takes a lot to rattle me, but wow, did Beck manage it. He fucking shook my entire foundation, then tried to escape unscathed. I never understood the expression "hell hath no fury like a woman scorned" until the moment my suspicions were confirmed. Some will call me a psycho, but I don't really give a shit.

I exit the Tube at Notting Hill and begin my final small walk home. I pass the pastel buildings as my feet move along the paved streets, weaving among tourists and locals alike. In all my time I've lived here, there has always been a mix of both. I don't know if it's the movie-like tranquility that comes from this neighborhood or the Portobello Market that features a range of baked goods, antiques, and artwork, but something draws people in.

I'm about to pass my local chemist when I realize I'm out of shampoo, and if you've ever had bleach-blonde hair, then you know you don't skimp on purple shampoo. One wrong product and I could be rocking yellow hair. Not a good look. Plus, I need to get something to settle my tummy as it's been sensitive for a few days now. Coming down with something is not what I need right now.

I enter the store and go straight for the shampoo, then quickly find the other items I need. I should probably have gone to my own work to pick up these things, but I'm too exhausted from today to walk the extra four hundred meters.

It isn't until I pass the tampons that my steps come to a screeching halt. My mind begins to race as I look at the sanitary products I haven't actually needed for the past two months. I mean, it has to have been all the stress. I've never had a regular period and my birth control makes it infrequent. But coupled with the stomach aches and smell sensitivity, it gives me reason to pause.

Jesus fucking Christ.

I'm a pharmacist—it's literally my job to pick up on this. Yet here I am, seven p.m. on a Saturday, questioning if the reason I've been so off kilter these past two months is because my cheating ex-boyfriend knocked me up and I've been too daft to notice it.

Okay, there is a logical way to figure it all out.

I walk two isles over to the pregnancy tests, then make sure to scan my surroundings before grabbing four, as if some alarm is going to go off with a big flashing arrow pointing my way just for touching the things.

While paying for my supplies, I'm thankful that I don't recognize the pharmacist behind the counter. I don't miss the look he gives me as he scans each test. I ignore it, muttering thanks before shoving them into my bag and bolting.

I race home as the night sky darkens, no longer taking the time to appreciate my neighborhood and all its beauty.

"Shit. Motherfucking shit fuck," I yell at the white stick. There is no way in hell this can possibly be happening to me. My hands shake as I put it on the sink, lined up next to three other identical tests. There is no denying what I'm seeing, yet my mind can't seem to comprehend the drastic reality that is displayed in front of me.

I'm pregnant.

Twenty-five years old, single, and now a looming pregnancy I'm nowhere ready for. I haven't once held a child. My life consists of my job and my friends—no real responsibilities. How the bloody hell do I fit a child into that mix? I don't know the first thing about babies. I'm not equipped for this.

If I'm honest with myself, the signs have been here for the past few weeks, but I've been so desperate to be wrong that I ignored them all.

"FUCK!" I scream into my little bathroom, deciding it's better to let it all out in one yell than go off like a madwoman for hours and scare the neighbors.

"How the hell did this happen?" I ask before wanting to whack myself.

Of course, I know how it happened. A late night after too many tears and a bottle of whiskey. Beck was there and I was leaving Edinburgh and despite the burning anger I felt inside, I just wanted to feel loved. I think some small part of me was trying to hold onto something we once had, trying to search for the side of him I'd fallen in love with, not the one that crushed my heart. Of course, all I got out of the situation was regret and despair. Well, I guess now this too.

Despite my unease over the whole situation, I pull myself off the bathroom floor, straighten my dress, and head back into my bedroom.

I pull out my mobile and dial Beck's number, something I never thought I'd have to do again. I sit on the edge of my bed, elbows digging into my knees as the phone continues to ring.

And ring, and ring.

Beck never picks up.

Three

I cancel my movie with Owen. I lie and tell him I have a stomach bug. He's probably skeptical, but I don't have the energy to care too much. Mostly, I've been centering my days around working and seeing the girls. I've been at Saint Street a few times in the past week since finding out, and things with Owen are luckily fine, him not bringing up our canceled plans.

I know I need to get to a doctor's office and confirm everything, but I've been a pharmacist long enough to know I'm definitely pregnant.

After Beck never called me back, I held off, but I think this afternoon I'm just going to have to bite the bullet and try again.

I'm halfway through breakfast with everyone at Saint Street when the smell of bacon sends me running to the loo.

I empty my meal into the toilet, my heaving a recent occurrence that has come with my impending motherhood. Groaning, I rest my head against the cool bathroom tiles, giving myself a moment to catch my breath. Who knew that a bacon-and-egg roll would send me straight to the bowl of a loo?

I give myself a few more seconds before standing, then turn on the water to slowly begin to piece myself together again. It would be an understatement that keeping this a secret from my friends is challenging. But the truth is, I'm just not ready to tell anyone. I don't think I've even accepted it, to be fully honest.

After rinsing out my mouth and fixing my makeup, I feel decent enough to face the music. Lord knows everyone probably thinks I've got some type of stomach issue, the amount of times I've run off to the bathroom recently. Good thing they all seem rather distracted by each other today.

Finally back to my usual self—well, minus the child inside of me—I pull open the door of the Saint Street bathroom. I quickly draw back when I find Owen standing in the narrow hallway, his usually goofy demeanor replaced with a flat expression.

"You scared me, puppy." I laugh, attempting to act casual by using his nickname.

He smiles, and it's small and says more than I care to admit. My defenses automatically go up.

"I didn't mean to loiter in the hallway. I just heard you getting sick and wanted to make sure you were okay." His stare is piercing, my stomach hollowing out.

"I'm okay. I guess I just ate something bad," I lie.

He nods. "I really don't mean to pry, Lottie. Your life is none of my business, but if you need anything at all, I'm here."

I keep my mouth shut, my sudden anger toward him taking me aback. Does he know? How could he possibly?

"I, uh—" I pause, unsure how to continue.

He holds up his hand. "I don't mean to put you on the spot at all. My mum used to get sick from the smell of bacon too when she had my brother. I was ten, so I remember is all."

I keep my mouth shut, unsure how to proceed. Unsure how to comprehend the fact that someone I've known less than two months is the first person to know about my pregnancy.

"I'm sorry, this is probably highly inappropriate, but I just wanted you to know I'm here if you need someone to talk to. Clearly you're keeping this to yourself for now, which of course is your right, and I'm probably overstepping every boundary ever created, but I've come to value you as a friend and I just wanted to let you know I'm here. That's all. I'm rambling. But yeah, sorry. And if I'm totally off base, then consider me highly mortified and accept my apologies." He looks around, seemingly uncomfortable with himself, unsure how to proceed. I can't help but laugh. It just jumps out of my mouth, my hand instantly covering it. None of this is funny. But all things considered, it is partly comical that Owen, of all people, is the first to know. Jesus, maybe I'm also losing my mind.

His expression is uncertain, my anger toward him suddenly gone.

"I'm sorry, I shouldn't laugh," I reply. "I'm not sure what to say if I'm being honest. I don't know too many men who are quite so perceptive." I keep out the part where I assumed Owen would be the last of anyone in the group to guess what's going on. He's got that "beautiful blond idiot" look to him, which now that I say it, makes me feel like the idiot, and an asshole.

He scratches his neck but continues to look at me. "Sorry, I didn't mean to put you on the spot. Ah, God, sorry. I feel like I've overstepped and now I'm saying sorry again."

"You're fine," I say, surprised I actually mean it. I'm not one to let strangers into my business, but there's a comfort that comes from Owen. "I would usually say now is a good time for a drink, but I guess we both know I'm in no position to be doing that."

He laughs, seeming to loosen up a little bit.

"We should probably get back to everyone," I say. "But yeah, um, it would be great if you could keep this to yourself," I throw in as I walk by him.

"I won't say a word."

I nod, my body shaking slightly. I dig my fingers into my bag and quickly exit the hallway, leaving Owen alone.

Two days later I'm sitting alone in my flat, drinking water that I wish would magically turn into wine. After having to call in sick to work, I'm already dreading how the next seven months are going to play out. If my calculations are correct, and they *have* to be, I got pregnant in July and since it's September, that means I'm two months along.

My phone pings, causing my heart to stop.

It could be Beck.

Beck. The lying asshole I gave over two years of my life to, even moved to Edinburgh for, before finding out he had been cheating on me for over a year.

Beck, who was the last person I slept with, the father of this little thing cooking inside of me.

Also, the same man who has been avoiding my calls for the past two days. It could be that he's still pissed that I sold his

TV to pay for my "emotional damages" as I claimed at the time. Or the countless other items I tossed out our flat's windows.

One might have lingering guilt, even offer to pay for it in the long run, but not me. As far as I'm concerned, that fucker can rot in hell. Well, that was my thought process before all of this.

Now I still want him to rot in hell, but I also need him to step up for our child.

Ugh, even saying the words "our child" hurts my soul. I pray to the universe that he's going to be a better father than he was a partner; otherwise, we're both screwed.

Letting out a breath, I place my water on the table and check my message.

I try to blink away the frustration I feel when I see Stana's name instead of my ex's. He may be a cheating asshole, but not once over the past few days did I think he'd ignore my calls, ignore the fact we're having a child together.

It was never something I wanted to tell him over the phone, but after countless unanswered messages and straight-to-voicemail calls, I'd had enough. I told the daft prick I was pregnant, and he better call me back.

That was over twenty-four hours ago. And if I know Beck, which I do, his mobile is never more than a meter away from him.

"Lousy, no-good bastard," I mutter as I get off the couch, deciding to call Stana later. Keeping this secret from my friends was never the goal, but as the hours pass me by, I can't seem to get the guts to call them.

I've never been a secretive person. Sure, I'm loyal as hell and would keep a secret for a mate, but keeping them *from* a mate, not my style. But I suppose I've never had something to really keep from them.

I've lived a good life. Up until I was twenty-one, I lived with my parents here in London before they decided to move to France nearly four years ago. Their leaving didn't come as a surprise to me. Like my mum's brother, Stan's dad, my parents could never sit still. I'm surprised they lasted in London as long as they did.

Their departure left me with my own flat in Notting Hill and a comfy pharmacy job down the road. I've never really known hardships like my friends. Ali and Em's parents died years ago, Reeve's dad was never in the picture, Owen's dad died before he even knew him, and although Stana has both her parents, they could use a little assistance in the parenting department.

But not me. My parents' desire to leave London wasn't to get away from me, just to begin a new adventure. I've never lacked in love or material things; my life has been relatively normal. That is, until now. Here I am, newly twenty-five and alone and pregnant.

And no one knows, except me, Beck, and bloody Owen.

My front-door buzzer goes off despite the fact I'm not expecting anyone.

Who the hell is buzzing at this time?

I peel myself away from the comfort of my couch, cringing slightly at the pajamas I'm still in.

"Hello," I call through the intercom.

"Hi, it's Owen."

I eye the speaker, as if he could possibly see my uncertainty.

"Um, can I come in?" His voice breaks through my mind and I reluctantly press the buzzer and walk to my front door.

After a few moments I pull the door open, Owen's face greeting me.

"Uh, hi?" I laugh, feeling awkward and unsure.

"Do you mind if I come inside?" He lifts his shoulders and I notice the two full grocery bags in his hands. Uncertain how I can say no, I open the door wider, signaling him to enter.

"Thanks," he says as he walks into my home. It's not a huge space. There's a bathroom to the left of the front door, and my bedroom is off to the right. Both doors are closed and my small kitchen is straight ahead, open, looking into the living room.

It doesn't take Owen even a moment to get to the kitchen, where he places the two bags of stuff on the bench.

"Uh, it's not that I'm unhappy to see you, puppy. But what are you doing here?" No need to beat around the bush.

Owen takes his attention off my modest living room. It could have a bit more character, but I've yet to take the time to furnish it more than the tan couches and TV. Lord knows it needs some love, but working and having a semblance of a social life take up most of my time. I can't even imagine how it will be after the baby arrives.

The baby. It's a sobering thought that leads me right back to Owen. One of the only people who knows about the baby. He wasn't showing up at my house before he found out, so my only guess is that he's here for that reason.

"I've been thinking," he starts, looking down at his brown boots before returning his attention to me. "Is it okay I wear shoes in the flat?" he asks, as if he's possibly broken some cardinal rule by crossing into my flat in shoes

"You're fine," I assure him. "Back to what you've been thinking?"

He nods, seemingly glad he hasn't upset me. I guess his mother really did raise him right. Stana always told me behind his playboy persona Owen was a mama's boy.

"Right, anyway, as I was saying, I've been doing some thinking. And…" He pauses, looking me over. "Sorry, do you want to sit down? I could make you a cuppa and some—" His forehead creases as he paces back and forth. "Perhaps a biscuit, or if you're hungry I could throw together some lunch?"

"Owen!" I can't help but choke on a laugh as I say his name. I don't think for a minute that he's stalling; he just genuinely wants me to be comfortable. "I'm fine. Let's sit down and you can tell me what's going on."

I move around the couch before sitting down, motioning for him to sit across from me. He's not a small guy by any means. Tall, golden, and I reckon under that white T-shirt, he's probably fit as fuck. *Shit. Lottie, no!*

He sits and I wait for him to begin, feeling I've probably said enough.

"Okay, sorry, I don't mean to come across as a worrywart. I just know how rough it can be in the first trimester. Mum was always so sick, and I didn't want you to be standing listening to me go on and want to be sick or something."

I bite my lip to keep from smiling at his terminology. For a tall, sexy drink of water, sometimes he can sound like my nan.

"Anyway, the real reason I'm here is that I want to help you, Lottie. I know we aren't exactly close, but it's clear we get along. What's also clear is you're going through this alone and that can't be easy on anyone. I know this might come off as weird or pushy. I'm not trying to put the moves on you or anything; I want to help."

I sit back, attempting to process his words. I don't really know men like Owen. To be completely honest, I wasn't sure they existed at all.

"I'm a very vocal person, Owen. It's rare for me to be speechless."

He nods. "Good or bad speechless?"

Lifting my shoulders, I swallow. "I don't know. This is a deeply personal time in my life, clearly something unexpected. Being blunt, you're not exactly the first person I would think to call, let alone tell. It's a lot."

"Okay, well then, I'll go." He runs his hands along his jeans, his movements reeking of hesitancy.

"Okay," I reply, still unsure what else to say.

"But before I go, I just have one question. Are you okay?"

I pause, his words catching me off guard. It's the first time I've been asked that. Well, obviously, because I haven't told a soul. I don't have it in me yet. And I think that fact alone tells me all I need to know. So, in a moment of utter surprise not only to myself, but also to Owen, I open my mouth and answer honestly.

"No, Owen. I don't think I am."

"It's okay to not be okay, Lottie. Everyone needs someone every once in a while."

He moves of his own accord, each step drawing him closer. Once he's in front of me, toe to toe, his arms coil around me and pull me into him.

It isn't remotely romantic, and despite not knowing him too well, I sink into him. His fresh T-shirt smells like laundry detergent, and it's comforting, peaceful almost. I want to crawl inside whatever has made him so calm while I can't seem to stop the storm brewing inside of me.

His hands tighten around my back, not so much that he's hurting me, but enough for me to feel a level of safety in his grip. Like the first few times I met Owen, I get that familiar sense of ease and familiarity that accompanies his presence.

It's those feelings that I use to convince myself to let Owen stay for another two hours. We don't discuss anything baby-related. We simply sit and watch Star Wars. And honestly, it's one of the best times I've had in months.

Four

"Are you ready?"

I look up at Owen, because he's just about a foot taller than me, before nodding. The big white building looms in front of me. People walk in and out, some carefree, others crippled with fear. I think I'm stuck at that in-between phase of just feeling royally fucked, and not in the fun way.

"I guess I don't really have a choice, puppy," I admit. "I can't keep ignoring this. I need to woman up, and this is the first step."

He eyes me thoughtfully, the deep depths of blue swirling around like a torrid ocean. *He's like a Ken doll*, I think to myself, but I refrain from saying that aloud. I'm sure that would only piss him off.

Over the past few days Owen's been keeping a close eye on me, offering to help at any small inconvenience. And he's the one who has been pushing that I see a doctor and get this confirmed.

"I can hold your hand if you want," he offers, trying to lighten the mood. He knows that isn't my style.

I look up at him and he's grinning, so I shove his side. "Fuck off." I laugh and he chuckles as we walk into the doctor's office.

We check in, and I can't help but scan all the patients in the waiting area, my eyes locking onto a young mother, her stomach protruding, clearly about to burst any moment. Her partner sits beside her, the two of them holding hands.

Other couples sit together, too, their arms touching and voices hushed as they speak. A small pang of jealousy pricks my heart at the sight. I won't get those moments. The moments of being together, comfort filling every word.

But that's okay. Lots of women do this alone. I won't be the first or the last.

Owen and I sit down on the hard plastic chairs, his long legs hanging into the walkway despite how hard he tries to pull them in. I laugh and he glares at me, only making it all the more hilarious.

"Ms. Knight." My name is called out after twenty minutes, and we are ushered into a waiting room. It's stark white and sanitized, smelling of antiseptic wipes. Not too different from parts of the pharmacy, so oddly, I feel at home here. Owen too seems surprisingly comfortable, but then I remember he's done this before. With his mum.

The door opens and a petite woman sticks her head in. Her deep brown hair sits just upon her shoulders while her coat seems to swallow her. I'd assume she's in her late forties, maybe early fifties. A huge diamond sparkler sits on her ring finger, glaring at me when the sun hits it.

"Good afternoon, I'm Doctor Estelle Montgomery," she introduces herself, and I'm quick to do the same. Having seen enough movies that I know she will assume Owen is the father, I beat her to the punch by telling her he is a friend.

She doesn't waste any time, moving around the sterile room, her steps barely audible as she brings over a machine twice her size. "Now, it says here we're thinking we're pregnant?"

I nod. "I took a test and it came back positive. I've had all the symptoms, so I just wanted to get it confirmed. I'm also a pharmacist, so I used all the tells I know to self-diagnose. I get that's probably the wrong way to do that, but I'm also assuming I'm around ten weeks along."

She looks at me for a moment, taken aback, before schooling her features. "And when did you suspect?"

"A little over a week ago."

"Okay, well, usually we would do a blood test to confirm, but since you're assuming you're at least two months along, we might as well use the ultrasound machine. Let's lift up your top a little. Now be aware, this will be cold, but nothing painful."

I nod, little pinpricks of anxiety crawling up my spine as the reality of my situation begins to set in.

With shaking hands, I pull up my white T-shirt. Owen moves closer to me, my gaze quickly darting to his.

"Ugh, now might be a good time to hold my fucking hand," I whisper to him, realizing I'm not as tough as I thought in this moment.

He doesn't joke with me, knowing now probably isn't the time. Instead he grabs a stool and plops down, then pulls his body forward till he's next to me. His large tan hand comes out and laces our fingers together as Dr. Montgomery begins to move the wand around.

Suddenly the silence of the room is filled with a soft thump.

Boom boom. Boom boom. Boom boom.

"Holy fucking shit," I say, not caring if my sailor's mouth offends the doctor. Those are about all the words I can manage, emotion clogging my throat while water seeps into my eyes.

"Well, you were correct, Lottie. Looks like your little one is around ten weeks old, making your due date end of March, the twenty-eighth."

She pauses, giving me a minute to collect myself with all this news.

"Can she find out what she's having yet?" Owen asks, his voice slightly different from usual.

"Science has come a long way in the last few years, so now we can do a blood test at nine weeks to determine. That is, if you want?"

I nod quickly, suddenly desperate to know if it's a little girl or boy.

"Okay then, let's finish up here, and then we can get to work on drawing blood." She talks to me a little longer, going over basic prenatal care and what to do and not do. I try to take it all in but know I must be missing a few things. Luckily, Owen's taking notes on his iPhone. I don't let myself think about how most dads don't even do that. The girls were not lying to me when they said Owen was special.

"It will take a few days for me to get back to you with the results, so after the nurse has finished with you two, you're free to go."

We say our goodbyes before she's off checking on another patient. I'm still speechless, trying to comprehend the gravity of everything finally sinking in.

This is real. I'm going to be a mother.

And for the first time, the fear of that concept doesn't send me into total panic.

We're in the office for another twenty minutes before everything has finally wrapped up, Owen and I free to go. It's as we're exiting the room that I realize Owen has been holding my hand the entire time.

He pulls away from me to open the door, and I take the opportunity to rub my hands down my sides. Owen catches me and smiles. I, of course, roll my eyes.

As we get back into the car, Owen in the driver's seat, I realize the entire dynamic between the two of us has shifted. Despite the little time we've known one another, there is a closeness and comfortability that time just can't buy. And for that, I'm thankful.

Three days later, I'm on my way to Saint Street to meet everyone before the guys' show, thankful it's only a five-minute walk from work. The best part about living in Notting Hill is that everything you need is here. But Lord knows that doesn't stop me from running off to Oxford Street for a shopping spree or to Shoreditch for a night on the town. Well, I guess the latter is no longer an option for now.

It's been days of anxiously waiting for the call to find out what I'm having. God, even saying it all aloud sounds so surreal. I haven't seen Owen since the doctor's office—we've spoken on the phone once, but both of our jobs have kept us busy.

Plus, he had to practice with Ali and Reeve for their performance tonight. I've only managed to see them play together a few times, but shit, they're good. Em says they could have made it big time, and I believe her, but none of them wanted that. Said it would make it all feel too much like a job, when the reason they do it is to decompress.

I'm outside of Saint Street when I spot Stana out front.

"Hey, stranger!" I call out. Her deep brown hair blows in the wind as she turns around, her signature smile in place.

A man walks in front of me, his side brushing my bag as I attempt to get to my cousin.

"Watch it!" he yells before muttering under his breath, "Women."

"Hey!" I shout back. "Why don't you watch it, asshole!"

Stana's eyes are wide as she watches the man retreat around the corner. She's never been one to really raise her voice or retaliate at strangers. Me, on the other hand... Well, it might have to be something I work at once I'm a mum. Hmm, or maybe not.

"Lottie!" she calls out as she meets me halfway in a hug. "That man could have been crazy or violent," she chastises, but I hear a slight laugh in her voice.

"He was a dickhead," I reply, pulling her in tighter. "Stana, I feel like I haven't seen you in forever. Work takes up all my time."

"And apparently Owen?" she says, attempting to hide a coy smile.

I pull back, brushing off the comment. "Owen's just a friend. Nice to know not all men are pure vile shit like Beck." I beam, linking our arms together as we head to Saint Street. For a smaller bar, this place sure draws a crowd when the guys perform.

Their band is called The R.O.A., literally all their first initials. Pretty basic, but not terrible. I like to think Owen could have done better.

"Well, let's get this show on the road," I say, pulling open the heavy door and entering.

"Tell me again why they didn't want a record deal?" I ask Em one more time as the guys transition into an original song. The three of them are incredible, Reeve up front singing, Ali playing guitar, and Owen fucking owning the drums. Who knew I'd love the drums so much?

"No interest," she says back, then chugs her last few drops of wine.

God, how I wish I could have one.

"They are bloody brilliant, I will say." I lean back, watching with pride as Owen smashes through each song with ease. His eyes catch mine every so often and he smiles. I grin back and motion to all the women and men fangirling over them. I can't be sure, but I think he rolls his eyes before getting back into the song.

It isn't long till it's past eleven and my body just needs a soft bed to crawl into. I say my goodbyes to everyone except Owen. He's chatting to a brunette by the bar who appears to be eating up everything he says.

Our gaze locks from across the room, and I give him a thumbs-up. It looks as though he's going to come over, but I hold up a hand to say otherwise.

I wink and slip out of Saint Street, trying not to read into the way my chest feels from seeing him with someone else.

It's a day after the guys' show when I get the call from my doctor to let me know what I'm having.

A little girl.

I sit down on the couch, attempting to catch my breath after we hang up, my fingers itching to call Owen and tell him. As if he's got some sort of telepathy, his number appears on my mobile, and I answer the call instantly.

"It's a girl!" I yell, unable to hold back my excitement.

"What?" he replies, seemingly taken aback. Oh yeah, I forgot to even say hi or give him context.

"My baby," I respond. "I'm having a little girl." I can practically hear the smile in my own voice. Pure joy.

"Wow," he whispers. "Wow, Lottie, that really is something. If anyone will be a great mum to a little girl, it's going to be you."

I smile, my cheeks suddenly feeling wet, so I brush my hand across them. I didn't even notice I was crying until now as my throat tightens and the small trickles dance down my face.

"Are you happy?" he asks, voice slightly hesitant, wary almost.

"Honestly, Owen, I was fucking petrified of having a child, but now that I've seen her heartbeat and know it's a little girl, it all feels so real. Sure, I'm still scared shitless, but finally I think I can admit, yeah, I am happy."

We stay this way for another hour, Owen listening to me like Stana or Em would as I rattle on about her. About all the things I need to do and places I will have to go. He lets me talk on and on, only occasionally throwing in his two cents.

And after we say our goodbyes, for the first time in weeks I don't feel so alone in everything. I feel as if I'm going to be okay. *We* are going to be okay.

Five

"Are you sure you can eat all that cheese?" Owen eyes my pre-dinner snack and I scowl at him, scoffing down another slice of cheddar.

"Yes, I'm sure. It's soft cheese I can't have," I attempt to reply, mouth full of food.

He doesn't respond, just goes back to his pot on the stove.

It's been two weeks since he found out, and since then something has drastically shifted between us. I've taken great comfort in Owen, and our semi-friendship has turned into something much more in such a short time. I've come to rely on him and confide in him, and with that, he's become a permanent fixture in my home.

Amid all of this uncertainty, our friendship has centered me when I feel as if everything is going to fly off course.

"So, I know it's been a while, but are you sure you don't want to talk to Stana or Em about any of this?" Owen's voice drifts out of the kitchen. I turn to look at him, his gaze already trained on me as he taps a wooden spoon against the rim of the pot.

"I'm going to tell them. It's more just a matter of when, not if." I pause, running my fingers through my hair. I'll probably have to hold off getting it done now. It's the little things you wouldn't even think about that matter.

"I'm not trying to pressure you, Lottie. I know you've got a lot going on. I just want to help you."

I smile, rolling my eyes playfully at him as he walks toward me, our meal in hand.

"Thanks, puppy," I tell him, taking the bowl he hands over.

"Anytime, Lottie. It's important you keep eating good meals. I was thinking—"

The ringing of my phone cuts Owen off mid-sentence, and I lift a hand to tell him to hang on when I see the name flash across the screen. The name of the person I've been trying to get in contact with for weeks.

My hand stills midair for a moment, my head turning to Owen, and I catch him eyeing the phone with disdain.

"I, um, I need to take this," I say quickly, picking up the phone with shaking hands.

"Hello?" I answer, my heart irregularly fast paced.

"Hey, Lottie, it's Beck."

I swallow. "Yeah, I know who it is. I've got your number, remember?"

He laughs through the line, and it's forced and awkward. I hate it. I let out a breath, feeling all too aware of Owen's presence next to me. I'm practically able to feel the anger coming off him in waves. To say he hates Beck would be the world's biggest understatement. Being completely transparent, I feel the same as Owen. But I won't let that cloud my judgment. Despite his cheating and his absence the past few weeks, he deserves a chance to be in his child's life.

"Yeah, um, sorry it took me so long to call. It wasn't exactly easy news to hear over the message bank."

I nod, even though he can't see it.

"I tried calling you multiple times. I obviously didn't want to tell you over a voice message, but you didn't really give me much choice." There is a burn to my words, little morsels of resentment peeking through.

"Yeah, I guess you're right." His voice is flat, devoid of his usual life and charm. Perhaps I only saw those things when I thought I was helplessly in love with him. What a joke. He was pulling the wool over my eyes the entire time, putting the charm on for me like he did with every other girl. I'm just sorry it took me so long to notice it.

"I know this is a lot to handle. I'm still processing everything myself, but we need to be adults about this and put our feelings for one another, no matter how bad, aside. We have a child coming end of March and even though we are not together, we have a lot to talk about."

He's silent on the other end, and my patience wears thin. "Hello?"

"I'm sorry, Lottie." His voice comes through weak, small. And despite saying nothing at all, he tells me the one thing I need to know.

"No," I respond instantly. "No, Beck. You don't get to do this. This child needs a father. You need to pull your shit together and be there for them. I don't care how I feel about you—I will do anything to make sure this baby has everything it needs."

"You don't need two parents in life, Lottie. Especially not a dad like me. I've had weeks to think about it and my mind is made up. There is still so much I want to do. I can't have a kid—I'm only twenty-eight."

"Are you fucking kidding me? You're only twenty-eight? I'm twenty-five, you dickhead. Do you think a child was part of my plan? Fuck no, but it's here and it's happening, so you need to pull your shit together."

"I'm sorry, Lottie. I've made up my mind, and I'm not going to change it. Trust me when I say you'll be better off without me."

My breath is choppy as I process what he's telling me. In all the scenarios I imagined, never once did I think he wouldn't show up for his own child. This information only solidifies the fact I never really knew him at all.

"Have you told her yet?" a female voice whispers in the background of Beck's call. I can tell from the rustling that he pulls the phone away, but the idiot isn't smart enough to mute it.

"I'm doing it now, Francesca. Just give me a minute," he whispers back, the dickhead forgetting to cover his microphone.

Francesca.

At the mention of her name, my spine straightens and my skin goes cold. I mean, who wouldn't feel this way when they find out their ex is with the girl he cheated on them with?

"You stupid fucking prick," I say on impulse, each word low and cold.

A warm hand covers my own, my attention snapping to Owen. He gives me a reassuring smile and I try not to cry at the warmth from it.

"Fuck, shit, Lottie," he pleads, "I didn't mean for you to hear her. I didn't mean for any of this to happen." He almost whines, like a small child who isn't getting a dozen new toys for Christmas. Images of Dudley from Harry Potter crowds my mind.

"I'm sorry my pregnancy is an inconvenience to you, Beck, but it's also my reality. Yet upon reflection, you're right. We don't need you, because there are millions of single mums in the world. In fact, one of the best people I know was raised by one." I pause, looking over at Owen. "So, you're right. We don't need you. I fear you'd only complicate it. Don't call me again— you had your chance." As I hang up, I realize whom I've been talking to all along: a coward.

With an extra pep in my movements, I slam my finger against the End button, then return my attention to the man next to me.

"I think that went well," I manage to get out before bursting into tears. As usual, Owen is there to catch me as I fall. He pulls me into him and rubs my back in silence, offering me the comfort that Beck should have given.

"Guy's a dickhead, Lo. As you said, I'm proof a single mum can raise good humans."

I look up at him through watery vision as he gives me his million-dollar smile. I can't help but laugh, wiping away the mess on my face.

"A total dickhead," I confirm, desperately wishing I could have a glass of wine right now.

Sitting up, I pull out of Owen's embrace, not wanting to accidentally cross any lines between the two of us. Things are already so complicated, and I don't have it in me to deal with more.

"Fuck, puppy. What the hell am I going to do? I'm single and twenty-five with a baby on the way. I'm going to lose my job and won't be able to support the baby or myself. I'm going to be a huge joke, and everyone will know." I hiccup, using the end of my jumper to wipe my face.

"Hey." His voice cuts through my small sobs, his hand finding my face and turning it toward him. "You're no joke. You're intelligent, kind, funny, and beautiful. I have no doubts that all of that will contribute to you being an amazing mother. I'm not saying we can work this out in a night—it will take time—but I promise we will."

I turn my entire body to face him, his hand leaving my face in the process.

"Why are you even here, Owen? I mean, this baby doesn't belong to you and you barely know me. Why are you being so kind and helpful? I'm not some damsel who needs saving. I can do this. I'm perfectly capable."

He looks at me with eyes I'd usually regard as pitying, but having come to know Owen, I know it's just sympathy and understanding. I'm not sure what I feel is worse.

"I think you're the last person on this earth who needs saving, Lottie. But sometimes, even the strongest people need a little help. I don't want to save you. I want to help you."

He's silent for a few moments, his deep blue eyes connecting with my own, as if some cosmic force is pulling us together. I would try to look away, but the truth is, I don't want to.

"When my mum got pregnant with my baby brother, she was all alone. I was the only person who could help her, and even I couldn't do everything she needed. It crushed me as a kid to hear her crying alone at night when she thought I was sleeping, or her panic to make sure she gave me as much attention as the new baby. It was hard on her, Lottie, really hard, and I never really forgot it."

He runs his hand across his mouth before he continues. "I'm not going to lie to you, Lottie. When I first saw you, you captured my attention instantly. You had this wit about you, and our banter just felt so easy. I was interested, but as soon as you shut that shit down, I saw the possibility of a friendship between us. Before Stana came along, Em was the only female friend I'd had. People see me and instantly assume that I'm either an idiot or a player. I'm not saying the latter hasn't been true, but there is more to me, and I felt like you saw it.

"So yeah, I was drawn to you. And maybe this whole thing is weird and unconventional because we haven't known one another for that long, but I don't care. I don't care because you've become an important person in my life, and I want to be there for you. So please, without an ulterior motive at play, *let me.*"

Stunned into silence for only the second time in my life, I eye Owen, attempting to process all he's just said.

"Okay," I reply honestly. "You can be here."

His lips, which were previously in a line, tilt upward at my response, his tall frame rising up from the couch.

"Great, because we still have the rest of the Star Wars franchise to watch and I wasn't going to leave anyway."

I toss a pillow at him, just missing as he dips into the kitchen.

"At least get me some popcorn while you're up."

"As you wish!" he calls back.

"Thanks, puppy."

I chuckle to myself as he groans in the kitchen, my earlier feelings of despair momentarily gone.

"Darling, are you sure you're okay?" Joan, the head pharmacist at the chemist, looks me over. Her bright red cat-eye glasses sit at the tip of her nose, her big brown eyes magnified.

"I swear I'm okay. I just skipped breakfast and it's made me a little dizzy." I munch on the muesli bar she handed me, attempting to keep it down. It's only a little over three months into this pregnancy, but so far I'm going through hell. The morning sickness is unparalleled, and don't get me started on the dizzy spells.

Joan looks me over one more time before going to serve a customer. I doubt she's fully convinced, but I'm not ready to spill the beans. She's been working here over twenty years and has four children of her own, so I'm sure she's clued in. But she would never ask, and therefore I don't have to tell...well, not just yet.

I scarf down the rest of my bar, feeling a little better before going back to serve the next person in line.

Henry's Chemist was the first place I got a job post-uni, and I stayed here until Beck swept me off to Edinburgh earlier this year. Luckily, Joan and I stayed in contact. Otherwise I'd be not only pregnant, but also jobless.

I quickly check myself over in my compact mirror, thankful my mascara hasn't smudged and that I don't look too disheveled. I pull at my sleeves, making sure they cover the tattoos on my arm. It's not a policy, but I know they prefer a more polished look behind the counter. My feet wiggle in my black combat boots, my only touch of personality in this entire getup.

I take a deep breath, centering myself, now ready to serve whoever comes my way.

"So, are you bringing Noel tomorrow?" Stana leans against the brown table at Saint Street, her vision directed at Em. I keep sipping my mineral water, thankful that my stomach hasn't decided to revolt against this morning's breakfast.

"I might be," Emilia replies, her voice coy in regard to the lad she is dating. Stana wants to cook dinner for all of us, a sort of pre-housewarming for close friends before the party they're having later in the month.

"I'm so excited." Stana beams. "Ali thinks I'm over-catering, but imagine if we didn't have enough food." The look of pure horror that crosses her face as she talks about her first dinner party that she's hosting tomorrow makes me laugh.

"I think you're going to be fine," I tell her.

"Are you going to bring anyone, Lottie?"

We're all quiet for a moment from Em's question, my mind wanting to yell, "Just bringing my baby!" But I hold off.

"Nah, just myself. I think it's going to be a while before I jump into the dating pond again." I mean it more in regard to the fact I'm pregnant, but since neither of the girls know that, I assume they take it to mean because of Beck.

"You'll meet someone extraordinary one day, Lo. I know it can be hard to see the light when you're used to so much darkness, but it will happen."

I smile at Stana and her words of reassurance, taking her hand in mine.

"I know," I confirm. "To be completely honest, it's not even Beck. I'm just not ready to jump into anything."

"What about Owen?" Em throws out, the time I've been spending with him apparent.

"We're just friends, honestly. It's been nice to be around a bloke who isn't a total lying snake."

They nod.

"Owen is good people, Lottie. People are quick to judge him because he's so attractive and chats up the ladies. They just assume there's no substance underneath," Em tells me, her voice fierce with the loyalty she holds for her friend. It only makes me love her more.

I think back to the first time I met Owen. I might have had similar preconceived notions, notions that now make my heart ache, because every word Emilia is saying is correct.

"I know, Em. He's probably one of the most compassionate people I know," I find myself admitting.

"Plus, he loves his mum!" Emilia adds in, a grin overtaking her face.

At the mention of his mum, Evie, my heart grows weary. I've yet to meet her and I worry she'll be cautious of me due to my relationship with Owen. From what I know, she's a surrogate mum to Emilia after the death of both of her parents, plus she has everyone over for Sunday dinners frequently. But she's been overseas the past year, hence why Stana and I don't know her yet.

"Very true," Stana throws in.

"Well, you'd know," I can't help but reply. When Stana first moved to London, Owen set his sights on her right away. Obviously things didn't work out romantically, but there must have been something there.

Stana turns to me, eyes wide. "Owen's like my brother, Lottie. I know it's hard to grasp because you only heard my side of it through the phone, but the fact we even considered a romance is laughable now." She brushes it all off and I know she means every word, but it's just that little nagging thing that rears its head in my mind every so often.

"It's true, Lottie. Everyone knew Ali and Stana were endgame. Owen will be the first to admit that now."

I avoid eye contact, trying to seem unaffected before I change the topic to tomorrow's dinner party, my mind lingering on how Owen rarely brings up Stana, yet I seem to be stuck on that more than usual these days. And it's I'm thinking about it at all that scares me.

My head hangs in the toilet as I wait for the rest of my lunch to come up. It's not long till I'm dry-retching into the loo.

"Jesus Christ," I mutter. "You just had to go and get knocked up, didn't you, Charlotte?" I scold myself, hating the morning sickness that just won't fuck off.

"I've got some tea here." Owen places the hot mug on the counter, thankfully the scent of chamomile not making my stomach dance.

"Thanks, puppy. But you really don't need to be here. Stana and Ali are having their dinner party tonight and you shouldn't miss it because I can't keep a meal down."

Finally feeling as though I'm not going to puke, I stand up, then rinse my mouth out at the sink before going for my tea.

Owen stands behind me, my body practically warming to his presence as usual. I stare in the mirror, hoping I don't look too disgusting. Slight bits of dark brown roots peek out from my head, the absence of my hair appointments already prominent.

"You look fine." Owen's voice is gentle in his attempt to calm me.

"Fine?" I laugh. "Puppy, word to the wise, no girl wants to be told she looks fine."

He grins back at me, giving as good as he gets. "We both know you always look great, Lottie. What are you worried about?"

I roll my eyes, unable to take his compliment, so I change the subject, something I've become quite good at recently.

"Anyway, enough about that. Back to tonight. I really think you should go."

He shakes his head, my gaze going to his freshly cut blond hair.

"Well, it's too late. I've already texted them saying I have to work."

"Owen!" I chastise him. "You didn't need to do that. You can't keep putting your social life on hold because some girl you know got pregnant." I try to push past him, but his warm hand covers my arm.

"We both know you're not just some girl, Lottie."

I lock eyes with him, nodding, because we both know it's true. Our strange relationship has become so much more than acquaintanceship, but it never crosses that invisible line. It's as if we've both acknowledged there could be more with one another, yet at the same time we've never actually said it aloud.

"I need to sit down," I say, changing the subject. "Want to eat shit and watch crappy TV with me?" I don't wait for his reply as I pull snacks out of the pantry before throwing myself onto my couch. A fuzzy blanket sits at my feet and my insides warm. Owen must have pulled that out for me earlier. As the month of October moves along, so does the chill that creeps into the air and my flat. London is all fun and games until the cold comes back, and that is most of the time.

"So?" I call out to him when he emerges from the bathroom and leans against my doorframe. I try not to let my gaze trail over the outline of his biceps against the T-shirt he wears, or the way his jeans meld to his skin without being obnoxiously tight. Or his tan skin against that golden-blond hair. *Nope. No, Lottie, pull it together.*

I avert my gaze to Owen's face, which now holds a smirk as he's caught me.

"Please, feel free to stare. I'm here all day."

I roll my eyes and throw the nearest pillow at him, then turn back to the TV to pick the newest *Real Housewives of OC.*

Owen's broad frame moves around my room before stopping in front of a photograph of me as a child that's perched on my mantle.

"This you?" he asks, staring down at two-year-old me. I'm flashing a big smile and in my favourite yellow dress with pigtails.

"The one and only," I confirm. "It was my second birthday and my parents had gone all out—Mum dressed me to the nines. She said I refused to take that dress off all week, and she had to wash it daily."

"You still have it?"

"The dress?"

He nods.

I shrug. "No. Mum kept all my baby stuff, but most of it was lost in one of their moves. We still have a few things, but not much. This little gal will be getting a whole new wardrobe." I grin, rubbing my flat stomach.

Owen smiles at the photo before placing it back with care and coming over to me. He loses the look on his face when he spots what we're watching.

"Oh God, Lottie, not Orange County," he begs, my couch dipping as he sits down next to me.

I grin, knowing this is his least favorite of the franchise. And I say "least favorite" because he does in fact have a favorite, although I'm sure he'd never admit it outside this flat. It's the New York housewives, if you're wondering. His mum, Evie, is obsessed, hence pulling Owen in with her.

"But I haven't seen this week," I say, pouting. "Please, just this one episode, and then we can watch Lord of the whatever or Star Trek."

He nudges my leg. "It's Lord of the Rings and Star Wars." He shakes his head, like how could I possibly not know. It's Owen's little secret that he's a nerd about superheroes and comic books. And I say "nerd" in a totally loving way; I think it's adorable. I'm not even sure it's something he hides. From what I've gathered, no one has ever bothered to really ask.

"Anyway, we have a deal?" I turn and give him my hand, waiting for him to shake it. Finally relenting, he connects his with my own, my mind not able to ignore how instantly my body reacts to him.

DANGER ZONE. ABORT.

I question if he sees it too, because after I pull away as if I've been stung, his hand lingers for a few moments, a pensive look crossing his face.

Neither of us says anything more as the episode begins, my body relaxing a little too much as my mind drifts off to sleep.

The last thing I remember is being lifted from one place of comfort to the next.

I wake up at ten the next day to an empty apartment, tucked tightly into my bed. I don't remember falling asleep or Owen leaving.

Instantly feeling bad for being such a dud, I pull out my phone and see messages from Emilia and Stana hoping I feel better, before I spot one from Owen.

Hey sleepyhead,
I let myself out when your snoring became too much for me to handle.
I've got some work on the next few days, but I'll message you.
O

I quickly reply, apologizing for my suckiness before pulling myself out of bed, my shift starting in two hours. Pulling off my pajamas, I stare into my full-length mirror, my pale skin bright against the darkness of my curtained bedroom. My hands can't resist slowly moving over my flat stomach. Not even a little sign there is a tiny human growing inside of me.

To be completely honest, the concept hasn't fully sunk in yet. I mean, I've had a few doctor's appointments and am taking care of myself, but besides that, I think I'm still trying to grasp the situation I've landed myself in.

I know absolutely nothing about children, and I'm pretty sure there are only so many books one can read before needing some real hands-on experience. I am not exactly maternal. I'm blunt and although it comes from a place of love, I don't think you're supposed to be that way with kids.

"Fuck," I yell out before wanting to chastise myself. You can't swear in front of kids; I'm pretty sure that's the number-one rule. And here I am like a bloody sailor.

Attempting to ignore my epic fails, I throw on some of my favorite black jeans that probably only have a month or two of wear left in them before I blow up.

My mobile goes off next to my bed as I'm attempting to pull a yellow sweater over my head. I grab it, righting myself before answering.

"If you called any later, I would have had to put out a missing person's report!" I yell into the phone, sitting down on my bed as I talk to my mother.

"Lottie, my darling, how are you?" My mother's cheery accent flows through the phone, and I can only imagine the shenanigans she's gotten up to. Despite my parents' departure from London three years ago, we've stayed close. This is the first time I've heard from her in a week, so I'd guess she's living her best life.

"I'm good, Mum. How are you? How's Dad?"

"Oh, Lottie, you wouldn't believe it. We've been on safari for the past week and had no service to call! I hope we didn't worry you, my dear."

I shake my head, despite them not being able to see me. "I had a feeling that was the case, Mum. You and Dad off on yet another adventure." I grin, happy the two of them can live their life to the fullest.

"I just wish you'd come with us one of these days. You really are missed."

There is something about the connection I formed with my parents being an only child. I really feel as if it can go one of two ways. Either you become close or the pressure pushes you apart. I'm lucky my situation was the former. Poor Stana hasn't been so lucky. Although my mum and her dad are siblings, there isn't a lot of similarity between them, travel probably being the only one.

While Stana's parents love her, their life has always been focused on the two of them. It wasn't abnormal for Stana to fit into their plans rather than them fitting in around hers, and occasionally they'd forget about her in full. Her mum sees what she wants to and while her dad is a nice guy, he's just as clueless. I know I'm probably a harsh critic of them, but they let Stana fade away in Los Angeles and never noticed anything was wrong. That bothers me.

While my mum and dad have their flaws, they've always put me first and taken care of me. Even now when I'm twenty-five, they still want me to gallivant with them on their global travels.

"You know I'd love to, but I have work and commitments here, Mum. I can't just leave it all."

She sighs. "Of course I understand. I'm so proud of you and all your accomplishments. I know this year has been less than ideal, but you're coming out on top, just like you always do."

At her words, a tightness climbs my throat. If only she knew just how much is going on, but like with the girls, I'm not ready to tell her and Dad. I've never been one to overly rely on others; I feel if I want something done, then I must do it myself. This situation is no different. Plus, I know my parents—they would take the first flight home and probably try to stay here until the baby comes, and that's the last thing I need.

"Thanks, Mum. It hasn't been the easiest year, but I'm lucky to have a home and great friends, so I can't fully complain."

"Oh, that reminds me. How is Stana doing?"

Mum is far too familiar with the situation between Stana and her parents.

"She's really good. Moved in with Ali and has gone back to uni for a master's."

"Good." I can practically hear her happiness through the phone. "I always knew it would work out for her. Things did get rocky there, but I think having you around is exactly what she needed."

I smile. "I think we needed one another."

Our call continues, Mum explaining her next dream destination, knowing her, I'm sure they will be going next year. I give her life updates, but the details all feel rather meaningless with the huge secret I'm keeping. And despite my mind screaming at me to be honest with her, I hold my tongue. Even though secrets can eat away at you, I'll let this one take a small bit of me because I'm just not ready. Not yet, anyway.

Six

The week drags on, work overtaking every aspect of my life, so I don't even have time to see the girls. It's been hard keeping this from them, but I know it's what I need to do right now. I attempted to call Beck again, figuring he deserved one more shot, but it's been over a month now since he found out and his tune hasn't changed.

I haven't seen Owen since I fell asleep during our movie, his work having become more intense than usual. I try to tell myself it doesn't bother me, that I need to get used to being alone, but the pang is still there.

It's nine p.m. when I decide to call it a night, after a day of doing nothing. I attempted to read a baby book but got distracted by my phone and here I am, a whole day later without accomplishing anything besides spilling dip on my top.

It doesn't take me long to get to sleep, my stomach no longer rioting against anything I've fed it. I'm finally relaxed, my body relishing in the quiet, when a loud *pop* pulls me out of my slumber, accompanied by the sound of water.

I bolt out of bed like the devil leaving hell, my mind in a panic over what's happened. Rushing out of my room, I shove my cold feet into my unicorn slippers, a gift from Stana for my birthday that she missed in June.

It doesn't take me long to figure out the noise is none other than a burst pipe in my bathroom, water spraying absolutely everywhere, saturating my pale pink bathmat and spurting all across the walls.

"Fuck, shit, fuck," I say, quickly jumping back from the mess. I may have scientific skills in life, but handy ones are out of the question. I have no fucking idea how to clean or fix this mess.

So, despite vowing I wouldn't call, I pick up the phone and dial the number of the only person I can think of to help. Well, more like the only person I want to help.

Thirty minutes later, Owen's standing in my bathroom, both of us looking at the mini pool residing on my floor. The liquid has seeped out of the bathroom and found its way into my bedroom, causing what I can only begin to imagine is a hellish list of problems if I don't get this fixed right. Can't mold grow this way? Or what if animals got in or bugs? My skin crawls at the thought of the long-term issues I'm going to have from five inches of water spilling out of the bathroom and into my home.

"Well, I've stopped the water from coming out, but it's going to keep leaking. You can't stay here tonight, Lottie. I can have a mate come fix this in the morning, but no one will be around for a reasonable price at this hour."

I tighten my dressing robe around myself, looking up at Owen. He still looks pristine, so I know he hadn't yet gone to bed, but I still manage to feel like shit for ruining his night.

"Fuck," I say, pulling on the ends of my hair, taking in all the mess that is my home. Of fucking course this shit happens. And Lord knows I'm going to need all the money I can get with this baby coming along, so paying double for someone to fix this all tonight isn't an option.

"I'll call Stana," I mumble, my feet doing a weird dance as I maneuver my way back to the dry area in the kitchen. My unicorn slippers take the brunt of the water, the little horns wilting from water retention.

"I'm here now," Owen says from behind me, the outside of his boots already a darkened brown from the water. "Pack a bag and you can crash at my place."

I shake my head, ready to protest. "Owen, I can't do that. I've already put you out enough, forcing you to drop your plans to help me. God, this is all so fucked."

"Lottie…" His softened voice catches me off guard. I turn, finally meeting his eyes. "It's okay to need someone else. I know you hate being helpless, and trust me when I say you're probably the least helpless person I've met. But you can't stay here tonight, and Stana and Ali are probably already asleep. We all know they're a hundred at heart."

I can't help but let a small laugh sneak through my lips. Stana and Ali are homebodies, that's for sure.

Owen smiles at me, warmth radiating off every ounce of him, and as much as I'd like to say "fuck this" and attempt to handle it myself, I realize the adult thing to do in this situation is ask for help.

So instead of fighting him, I nod, then dart back to my room to collect a few things I'll need for tonight. I see him on the phone when I come out, and he quickly says his goodbyes before we exit my flat.

I continue on with my silence, my mind unable to avoid the meaning behind me calling him tonight. I really could have called anyone else, but I chose not to. And I'm scared the longer I avoid being honest with Owen and myself, the worse any potential heartbreak could be between us.

Without asking, Owen takes my bag from my shoulder and slings it over his own. His tall frame mixed with the streetlamps casts a shadow against the dimly lit Notting Hill streets. My body warms from how comfortable and familiar being around him feels.

It's not till we're in the cab that I finally break the silence, somehow feeling as if the darkness will protect me.

My voice blends into the dullness of the radio, Moby's "Porcelain" our background noise. "I do like doing things on my own, Owen. But I'm also not too prideful to know when to say thank you. So, thank you. I really don't know what I would have done without you tonight."

Owen's hand comes to rest atop my own, giving me his version of comfort. "That's what friends are for, Lottie."

"You know, you didn't have to kick Reeve out." I attempt to keep a firm voice, but I can't really be mad at him. I look around his apartment, attempting to take it all in. It really is a mix of Reeve and Owen. There is a sterile aspect to it that I attribute to Reeve, very minimalist, while the wall has a few movie posters, one being *Wedding Crashers* with *The Godfather* posted right next to it.

"What's so funny?" Owen comes up beside me, handing me a water while he has a beer. That's one thing I appreciate about him; he doesn't treat me with kid gloves, apologizing that I can't drink and refusing to himself. I think he learned early on that would drive me mental.

"Your posters, they're kinda polar opposites, don't you think?"

He looks at the wall, his brow furrowed. "Nope."

"You're telling me, someone who doesn't even know film, that *Wedding Crashers* and *The Godfather* are on the same level?"

"Vince Vaughn and Owen Wilson are a masterful comedic duo."

Not able to hold it in any longer, I burst out laughing. "I'm actually not even a little bit surprised you like them. What I am surprised about is that Reeve let you put them up."

"It was a hard sell, but I managed." He grins, motioning toward the couch. I walk over with him, still finding joy in Owen's ability to positively look at life. He doesn't give a shit if someone will judge him, and I fucking love that.

Okay, Lottie, slow your roll.

I sit down on his black couch, placing my water on the empty coffee table. Both definitely a Reeve contribution.

"You think something's going on between Reeve and Emilia?" His question catches me off guard, especially his willingness to talk about his best friend with me.

"Um…" I laugh, unsure how to respond. "I never took you as one for a gossip session, puppy." I relax into his couch, my body sinking into all the right parts. It feels like a fucking cloud. Jesus, I could stay here all day.

Owen launches himself onto the other end, then moves his body until he's comfortable. He brings his beer up to his lips and takes a sip.

God, I wish I could have one of those.

"Oh, come on, Lottie. Don't play all innocent with me. I know how you operate."

I raise my eyebrows. "What's that supposed to mean?" My voice is playful, because Lord knows I'm anything but innocent. I think back to everything I did to Beck post breakup. Yep, not innocent, but it was certainly deserved on his part.

"Okay, maybe I'm not a poster child for good behavior, but I don't really think I'm in a position to be questioning anyone else keeping secrets right now. I mean…" I motion to my stomach, and Owen nods in agreement.

"It's not like I'm talking to a stranger; you're in our group now. Emilia's one of your best friends, Reeve's mine— hell, both of them are like family to me. Don't tell me curiosity hasn't gotten the best of you sometimes."

I purse my lips, figuring if there is anyone I can talk about shit with, it's Owen. He's loyal, definitely wouldn't tell anyone.

"Okay, I don't know anything, but yeah, I've questioned it. But Reeve is so silent and stoic, it's hard to know what the hell he's about all the time."

"That's just Reeve," Owen cuts in. "He's actually pretty chill when you get to know him better. But lately he's been on edge, so one can only assume it has to do with Emilia."

"God," I say, leaning back, "relationships are messy—I get that more than anyone—but this seems like we're reaching. I mean, Emilia is dating Noel!"

Owen eyes me. "I call time of death on that."

I can't help but laugh. "That's terrible."

"I'm not being mean, Lottie, but it's Em we're talking about. She's got too much life in her—Noel wouldn't be able to keep up. Trust me, I went to uni with the guy."

"I guess you're not wrong there. What about you, Owen? Any special ladies you're hiding from us?" The question is supposed to be lighthearted, a change of subject from our friends, but instead I think I've stepped in some quicksand and despite how much I want to get out of it, I'm stuck.

Owen's gaze connects with my own, his smile slightly falling, but he masks it. Not very well, though, might I add.

"I've never really been in a committed relationship," he admits, sparking my curiosity that always manages to get me into trouble.

"How come? I mean, I've seen you. You're not exactly hard to look at."

His gaze detaches from my own for a moment, as if staring into his hands will suddenly present him with the answers he needs.

"It's not that I have a hard time with women. I hadn't found anyone I wanted to bring home to Mum." He tries to laugh it off, but I see what he isn't saying.

"It matters to you," I whisper.

His eyes find my own again and he nods.

"You want the white picket fence and the two-point-five kids?" I lean forward, attempting to keep my voice casual, but I know I've pulled back a layer of Owen that not many people get the privilege to see.

"Is it so bad to want that?" he asks me.

I shake my head. "I think it's perfectly okay to."

"I could see how people would think that that stuff doesn't matter to me. I've never had a serious relationship, and I joke around a lot. It's easier to look at a guy like Ali and pinpoint him as the one to want that stable home life. But I guess since I grew up with such a powerhouse of a mother and was so close to my brother, it made me realize pretty early on that I want that, but I also won't settle for anything less. So maybe that's why I've yet to fully commit to anyone. I hadn't met a girl who I saw more than a weekend with."

Hadn't met.

Fuck me and my fucking brain for being stuck on the word "hadn't."

"You're a good person, Owen. You're incredibly kind and caring, far more than you'd ever take credit for. Hell, you befriended a pregnant girl for no other reason than the fact that you wanted to help."

"Hey," he says quickly, raising a hand. "I met you before you were pregnant, Lottie. And it was that ten-second introduction that told me all I needed to know, that I saw you as

82

someone who could be in my life. I never want you to think I'm staying here out of pity or obligation just because I'm the only one who knows. And if I need to, I'll dispel any other preconceived notions you have right now. That first night I met you in Saint Street, there was a connection there. You can deny it all you want, but we both felt it. It was that connection that made me want to know you. So yeah, you ended up finding out a life-changing revelation a few weeks later, but either way, whether you're pregnant or not, I want to be in your life. I just think the capacity of how much you'll *let* me be has to shift."

"I remember hearing all about you from Stana during her first few months in town." I fiddle with my glass of water, my stomach suddenly rejecting anything else.

Owen looks up at me, his dark blond eyebrows coming together, yet he says nothing. Sure, maybe this was the wrong thing to say after what he's just put forward, but the nagging question pulls at my mind. I've always been the spokesperson for if you have something on your mind, say it. But right now, I feel as though I might have entered a danger zone I can't get out of.

So I smile, my attempt to keep things lighthearted. "You had quite the fascination with my cousin." My voice isn't dark or deepening, each note with more cheer than intended so he doesn't think this is some kind of interrogation. Hell, Owen and I are friends despite those underlying feelings yelling that it could have been otherwise. Yet we both know I'm in no position to reach for something else with him. But alas, my entire life I've had an illness called curiosity. Mix that with my big mouth, and I can't exactly stay quiet about my questions in regard to his feelings toward my cousin.

"That was a long time ago, Lottie," Owen replies, his smile fading. I focus my attention on my nails, still keeping up the smile.

"Less than a year," I reply, even though I agree that that life feels like decades ago. How so much has managed to change in so little time… I didn't even know Owen at the start of the year, and now I can't imagine a life without him.

"A lot can change in a few months. I think you know that more than anyone, Charlotte." His gaze is piercing, making my body squirm and my hands dig into my legs. Owen never calls me by my first name unless he's feeling serious, I've come to learn, and with him, it's almost always jokes.

"Very true," I say, appeasing him, no longer satisfied with myself for beginning this line of questioning. Again, I try to change the subject, as if the mere action can brush off the feelings I'm starting to have a very hard time avoiding.

"Hey," he says, his hand suddenly on my leg, pulling me away from my thoughts. I turn to him, the look of determination in his eyes scary.

"It would be a lie to say I wasn't drawn to Stana and yes, I did pursue her."

My chest aches, a realization that knocks the air right out of me. I'm not a jealous person, but the thought that Owen would want to be with Stana does something disastrous to my insides.

"But nothing ever happened. It was a few weeks out of my entire life, and it's clear to me now, more than ever, that what I was feeling for her was friendship. I'd never want to change how things turned out, Lottie. Stana's like a sister to me, nothing more."

I place my hand on his leg. "You don't have to explain yourself, Owen." I attempt to reassure him, suddenly overwhelmed by the weight of the conversation we've ended up in.

My other hand rests upon my still-flat stomach, my personal comfort when everything feels so uncertain. I don't usually realize I do it, but more often than not, I look down and there is my hand.

He looks as if he wants to say more, so I pop up from the couch, deciding to retreat to the kitchen. "I'm going to make a cuppa. Want one?"

Not able to stand the dejected look on his face as he shakes his head, I focus all my attention on making my tea, pushing out all thoughts of why in the hell I started up this conversation to begin with.

Seven

"You know, I've been thinking about it, and I'm surprised we never met before Stana introduced us." Owen carries over a Coke for me and a beer for himself. My mind questions how he can still wear a white T-shirt when it's so bloody freezing out.

"I mean, London isn't exactly a small city." I nod in thanks when he passes me my drink, thankful no one questions why I'm not drinking. Em and Reeve both have other work commitments, so it's just Stana, Ali, Owen, and me this afternoon. We've still got a few hours until Saint Street opens, all of us reveling in the peace.

"Actually, that's a good point," Stana adds in, her body angled into Ali. He runs his hand up and down her shoulder in calming strokes.

"It is?" I ask her.

"I mean, think about it. You're who introduced me to Saint Street. I'd never have come here if you didn't first," she says.

At that Owen's face perks up. "You used to come to Saint Street before we met Stana?"

I nod, my mind drifting back to the days when I'd come to see the guys perform with girlfriends or even Beck.

"And when I first moved here, she told me it was her favorite pub, plus they had a killer band." The cheer in her voice makes me seem like a little fangirl. Jesus Lord, help me.

"I don't think I said it like that," I protest, my gaze digging into hers.

"No, I'm pretty sure those were your exact words."

I roll my eyes at her before taking a sip of my drink.

Owen, who can't seem to get enough of this development, turns to me. "A fan, huh?" He grins at me while I resist the urge to shove his arm.

"I think that's taking it too far," I tell him. "I used to come here with some friends occasionally, and it just happened to be a lot of the time you were all performing."

"So, you already kinda knew us when we met?" Owen says.

I rub my hand over my wet glass, my fingers picking up the condensation. "I mean, I didn't *know* you, but I definitely recognized you."

"I can't believe I never saw you before," he says more to himself than anyone else.

"Heaps of people come to see you guys perform. It's really not that surprising. Plus I was always with people, so…" I shrug, not really sure what else to say.

"Ali"—Owen turns to him—"did you recognize Lottie?"

Ali leans forward and places his beer on the table. "I'd never formally met her, but I'd seen her around," he says, surprising even me.

"Really?" Stana asks him, smiling.

He nods. "I've always got to keep an eye on the place. You remember some faces more than others. Plus, I saw her the first night she brought *you* in here."

Stana beams, clearly thinking back to her first night here. Her first sighting of Ali.

"Huh," Owen mutters to himself.

"Owen," I say, touching his arm, smiling, "it's honestly not a big deal you don't remember me. We're friends now and that's what matters."

"Of course." His voice is casual as he leans back in his chair. I try not to read into why it bothers him so much that he doesn't remember me from my frequent visits to Saint Street.

The next day, I'm heading to work after finally getting a good night's rest.

"Do you need me to pick anything up?" I speak into my mobile as I cross the paved street of Notting Hill, making sure to look both ways so I don't become roadkill.

"No, I think Owen is handling most of it. It may not always seem like it, but Owen has a tendency to go above and beyond, especially for birthdays. Lad can never pass up the opportunity for a party," Em replies, an airiness to her voice. The other night Owen had the idea to throw a joint birthday for Stana, Reeve, and Ali, despite Ali's birthday not being until early Jan, at least two months away. I think Owen just wanted a reason for us all to get together. If I weren't pregnant, I'd jump at the idea of drinking with my mates, celebrating. But this year it feels a little somber, my mind still not thinking this is the right time to come clean.

"I'm starting to learn that." I laugh, finally arriving at work, slipping past the small queue of customers and into the back room. I still have ten minutes before my shift starts, so you best believe I'm taking my time. Joan sees me as I sit down, giving me a small wave before disappearing to the front.

Em and I speak for a few more minutes before I have to go, my shift starting in five. We hang up with our plans finalized to see one another tonight at the party.

I lean back against the metal chair, a sliver of my wool jumper riding up, exposing skin on my back to the cold rod. Attempting to get more comfortable and relieve my back pain, I move around, but it's too little relief. Despite only being twenty weeks pregnant, my body feels as though it's going to crap out on me at any moment. I've even started seeing the physical changes this month. My previously flat stomach has rounded slightly, but it's still subtle enough that I can easily hide it.

Thankfully the morning sickness dissipated when I entered my second trimester, making me able to do longer hours at work. I know Owen thinks I need to take it easy, but he isn't the one bringing a baby into the world alone. He never says it out loud—it isn't his style to outwardly judge—but I've come to learn his tells. Like that he's almost too quiet when I talk about things he disagrees with.

It's funny, I think so many people look at Owen and see this big sexy goofball, and sure, he definitely is, but there are so many layers to that man, I could start peeling them back today and I don't know if I'd ever get to the center.

"Lottie?" Joan's voice jerks me out of my Owen-centered thoughts and I quickly stand, making sure my jumper is pulled all the way down.

"Sorry, hun, but we are so swamped. Do you mind helping out Ms. Meyers?"

I nod and head over to the counter, ready to earn every single dollar.

"Are you sure it's okay I crash?" Although it's probably too late to ask the question, as we're already in the car, I can't help myself. Intruding on Owen's family lunch feels weird, especially since I've yet to meet his mother, stepfather, or younger brother. But from what Owen has said Hugo won't be here today, so I guess it's meet-the-parents day.

"Lottie, relax," Owen says next to me, a grin still plastered to his face over the fact he's driving my parents' vintage BMW. Mum called me a few days ago and said I need to use the car more to make sure it keeps running smoothly. I'm not sure if that's an actual thing or if she's just being generous, but I didn't need to be told twice.

So this morning when Owen surprised me with news I was meeting his family, it didn't take me too long to decide we'd take my car.

"I just don't want your mum to feel like I'm intruding on your family time. I know she's been traveling the past year, and

I don't want it to seem like I'm running her time with her children."

"Lottie, are you nervous?" I don't need to look at him to see he's grinning, showing off all those pearly whites. I hear the smile in his voice.

"Well, duh, Owen. She's your mum. Of course I'm nervous."

"She's been home for a while—she's fine. Plus she really wants to meet you."

I freeze up at the statement, clutching the silver door handle next to me.

"Does she know?" I ask, my voice low, almost a whisper. Owen knows this secret about me, he's the only one, and although I'd understand if he wanted to confide in his mother, it's not something I would want. I don't need pity or charity, especially in the form of a Sunday lunch. Yes, I know I sound like an asshole, but if Owen's spilled the metaphorical beans, then I fear this will be me dropping him off and speeding back to my flat.

I must have gone silent, because Owen's hand leaves the wheel and comes to rest upon my own that's sitting on the center console.

"I'd never break your confidence like that, Lottie. Mum just knows we're new friends and to be totally honest, she's a bit of a busybody. She thinks of anyone I care about as a surrogate child at this point, so it isn't a shock to me she wants to meet you."

I try not to let my mind linger on the "care about" aspect, knowing I'm already far too invested in this friendship with Owen. Now I'm meeting his mother and this could really go one of two ways. I just hope she doesn't view me as someone stringing her son along. Guess I'll find out in less than twenty minutes.

Evie is probably the kindest human I've ever met. Plus, Owen is her spitting image. Her blonde hair is pinned up in a twist while black glasses frame her blue eyes, exact replicas of Owen's. Being a family lawyer, she's probably one of the calmest, most centered people I've had the pleasure of meeting.

Despite my initial hesitance about meeting her, as soon as she tugged open the door to her flat, she pulled me into a hug, going on about how excited she was to meet me. It didn't for one second feel disingenuous.

"So, Lottie, Owen tells me you're a pharmacist?" Steve, Owen's stepfather, takes a sip of his wine, looking at me from across the table. He isn't the father to Owen or Hugo. With Owen's dad having passed when he was little, Evie thought she wouldn't meet anyone else, so she decided to do IVF and that's how she got Hugo. Then she eventually met Steve and the rest is history.

"I am," I confirm after swallowing another roast potato. *These are the best fucking potatoes I've ever had.*

Steve smiles at me, his salt-and-pepper hair giving away the ten years he has on Evie, although neither of them looks their age. From what Owen's told me, his mum must be at least fifty, but I would easily say forty.

"I can't say I know many young people becoming chemists these days. It's very impressive." Evie's head nods with Steve's, a small smile tracing her lips.

"Thank you," I say, then take a gulp of my water. Owen sits next to me, digging into his mountain of food Evie served him. She really is a mum, feeding us all and already telling me she wants me to come back soon. It's hard to feel uncomfortable here.

"And you met Owen through Emilia and Alistair?" Steve asks, genuinely curious.

I tilt my head to the side. "Kind of. My cousin, Stana, is dating Ali so I met everyone through her, but I've been lucky enough to become very close with Emilia."

"She's a good girl, my Em." Evie has the look of love and tenderness at the mention of Emilia, who I know is like a surrogate daughter to her.

"She's the best," I confirm.

"Well, we feel very lucky to know you too, Ms. Lottie. My son has only had great things to say about you. And you should know this is the first time my Owen has ever brought a girl home." She winks at me before finishing off the wine in her glass.

I try to swallow the chicken in my mouth, but it suddenly gets stuck, like trying to push a leather shoe down a dry slide.

"Mum," Owen says from next to me, turning to pat me on the back a few times, his face slightly flushed. I take a gulp of water, trying to calm my mortifying coughing fit.

"Sorry," I say, placing a hand against my chest. "Wrong pipe." I grimace, suddenly feeling strangely hot and flustered.

"Don't worry, darling. Steve, get Lottie some more water. Once we finish here, I've got Owen's special chocolate cake for dessert!" She pops up from the table and tries to carry the plates before Owen's much taller form stops her. That's probably the only difference between the two—Owen has at least ten inches on his mother.

"Mum, you cooked. I'll clean." His voice is firm and it's clear he won't take no for an answer.

She pinches his cheeks, scrunching up her face before sitting down.

I stand, then collect what I can as I walk behind Owen to the kitchen. I spot all of Evie's little knickknacks along the way—small collections of trinkets from her life and abroad. I like that about Evie; she isn't cohesive. She's this big bright mixture of everything.

"Lottie, you're a guest. There is no way I'm letting you do the dishes." Owen grabs the dishes from my arms and despite wanting to snatch them back and tell him I can help if I want to, I resist. Instead I sneak back into the dining room and try to collect what is left. Too bad Steve has me beat and nods for me to sit down, both of his hands full.

"I feel like a bit of a leech not helping," I tell Evie as I sit next to her, then grab my water glass and have a few more sips.

"It's the fact you asked to help that matters, Lottie. Owen and Steve can handle doing the dishes." She offers me some wine, which I decline, thankful she clearly has no idea about my condition.

"So, darling girl, tell me about yourself. I want to know it all!"

I laugh and take a sip of my water. "Well, I've lived in London my whole life, only child. I'm a pharmacist, and much to the chagrin of your son, I'm not a movie person."

Evie laughs at the last part. "Well, that tells me you must be special if Owen still keeps you around even though you don't like movies. I'll tell you, Lottie, ever since he was a boy, I could never keep him interested in anything if it wasn't related to film or the drums. Every birthday party he had till he was twelve was superhero or Star Wars themed."

"Really?" I can't help but smile when thinking about a younger Owen and how his obsession has only increased as the years go on.

"Oh yes. Owen once made his entire party watch *Jurassic Park* despite half of them wanting to run for the hills. In hindsight, I suppose that might have been scary for eight-year-olds, but what can I say? Owen knew what he liked."

"He still does," I confirm.

She nods thoughtfully, her lips tilting up at the sides from memories. "I'm sure he's tried to pull you down the rabbit hole?"

I playfully roll my eyes. "You have no idea. I swear I've never watched as many movies in my entire life as I have over the past few months. Half the time I have no idea what's going on, but I don't have the heart to tell him that."

"Oh God no," she jokes. "Would break his wee heart."

We spend the next fifteen minutes laughing with one another, her relaying stories of Owen's childhood as I reveal small bits about myself.

"So, Owen told me your parents live in France?" Evie swirls her glass of wine as she looks at me, her warm blue eyes hauntingly similar to Owen's.

I nod. "Yeah, Mum and Dad moved there nearly four years ago now. We'd lived in London my whole life, but they needed a change and I didn't, so I stayed."

"Do you see them much?"

"Unfortunately, I haven't seen them since Christmas. I've had a lot going on and they're traveling, so we just haven't found the time. I'll probably go visit them in February or something."

As soon as the words leave my mouth, I realize how impossible that visit will be. I'll be nearly eight months pregnant by then, so travel will be off the table. A slight touch of sorrow mars my heart at the thought of it being over a year since I've hugged my mum and dad.

Evie's hand comes to rest atop mine on the table, her array of rings glittering in the light.

"It's hard being without your parents. I don't think it ever gets easier, not at any age. That's probably why I've adopted so many of Owen's friends as my own. I think everyone needs a mum on call when theirs can't be there."

I nod, my throat tightening with emotion.

"You need anything, you call me, okay? I know we just met, but my son doesn't invest time in just anyone, and that tells me all I need to know."

I smile, nodding because once again the Bower family have left me speechless, not an easy feat.

"Now, darling, you said you're seeing your parents next year. What does that mean for your Christmas? Are you staying in London?"

I avoid her sympathetic eyes. "I haven't actually thought about it, to be honest. I'm not sure what Owen's told you, but this year has been pretty challenging for me. I'm still trying to get my bearings. Christmas has been the last thing on my mind."

"Well, it would be an absolute pleasure to host you here, Lottie. I know you don't know me very well, but something tells me we are going to be great friends."

The men come back into the room at that moment, Owen's gaze going straight to where my hands are locked with his mother's, then darting to my face.

He gives me a look to ask if I'm okay, but I nod, letting him know I'm indeed okay. I'm actually more than okay.

"Ooh, cake!" Evie interrupts, clasping her fingers together. "Lottie, you should know this is Owen's absolute favorite chocolate cake in the whole universe."

"Well, I'm excited to try it then." I lean back in the chair as Evie doles out huge slices of chocolatey goodness to everyone. I take a bite and indeed, it's the best fucking cake I've ever had.

I look around Stana and Ali's Shoreditch flat filled to the brim with faces, some familiar and some new. They've been living here for two months now, and this is only the third time I've been able to come over. I feel bad about being a bit absent, but it's clear to me everyone has their own things going on.

Stana is busy finally enjoying her life, being all loved up with Ali and going back to uni. Em is busier than ever with her work, having acquired a big hotel as a client to paint some pieces for. Reeve, well, I'm still not sure about him. Yeah, we're friends, but he's seemed even more distant and aloof than usual. Perhaps it's because I don't know him like I do everyone else, but my mind tells me something is going on there.

I just don't have the energy to dig too deep into it. Lord knows I'm hiding my own secrets. The last thing I need to do is pry about others.

I grin as I watch Stana fling herself at Ali, her hair flying around her face. They are definitely in love, and I don't know if anything could make me happier. Stana hasn't always had the easiest run, so seeing her get this, it's fucking magic.

"She's wasted," Em says from next to me, a slight sway to her words. "And I also might be a tad wasted." She starts nodding, her curly hair pinned up with pieces sticking out. Definitely rocking the sexy art-teacher look, despite not actually trying to. I attempt not to laugh at her, my mind knowing I'd miss all this if I too were drinking. I guess being the sober one has its perks. Does that mean I'm going to stay sober once the baby is born? Fuck no. I need a glass of wine like there's no tomorrow.

"It's a party. You might as well celebrate," I reply, hating how my head automatically scans the crowd.

"Owen's in the kitchen," she tells me, then chugs the rest of her drink. I keep my features neutral as I respond.

"I wasn't looking for him." My voice comes out level, sounds truthful even.

"Okayyyyy," she drawls, "but you know, if you were looking for him, that would be okay too. You know that, right, Lottie? I've seen Owen around you. He cares."

I try to smile at her, but it feels forced, sad.

If only she knew.

Sure, if there were no baby, maybe Owen and I would have had a chance, but that isn't my reality. And now that I've accepted this baby, there is not a single thing I'd do to change the path I'm on.

Turning to Em, I place my hand on her arm. "I know he cares, Em. That's probably his best and worst trait. How much he cares about people." I decide to be truthful for once, because dismissing Owen's attributes feels as if I'd be doing the universe a great disservice. And as much as I can lie about myself, I just can't lie about him.

"Huh?" Her face twists up and I realize I probably shouldn't be going deep while she is three sheets to the wind.

"I'm just being dramatic." I finish my Coke, ready to leave soon. I spot Owen through the crowd of people, walking toward me. He's got a goofy grin on his face, his eyes giving away how much he's had to drink. Good, I'm glad he's letting loose. I worry all he does these days is try to cater to my every need despite my insistence that he live his life.

He's in front of us the next minute, lifting me off the ground and into a big bear hug. Even drunk, he's careful of my stomach. He smells of pine and whiskey. My mind wants me to cling to him and run at the same time.

"Having fun?" I ask, looking up at him.

"Indeed, I am." His big dopey smile is directed at me, and only me. I don't miss how my body warms to him. But tonight only shows me that I need to prioritize my feelings for him. He's got so much life to live and although we can be in one another's as friends, it's important I convince myself of that.

"I'm actually gonna head home, though," I say, not wanting to spoil his fun.

"What, why?" The concern is clear in his gaze as he looks me over, his eyes asking the questions his mouth can't.

I pat his arm, letting him know I'm okay.

"I'm just tired, Owen. It's been a long day and I've got a shift tomorrow morning."

He nods, looking down at my hand resting upon him. Shaking his head, he stands a bit taller. "Yeah, of course. Just give me five and I'll walk you."

"No way, Owen. This party was your idea—I'm not gonna pull you away from it all just because I need to go to bed. I want you to stay, please."

He doesn't reply, pursing his lips as he looks to the ground before coming back to me.

"I'm serious, Owen. I'm fine, and I don't live far anyway. I'm just gonna hail a cab."

I refuse to let him leave, so drunk or not, he'd better understand I'm still my own person. If I tell him I'm leaving alone, he will listen.

"Okay," he finally relents. He smiles, but it doesn't reach his eyes. "If you're sure."

"I'll be fine. Give my love to everyone—I think they're all too wasted to even notice I'm going. I'll call you tomorrow," I say to him and Em.

She gives me a quick hug before walking over to Reeve, each step a little shaky.

"Lottie," Owen finally says to me now we are alone. Well, as alone as you can be in a room full of people.

"Puppy…" I put up my hand. "Stop."

His eyes pinch together as he looks at me. I hate making him feel this way, but I need my independence and I need to reinforce some boundaries. It's a personal thing more than anything.

"I know you want to take care of me and make sure I get home okay, but you need to have fun tonight. Live your life like you did before I came smashing into it. I've spoken to Em and Stana; I know you used to go out all the time, and since we've met you never do."

"I never said I didn't like going out, Lottie. Am I not allowed to change?" His voice takes on a slight edge of frustration, and I know starting this conversation in the middle of the party is a terrible idea, especially when everyone has had a few drinks.

"I'm not saying that. You know I love spending time with you. You've been there for me more than anyone, and I just don't want you giving up things you love for me."

He's silent, his eyes no longer on me as he looks off. Guilt fills my body, and I want to kick myself for not doing this at a better time or place.

"It's just been a really long day, okay? I don't want to get into something now. I promise to text you as soon as I'm home."

I soften my voice, placing my hand on his arm as I silently plea for him to look at me. He finally relents, nodding.

"Okay, we still on for tomorrow?" he asks, voice hopeful.

"Of course. I'll see you tomorrow." Not sure I'd be able to let go if I hugged him right now, I pat his arm and leave.

Eight

I spend the next morning with Stana and Em at my flat, both of them attempting to convince me to head to Edinburgh for Christmas. But I can't seem to deny, even though I just met Evie, her offer has been at the forefront of my mind. Despite fully moving on from Beck and harboring no positive feelings for him, I'm just not ready to go back to Edinburgh yet, especially at Christmas.

After telling the girls it's just too soon, I see the understanding dawn on their faces. They won't push this, that I know.

I pick at Evie's chocolate cake I made this morning for their visit after realizing I'd stuffed up and my early shift was for tomorrow, not today. I swear pregnancy brain is a very real thing and I've got it.

"Where will you spend Christmas, then?" Em asks, mouth open, showing me bits of mushed-up cake. I've never been one to cook, but when Evie gave me her recipe as I was leaving, I couldn't exactly pass up a chance at making it. I may have texted her a picture of it, then received an image of her with a big grin and a thumbs-up.

My face heats slightly as I reply. I try to keep my voice level; otherwise, I know the two of them will jump down my throat for details.

"Uh, Owen's mum asked if I wanted to spend Christmas day at their house."

Stana stops mid-bite, while Em starts coughing, seemingly choking on hers. "Sorry, what?" Em says.

"It's not what you think. Owen and I are just friends, I swear. He wanted me to meet his mum, so we went by and we just really got along." I continue to focus on the food.

"Lottie, you know you could tell us if there was something going on with Owen. He's an amazing guy, we love him, and we'd love you two together," Stana adds in, but I quickly cut her off, shaking my head.

"I mean it when I say we're just friends. After everything that happened with Beck, it was nice to know that not all men are the spawn of Satan. There are so many other factors that go into why we would never work in a million years, anyway. Plus, I'm clearly not ready."

"Is this more you don't want it to happen, or you're scared of what could happen if you tried? Because girl, Stana and I have been there and it's better to take the risk."

"It doesn't matter. All I know right now is that Owen and I are better as friends. Everything is already so complicated; I don't want to lose him. I won't." Even the thought of losing him scares the shit out of me, and the fact that it scares the shit out of me scares the shit out of me even more.

"Lo, is there something else? Something you're not telling us?" Stana leans forward, placing her hand on my knee. In this moment I feel incredibly guilty about the secret I'm keeping at bay, but it's just not the right time or place. Being so close to so many birthdays and Christmas, I don't have the energy to monopolize everyone's time and conversation. I'll tell them in January. That I know.

"I'm just having a hard time, that's all. The new year is coming, and it will all be okay." I smile at them both, putting on the bravest face I can muster. I'm not usually the damsel in distress. I'm usually breaking down the door and hauling the girls out of shit, but I guess you can't play that role in life forever.

"But enough about that. Stana, how is uni going? And Em, are you still on deadline for the hotel?"

My change in topic seems to grab their attention, Stana gushing about her master's degree in psychology. It appears that a once-unknown depth of life has bloomed inside of her— something I had yet to witness in my dear cousin before her departure from Los Angeles. I guess it's true; London really does hold that extra spark of magic.

"I am loving it, Lottie." Stana beams. "Don't get me wrong, it's bloody difficult, but so worth it. Plus, Ali is such a help. I never knew it could be this good. I think a part of me had grown resigned to the fact that maybe I wouldn't get this in life, but here I am."

At the mention of her handsome lad, she brightens even more. It's in these moments I know I've made the right choice to keep the pregnancy to myself. This is Stana's time to shine in life, and I refuse to be the one to take that from her a moment too soon.

"I can't tell you how happy that makes me, Stana. I knew London would be the exact dose of medicine you needed," I tell her.

"I think Stana moving to London was what we all needed," Em adds in.

"Amen to that."

"What about you, Em?" Stana asks. "How's work going for you? Still stuck working with that hideous man?"

Stana doesn't mean "hideous" in the physical sense, but I would bet money that his outsides match his insides. Bloody gross.

"He's a right wanker, Em," I toss in for good measure. Emilia has been commissioned to do some artwork for the Wentworth Estate Hotel, a top-tier chain in Covent Garden. Her only issue is the man who hired her. Basically, he used any excuse to be a dickhead and refused to give her name to clients who wanted to commission work from her.

She nods in agreement. "Hopefully I don't have to deal with him for much longer. I'm working with another woman, Ms. Brown, and she is yards better so hopefully it stays that way."

"Thank fuck for that," I say, to which the girls laugh. They can always count on me for a bundle of swears.

We spend some more time catching up with one another, luckily avoiding any landmine topics. The girls eventually have to go, and I have no doubt their walk to the Tube will include the topic of Owen and me, but I push it down. I know if roles were reversed, I'd be the exact same. It's their way of showing they care.

I spend ten minutes cleaning up before exhaustion takes over, my body desperate to lie down, even just for a moment. As soon as my head hits the pillow, it's lights out.

"So, do you think you're going to go?" Owen's question pulls me away from the baby book I've been distracted by for the past hour. I raise my eyebrows at him, unsure what he means. He stopped over about two hours after the girls left, finding me still asleep. If I sleep tonight, it will be a miracle.

He leaves the kitchen and walks to me, his steps almost silent for a man his size.

"Edinburgh," he clarifies. "Stana, Em, and Ali were talking about going for Christmas."

I nod, the conversation fresh in my mind. "I don't think so," I tell him honestly. "I mean—" I pause, patting the fabric softly for him to sit before I turn my body toward him.

"It's not that I don't want to go and be there for them. I know that Ali and Em were born there and it holds a lot of great memories for them. But it's different for me. Beck managed to taint that place, and no matter how much I hate giving him that power over me, he has it. I don't want to go back there, Owen. All that place holds for me is negative memories and heartbreak."

He's silent for a few moments, yet I don't say anything to fill the quiet. That's one of the great things about him—Owen speaks in his own time. No awkwardness, no need to fill the silence with useless chitchat.

"I get it. I was surprised you even said you'd think about it, if I'm being honest. That's kinda why I wanted to talk to you about an alternative."

"Okay?" I lean forward.

"So, I know it might seem like a lot, but my mum does this big thing with our family every year. There aren't a lot of us, but we make it a good time. My brother, Hugo, will be here for two weeks. So, I've already talked to her about it, and she'd love it if you'd come."

I unsuccessfully try to hide my grin.

"What's that face for?"

I laugh. "Your mum already kinda invited me at lunch the other day."

Now it's his turn to laugh. "Of course she did."

"What can I say? We're fast friends. Who knows, she probably likes me more than you now," I tease.

"I wouldn't put it past her. It's not that hard to see your charm, Lottie."

"Me?" I scoff. "I've got about as much charm as a stale slice of bread, Owen. I'm overly blunt, sometimes rude, and the mouth I have on me would make a sailor blush."

He pauses, looking at me, his features morphing into a soft smile. "Maybe you see it that way, but to others it's different."

"Uh-huh, and how is that?"

"You're not blunt but honest, you speak out against injustice, and you're not afraid to use your colorful vocab." He sits back on the couch, clearly satisfied with himself. I know he's keeping it light, but it's hard to ignore how my heart clenches at his words. Maybe it's all these pregnancy hormones, but his words manage to hit the chilly frost that covered my heart all those months ago. Now that I think about it, he's been melting that for some time.

"Well," I say, letting out a breath, "that's one of the nicest fucking things I've heard in a while."

"I wasn't trying to be nice, just truthful."

I shove his side. "Stop it!"

His eyes scrunch together. "What?"

"Stop being nice!"

He laughs. "I'm just saying it how it is, Lottie."

I grab a pillow from beneath me and toss it at him.

"Are you crying?" Suddenly he's serious.

"No!" I shout, getting off the couch, trying to hide the emotion from his kind words.

"Lottie!" He's half laughing, but I hear concern.

"It's all these hormones." I wave my hands in front of myself and my small rounded belly. I can only wear tight clothes in the house because I don't want anyone finding out.

Owen gets off the couch and comes over to me. He invades my space, but I let him, knowing I'd probably let him do a whole lot more if I weren't up the duff.

Ever so softly, he grabs my arm and pulls me into him. His hand comes up to cup my face, and it takes everything inside of me to keep breathing.

"I didn't mean to make you cry. But it's important you don't pick apart aspects of yourself you don't like. You're a strong, badass woman, and pregnancy doesn't change that." He looks into my eyes, his own a swirling hurricane. "Badass women also cry," he adds before catching one of my tears with his thumb.

"I know," I confirm. "I guess I'm just not used to someone hyping me up all the time."

He grins. "I can hype you up every day if needed."

I laugh, burying my face in his warm, hard chest. His arms link around my waist, our fronts aligned. Although Owen and I are close, this type of hug doesn't really happen. Correction, it never happens. This spells out intimacy, not friendship. Yet I can't seem to pull away despite a million warning bells going off in my mind.

We stand here for a few more minutes, Owen's hands rubbing up and down my back, my mind knowing it would only take a small movement for my head to tilt up and our lips to meet. When that thought crosses my mind, I quickly pull myself out of his grasp.

"Better?" he asks, his gaze lingering on me for a moment too long. "So, about Christmas?"

I smile up at him. "I wouldn't miss it."

Grinning, he leads me over to the couch, where we watch some Vince Vaughn movie. On opposite ends of the couch, all my doing. I couldn't tell you what we watched specifically or what it was even about, my mind running with tonight's events.

Owen and I nearly crossed a line tonight, yet fear of losing him, losing this stops me from acknowledging it aloud. What's the saying? Ignorance is bliss. For once I'm fine being a happy pig rather than an unhappy Socrates.

Nine

The rest of November and most of December flies by, with work busier than usual and my belly growing by the day. Before I know it, Owen and I are driving to Evie's for Christmas, with Ali, Em, and Stana all in Edinburgh for the holidays.

After accepting Evie and Owen's invitation, I didn't have one ounce of regret. I knew going to Edinburgh would have been a huge mistake, and I'm glad I trusted my gut.

Things with Owen have been the same since that night in his apartment, both of us going back to our normal behavior, but is it really that normal? With my due date only three months away, I can't help but overthink every little thing between us. How he's basically given up any chance at a relationship and social life, dedicating all his time to me.

I know I need to set better boundaries, not just for Owen's sake, but for my own too. He won't always be here and it's not healthy for me to depend on him for everything. Once the baby arrives at the end of March, it will just be the two of us, and I need to start preparing for that.

But that's an issue for me to tackle in the new year. Selfishly, I just want to enjoy our time together now and keep the peace.

"So, have you spoken to your parents?" Owen asks, his voice cutting through the music. I know what he's really asking—when am I going to tell them about the baby? But he won't outright say it for fear of overstepping.

"Actually, I have," I reply. "I spoke to Mum this morning. She's happy I've got someone to spend Christmas with, especially after I declined Stana's invitation. I know she wanted me to spend it with them in France, but for obvious reasons..." I motion to my growing stomach, despite Owen's eyes being on the road. "And I've made a decision about telling them. Well, telling everyone really."

"And that is?" he asks.

"In the new year. I refuse to monopolize everyone's Christmas and the devil knows if I told Stana before her trip to Edinburgh, she'd track down Beck and give him the beating he deserves."

"Stana as the violent type?" Owen laughs, clearly having a hard time imagining it.

"Well, maybe not violent, but I'm sure she'd give him a good verbal serve." We both laugh, my mind imagining kind Stana giving someone an ass beating. Definitely more my scene. Well, maybe not now.

"I think telling everyone is a great idea, Lottie. You know I'm here for you every step of the way."

"Thanks, puppy. I really don't know how I would have done any of this without you. I know I don't always say it enough, but thank you."

I risk looking at him; a small smile is tracing over his lips.

I turn back in my seat, facing forward, the expensive leather beneath me squeaking as I go. Then I reach for the radio and turn up the volume, not minding what's on. I'm not really picky when it comes to music as long as it's not country. If someone puts that shit on, I'm out.

"Fancy" by Iggy Azalea comes on, my hand tapping on my leg to the opening beat. I stare out the window as Iggy starts singing and nearly drop dead when I hear another voice singing along to the opening rap.

I turn, my eyes not believing themselves as Owen, all wrapped up in the song, sings about being a bad bitch, and I nearly lose it.

His shoulders move up and down to the beat, him not missing a single word of the rap. He's so into it I don't think he notices me staring, mouth on the floor.

"I'm sorry, what is going on?" I can't stop laughing, tears forming behind my eyes from it all. Owen keeps going, finally turning to me when the chorus starts. I assume he'll be embarrassed at getting lost in the song, but he just grins.

"Oh, come on. Tell me this song isn't catchy," he says, his body still moving around. He reaches for the volume and turns it up to max as he continues on.

"I'm so fancy!" Owen yells, to which I join in, no longer wanting to be out of the fun. We both piss ourselves laughing, but he doesn't lose a single note in the chorus.

Owen turns to me, face serious when the second verse comes on, my body shaking with giggles as he goes off again.

He sings and I join in, surprised I still know all the words. We pull up to a red light, both of us probably looking like loons as we have a rap-off.

I start moving my shoulders to the right then left, and Owen catches on quickly, our dance moves now in sync.

"It's just the way you like it, huh?" he sings to me and I tap out, no longer able to participate as I've died from all of this.

The song finishes up while I'm still in tears, and Owen is looking like the cat who got the cream.

"I have no words," I tell him, wiping my eyes.

"Who doesn't love a good sing-along?" he replies.

"What would Ali and Reeve think of your taste in music?" I tease.

He shrugs. "I'd probably be kicked out of the band, so let's keep this between us two."

"Your secret is safe with me."

A Destiny's Child song comes on and off he goes again, giving me the best ride of my life. Car ride, that is.

After arriving at Evie's, we settle in quickly, with champagne and nibbles all coming our way. I obviously decline the former, feeling slightly guilty at the fact I have yet to tell Evie. It's a weird feeling considering my own mother doesn't know about my pregnancy, but one that tells me all I need to know about Evie. She's comfort; she's safety.

An hour into the day, we're sitting in the living room, which is filled with two differently patterned couches and knickknacks littering the walls and side tables. It's not that it's messy—Evie would never keep that kind of household. It's just oozing with character and, well, Evie.

"I can't believe your brother is late," Evie says, her face cross.

"What do you expect, Mum?" Owen replies from next to me. "He's nineteen."

She shakes her head, shoving anther puff pastry thing into her mouth. I don't actually know what they are, but they're delicious.

"He'll get here, darling," Steve coos as he comes to sit by her side, topping up her champagne. Smart man.

As if Hugo's ears were burning, we hear the front door open, and a little replica of Owen walks inside. Hugo is tall and trim but not scrawny, having a mop of golden-blond hair on his head and dark blue eyes like his brother.

But where Owen has the maturity of his twenties and defined angles to his face and arms, Hugo still has that air of youth that hasn't fully gone away. I have no doubt he has success with the ladies, the smile he gives his mum charming.

"You didn't tell me your brother was a mini version of you," I whisper to Owen, grinning.

He gently shoves my side. "I'm more attractive. Remember that."

I roll my eyes before standing up, ready to meet Hugo. I make sure to pull my jumper down, thankful for its heavy knit.

"You must be the famous Lottie I've been hearing so much about," Hugo says as soon as he stops before me. He gives me a massive smile. Yep, definitely Owen's brother.

"Only bad things, I hope," I joke as I cross the room to meet him. He goes in for a bear hug, my mind only catching up as his arms circle my waist. I internally panic before he pulls away and says hi to Owen. Thank God for nineteen-year-old boys. He probably just thinks I've eaten too much over the holidays.

"Sorry I'm late. I missed the earlier Tube and couldn't get back in time." Hugo studies at Oxford, so he isn't around as much as Evie would like, but he's definitely here more than Reeve's brother, who studies in America.

"You get a pass just this once because it's Christmas," Steve says, winking over Evie's shoulder at Hugo. Despite Owen and Hugo having different fathers, neither of which were Steve, the four of them are a family. That only further proves to me there is no special formula to creating the perfect family. It gives me a little bit of reassurance that I and this baby are going to be okay without her having a stable dad in her life.

"Okay, should we do presents then?" Evie clasps her hands together, joy radiating from her as she looks upon everyone in the room. Despite me not being a member of this family, she really has a way of making me feel welcome.

"Can I go first?" I ask the room, grabbing the bag I snuck in with me.

"You know you didn't have to get us anything," Owen says in a low voice from next to me. I shush him by handing him his first, then giving Steve, Hugo, and Evie theirs. I don't have many artistic skills in life, but wrapping presents is one of them. Each is in shiny red wrapping with gold ribbon that has holly attached to the top. I'm quite proud of it if I say so myself.

"Darling girl, you're far too thoughtful," Evie says as she unwraps her gift.

"It's nothing," I tell them, secretly hoping they like it. I don't really know Steve or Hugo well, so I went with a nice bottle of wine for Steve and a gift certificate for Hugo.

"Lottie, this is far too generous," Steve tells me as he unwraps the bottle of Pinot.

I smile at him. "It's one of my parents' favorites."

He pulls out his glasses and places them on the tip of his nose. "An excellent vintage," he confirms.

"I'm glad you like it."

"Brilliant, Lottie," Hugo says, standing up and coming over to hug me. "Thanks."

"It's just something small to say thank you all for having me."

Evie is across the room, holding the teacups I found at a vintage store in Notting Hill the other week.

"Oh, Lottie," she whispers, tears in her eyes. "This means so much."

"I noticed you had the teapot and when I saw the cups that matched, I had to get them for you. I mean, what are the chances?"

She smiles at me, and it's filled with warmth and love. "It was fate."

I nod, suddenly feeling a bit emotional myself.

Trying to brush it off, I turn to Owen, hoping he likes his gift. But to my surprise, he's yet to open it. His eyes are already locked onto me, gaze probing as though it's reaching into my soul. It's intense, uncomfortable, and all too wanted at the same time, so I look away. I point to his gift. "Open it."

Nodding, he begins to pull off the ribbon. I glance around the room, seeing Evie and Steve in conversation with Hugo, Evie's gaze briefly finding my own before returning to her son. A small grin settles on her lips.

"Jesus, Lottie." Owen's hushed voice pulls me back to the present. He can't seem to look away from the signed movie script for the first Lord of the Rings film. It took pulling a few strings and calling some people my parents know, but I finally got my hands on it last week, just in time for the holiday.

"Are you for real?" he asks, his face still in awe. Suddenly unsure how to process all this, I bite my cheek, an awkward smile overtaking my face. Was this gift too much? Should I have just gone with a gift card? Fuck, shit, fuck.

"It's really not a big deal," I insist.

"Lottie, you got me a signed script of my favorite film of all time. Not to mention literally every bloody name is on this. It's a *huge* deal."

I begin picking at the end of my fraying jumper, wrapping the loose thread around my finger until almost painfully tight.

"Hey." His hand touches mine and I return my stare to him. "This means a lot to me, thank you." He runs his thumb up and down my hand before pulling it away.

"Well, you're welcome," I manage to get out, feeling a bit stupid for my dramatics over the gifts. Friends get each other nice things; this isn't out of the ordinary or weird. Yep, totally normal to spend a hundred pounds on your friends' mother.

Oh God.

"Well, Lottie, I think I can speak for the entire family when I say you're far too generous but with gifts like this, definitely welcome anytime," Hugo says to me. Evie reaches over and smacks his arm.

"You're welcome anytime, with or without presents," she cuts in.

I can't help but laugh, thankful no one except me is reading into this.

"Now it's my turn," Evie says. She gets up and begins to distribute everyone's presents.

"I sort of have to give you your gift in private," Owen whispers to me while Evie's attention is on Hugo. The warmth of his breath sends goose bumps sprouting across my arms.

"Sorry, what?" I say, eyes wide in alarm as I look to him.

"Oh God, not like that, Lottie," he responds, face blooming with red.

Ah yes, because who would want to do dirty things with the pregnant girl?

And that's how my fucked-up mind takes his response. Instead of thinking, *Fuck, he's my friend,* I'm offended he doesn't want to. I need to get my head screwed on.

"It's just something to do with—" His head motions toward my stomach and I instantly understand.

"Oh yeah, no problem," I say quickly as Evie is at my feet, handing me a pink box with ribbon.

"Evie, I'm your guest. You're not supposed to get me anything," I tell her.

She shushes me before giving Owen a small bundle of things.

I avert my attention to the gift at hand, opening up the wrapping to unveil a stunning pale pink jumper and an assortment of bracelets. It's all very different, all very me. I run my hands over the soft material of the jumper, instantly knowing it's cashmere. Christ, that isn't cheap. Now I'm thankful I didn't go for a box of chocolates for their gifts.

"Evie, this is so beautiful," I tell her, already knowing what boots and skirt I will pair it with.

"Oh good, I'm so glad you like it. I know clothing is always a gamble when it's for other people, but as soon as I saw it, I knew you'd look amazing in it."

"It's perfect," I reply, wishing I could try it on right now. But alas, that would give away my nearly six-month belly.

Everyone continues to open their gifts, Owen and Hugo bantering back and forth while Steve inspects each gift, always deeming it perfect.

An hour later we're at the table, feasting on roasted turkey, potatoes, stuffing, peas, and heaps more things I don't think I'll even make it to trying.

The dinner is filled with conversation, laughter, and a fair bit of teasing one another. It's as if I've been a part of their family my entire life, all of them making a conscious effort to keep me engaged without it feeling forced. It's special, and to be honest, one of the best Christmases I've had in a long time.

By the end of it, my back is sore from sitting in a chair for a few hours and my stomach is filled to the absolute brim.

After Owen and Hugo clean everything up, refusing to let me help, Evie ushers us into the living room, where my back rejoices at the pillow-soft couch.

"Tell me you've at least seen this movie?" Owen asks as he dives for the seat next to me. Evie tucks herself into Steve on the other couch while Hugo takes the floor, his tall frame stretching out with a pillow Evie tosses him.

"*Love Actually?*" I reply to Owen.

He nods.

"I actually have. Christmas movies are the only movies I religiously watch."

Owen grins. "Well, that's good because Mum makes us watch this film every bloody Christmas, so at least we know you like it for the future." He relaxes, his taut body moving about, adjusting his comfort to the couch.

I, on the other hand, am still caught up in what Owen was implying. That I will be here for future Christmases.

It should be a scary thought, that he considers me important enough to be here next year, but instead of reading into it too much, I sit back, grabbing the packet of Maltesers from Hugo when he offers.

And for the next two hours, I don't worry about myself or the baby or telling everyone. I just sit and relish in the simple joy that is Christmas with Owen and his family.

"Thank you for bringing me tonight." My voice is soft as it fills the car, only the sounds of Cat Stevens in the background.

Owen turns his head quickly, that pretty-boy smile upon his lips. "I'm glad you had a good time. My mum's practically adopted you, just so you know, so I doubt it will be the last time I have to drag you over."

"I can think of worse things than Evie being my second mum," I tease.

"She's not too bad," he quips back.

"She really is something special, Owen." My voice is still soft as I think about everything Evie has accomplished despite having to do most of it on her own.

"Tell me about it." He rubs his lips together before shaking his head. "Everyone always calls me a mama's boy, but when it comes to Evie being my mum, I'll take that name any day. I know it couldn't have been easy for her when my dad passed—she was in her early twenties, alone, and trying to become a lawyer and be a mum at the same time. Then she actively chose to do it all again with Hugo." He pauses briefly.

"And having seen all of that, I know you're going to be okay, Lottie. Neither Hugo nor I had a dad, but I like to think we turned out all right." He lets out a quick laugh at his last comment. It's not filled with humor, but rather marvel that it all worked out so well for them.

"Well, I can tell you from knowing you and meeting your brother tonight, you turned out more than okay. There aren't many men like you, Owen Bower."

"We're not that great," he cuts in, trying to make a joke.

"No, Owen, I mean it. You should be proud of yourself. It's not just Evie who's come a long way. You had every obstacle placed ahead of you growing up. Seriously, what ten-year-old can take care of an infant?"

He's silent at my question, and I suddenly understand that Owen is always so quick to praise everyone else, but reluctant to accept the same for himself.

"None. That's the answer, Owen. No ten-year-old can do that. You're a one-in-a-million type of human, and if I had known Stana going to Saint Street a year ago would set off the chain of events that led me to meeting you, I would have gotten her there a lot sooner."

My voice has risen slightly, and although I'm vehemently going on about this, I won't back down.

"So instead of brushing it off, I want you to acknowledge, right now in this vintage BMW, that you, Owen Bower, are fucking awesome."

He turns to me, a confused smile on his face, as if perhaps he doesn't actually think I want him to say it.

"Say it, Owen. Say it or I'm not accepting the Christmas gift you got me, and if I know you, which I do, I bet it's pretty great."

"You actually want me to say this, don't you?"

He shakes his head, a chuckle leaving his lips. "Okay then. I, Owen Bower, am fucking awesome." His chest moves up and down as he tries to suppress his laugh.

"Happy?" he asks me.

Although his delivery needs a bit of work, I nod.

He leans forward, turning up the radio as we drive back to my flat so I can get my final Christmas gift of the night.

And I have a feeling it will blow all the others out of the water.

I eye the small silver box in front of me, assuming it's baby related since Owen insisted on giving it to me in private. I've yet to purchase anything on my own; I guess a part of me is waiting to tell everyone before I do.

"Well, open it." Owen motions to the box.

Smiling, I tug off the lid and toss it aside on my couch. When I pull back the soft layers of tissue paper, a folded yellow dress sits below. My heart lurches as I carefully take it out and unfold it. Before me is a small yellow smock dress with puffy sleeves and a white collar, detailed flowers embroidered across the chest.

Oh my God.

My eyes fill with tears as I look it over, the tiny thing almost an exact replica of the one I wore as a child. The one I told Owen about all those months ago.

"How did you get this?" I ask, my voice soft as I stare at the gift in awe.

"It's not the exact one you wore, but I took a photo of your picture and sent it to a friend of Mum's who makes dresses. This should fit the baby when she's around one."

Without thinking, I lunge at Owen, wrap my hands around him and bury my face in his neck. I hear his quick intake of breath before his arms surround me.

"I take this to mean you like it?" he asks, his breath warm against my skin.

I nod. "I like it. Fuck, puppy, this is the best gift anyone has ever given me." I pull back and look at his face, a face that only ignites feelings of familiarity and comfort. One that's safe. Although Beck and I shared two years together before it all went to shit, he never once gave me something this thoughtful. And I guess that's where my issue lies. I compare Owen to Beck, and

Owen isn't my boyfriend. Yet another thing to add to my list of fucked-up problems.

"I know it's not really for you, but I noticed you hadn't gotten anything for the baby yet."

"I was waiting to tell the girls. If I know them, and I do, they're going to go crazy buying shit, so I don't want to go overboard. Plus, have you seen my flat?" I wave my hands around my living room. Although it isn't dirty, it's messy as hell. Filled with useless shit I've acquired over the years and useless knickknacks I will never use. My bedroom is another story.

"Nothing some cleaning won't fix." Owen shrugs as though it's all an easy solution.

"I guess, but I've got a small human coming in three months and I'm starting to realize I'm a lot less prepared than I should be. I mean, I haven't fully read one of the baby books that sit next to my bed gathering dust. And I don't even have a long-term plan. I mean, what happens when she's one and needs her own room?"

"Then you move. And you're a pharmacist, Lottie. It's not like you haven't helped hundreds of mums who've come in needing it. There is no formula to having a baby, no rulebook. Trust me when I tell you that you're going to be fine. Sure, there are a few things to work out, but we can do that this month. You've still got plenty of time."

I nod, knowing deep down he's right.

"I think I'm feeling emotional." I blink a few times. "Not in a bad way or anything. I'm not used to this level of love I saw with your family tonight. It's been so long since I've been with my parents, and I've never had any siblings."

Owen stays silent next to me, just listening.

"I guess it made me realize that no matter what happens, I'm going to be okay, you know? Your family is this incredible mix of humans and I think deep down I've been scared that Beck fucking off would somehow ruin this baby's life by leaving her without a dad. But all I need to do is look at you, Owen. Your mum raised one of the best people I know, and she did it on her own. And that alone gives me hope to think I'm going to be okay.

"Don't get me wrong, I'm shit scared, but I think I've finally gotten to the point of understanding that this is going to work out."

"You're never going to be alone in this," he says, his voice deep and gravelly.

"I mean, it's easy to say that, but at the end of the day it's just me and her, Owen. Everyone has to go home eventually."

He's silent, and my only indication that something is bothering him is the blank look coating his face. My insides twist at the sight, my brain pushing me forward to comfort him.

"Hey." I nudge his side until our eyes meet. "If I'm not worried, then you shouldn't be." He smiles, yet it doesn't reach his eyes. "I know it's late, but I wouldn't be opposed to watching *Wedding Crashers.*" I put on the best puppy-dog eyes I can until he relents.

Without any snacks, because we're still full from today, Owen and I get comfortable on the couch and dive into a movie I'm certain will cheer him up. But as we watch and he eventually begins to loosen up, I can't seem to stop thinking about the look on his face earlier, and worse, what it might mean.

Ten

A few days later, I'm just putting myself to bed when my phone lights up. I don't hesitate to pick up, wanting to make sure Em's having a good break.

"Someone's up late," I say, grinning into the phone.

"The guys decided to do an impromptu gig at the pub their mate manages," Em tells me, her voice slightly off. It's absent of her almost permanent cheer.

"If they're at a gig, why aren't you?" I ask, my concern rising. Em almost never misses out.

"It just ended. You know how full on those venues can get. I needed some air."

"I get that."

"What about you? How's London treating you? You know you're very missed here."

I laugh, thinking of the shit weather we've had over Christmas and the slight loneliness I've felt without my girlfriends. It's a bit of a joke how crap the season turned, but I can't fully complain; not everything has been terrible. In fact, my usually cynical self realizes it's actually been quite the opposite.

"The weather is shite and my apartment is bloody freezing, but Owen's mum made a delicious Christmas dinner, so it's not all bad. I miss you girls too."

"It's the dead of winter here. Thank God for heating."

She laughs, and it's abrupt and lacking warmth. I decide to pry, my gut telling me that something isn't okay. And I'm guessing that something has to do with Reeve. Unfortunately for Em, the guy who manages a large portion of her happiness also has the same power over her sadness.

"Is everything all right, Em?" I keep my voice soft, not wanting to scare her off.

"Yeah, I'm okay," she responds, voice low and breathy. She's silent for a few moments before continuing. "I just miss you, that's all. The holidays are always hard for me."

Fuck, here I am thinking about her being upset at Reeve when it's Christmas and her parents are gone. Instantly I feel horrible for missing the trip to Edinburgh, but I know deep down I'm still not ready.

"I can only imagine how hard this time of year is for you, Em. I'm really sorry I wasn't there for Christmas."

"Oh my God, don't be sorry. I wouldn't want to come back to Edinburgh either if I were you. You have nothing to feel bad about. I just was in a shit mood and wanted to call and hear your voice." She tries to put on the cheer, but it feels forced.

"It's okay to be in a shit mood, Em. As long as it doesn't take over every aspect of your life. Shit happens, moods happen. Accept it and it will go away eventually."

"You're right, Lo. But enough about me—tell me about Christmas with Owen. Did Evie make Christmas pudding?"

I can't help but grin at the mention of Owen and his family. Meeting Evie felt as though I were officially in a secret club that only the most special attend.

"Evie's great," I gush. "She welcomed me with open arms despite not knowing me from Adam. I'm really thankful Owen took me with him."

"That makes me so happy, Lottie. If anyone deserves a good holiday, it's you. And tell me, did Evie put on *Love Actually* for everyone?"

"Yes!" I reply. "I think it's the first time I've ever seen Owen shocked that I knew a film." I laugh, thinking about the look on his face.

We speak for a few more minutes, filling one another in on everything we ate. It makes my stomach rumble, but I push down thoughts of more food. Ever since this baby came into the picture, I've been a nonstop eating machine.

A week later, everyone is finally back in London. My feet practically trip over one another as I race to Saint Street, wanting to punch the entire rush of customers that made me have to stay late at work. Okay, maybe punching them is a little extreme, but I have plans!

I tug at my oversized hot-pink sweater, thankful it's winter and I don't have to worry too much about hiding my bump. I'm going to tell the girls next week—I just hope they don't murder me for waiting so long. I've got my bag full of shit from work, my entire demeanor a bit frazzled.

Finally here, I hastily lug open the big red door and barrel down the stairs, my black-and-gold combat boots thudding with each step.

"I'm so sorry I'm late. I got stuck at work," I call out, noticing everyone when I'm halfway down the stairs. I spot Owen, my chest doing its usual dance at his presence. I must be overly flustered from everything, because the next foot that hits the carpeted steps misses, my leg collapsing under me as my purse jolts me forward.

As if it's happening in slow motion, I lean my weight to the side to avoid my stomach. I slip down the last few stairs, and my side takes the brunt of my fall as I connect with the ground. Someone calls my name, but I stay silent, attempting to assess how badly I've hurt myself.

I wince when I touch my side, and fear quickly overtakes any other thoughts or feelings. What if I've hurt the baby? Panic floods my system at the possibility.

"Shit, Lottie, are you okay?" Stana asks from across the room, but I don't reply. It's a matter of seconds after my body meets the floor that Owen is by my side, his hand on my head while the other pulls me into an upright position.

"Call 999," he shouts to someone, probably anyone. I'm still silent, in shock. Well, probably not actual shock. Most people don't know this, but shock is a medical condition that your body goes into. People are just frivolous with the use of the term.

Okay, now I'm rambling. Maybe I am in shock.

Everyone is silent while they make the call, Owen not taking his hands off me. I use the time to reassess myself, pain only coming from my side where I hit the floor.

I look to Owen, panic etching every little space in his eyes, his grip on me unrelenting.

"It's gonna be okay," he whispers so softly to me, I question if he's trying to convince himself.

With an operator on the phone, Owen rushes to Emilia and grabs it out of her hands.

"She's fallen down a flight of stairs. I'm not sure if she's seriously injured," Owen says, voice firm but I hear the panic. Then he utters the words that will change everything for me, but keeping secrets is not a priority. "But she's twenty-seven weeks pregnant and twenty-five years old."

I hear the girls' gasps, not daring to look their way for fear of seeing disappointment or anger. I place my shaking hand across my rounded stomach, the jumper not doing much to cover it but the contact giving me immense comfort. My eyes begin to prick with tears, but I hold them back, refusing to let my mind wander to that dangerous place of what could be.

"No, there is no bleeding." Owen speaks into the phone as he walks back to me and links his cold fingers with my own. I close my eyes, unable to take it as I give him my hand, the other with my child.

"Okay, yeah, it's Saint Street in Notting Hill, the pub on the corner. You can't miss it."

Owen hangs up quickly, returning his attention to me, yet I just can't seem to open my eyes as we wait for the paramedics. I keep them shut so firmly I see stars. My hand, still linked with Owen's, is clutched so tightly around his own I feel his bones. He begins moving his thumb over my hand, back and forth, back and forth, while we wait.

It's five minutes, although it feels like a lifetime, later when the paramedics arrive. The room seems to disappear, along with everyone else in it, and I sit with the two men and they ask me basic questions about myself and the baby.

Owen doesn't leave my side for a moment, making sure to help me out if I pause or am unsure. Eventually I'm deemed okay, but a trip to the hospital is in order just to be sure. I'm thankful they recommend it, my mind still frantic despite their reassurances. I mean, what if they missed something? What if something is wrong with her?

"Are you okay to stand, miss?" One of them asks me the question—I'm not sure who because my mind has begun to race yet again.

I nod, but Owen slips his arm under me nonetheless, then lifts me to my feet and leads me out of Saint Street. I ignore the looks from my friends, not able to face them. I've never been a coward; I've always looked life and challenges straight in the eye, and some—okay, most—would call me a bull in a china shop, but since the baby has come along, a sense of caution and fear has invaded my system and I can't seem to escape it.

Despite everyone's reassurances that we are okay, the ride to the hospital is a blur. My mind is a fast-paced tornado of horrible thoughts and fears, questioning if I had done one thing differently today, would that have changed the outcome? But isn't that how it always goes?

Maybe if I woke up five minutes earlier, or didn't work late, or wore different shoes, none of this would have happened. But the reality is, it's very much happening, and no small difference of actions will change that now.

"It's going to be okay," Owen says next to me, voice firm and sure. I take his hand and give it a squeeze because something tells me he needs it a bit more than I do right now.

"I know," I lie. "It's just scary."

His eyes lock onto my own as he nods. Suddenly his attention drowns out the flashing red lights, smells of antiseptics, and pure panic.

I make sure to stay looking at him the rest of the ride, and it's not long before we're at the hospital. I'm quickly admitted and left alone with Owen in a waiting room until the doctor arrives. We say nothing, as he knows me, and one too many uncertain promises might send me over the edge.

The door opens and in comes a doctor in a white coat, clipboard in her hand. "Hi, I'm Dr. Stephans, and you must be—" She pauses, looking down. "Ms. Knight. It says here you had a small fall and are twenty-seven weeks pregnant?"

I nod. "I tripped on some stairs and fell on my side. I just want to make sure everything is okay."

She nods, the glasses sitting at the end of her nose threatening to fall off any second. Her big brown eyes turn to Owen, who is hovering by my side.

"And you must be Dad?" she asks him, seeming already sure that he is. I don't know why, but the question sends a pang to my heart. Owen stiffens slightly before relaxing when he sees my attention on him.

"Uh, no," I cut in for him. "Just a supportive friend."

"Oh, my apologies," she says before coming to sit next to me. "So, shall we take a look and make sure everything is tip top?"

I lie down and pull up the bottom of my jumper, exposing my rounded stomach. It's not huge, but definitely obvious I'm expecting.

"Okay, this is going to be a little bit cold at first, but I'm sure nothing you haven't already experienced."

The gel squeezes out, coating my stomach and sending a chill down my spine. Owen grabs my hand and looms over me while Dr. Stephans gets to work. It's no time before the deep thrum of a heartbeat echoes through the room, a gust of breath erupting out of me.

She's okay.

"You hear that?" the doctor asks me, her rose-colored lips tilting up at the sides.

My head moves up and down anxiously as I stare at the screen, seeing the little human looking back at me. My throat tightens, and I fear that if I speak even a single syllable, I'll lose it.

So instead I smile, reaching out to touch the screen.

"So, everything's okay?" Owen's voice is laced with panic.

"Everything is okay," she confirms. "But you're going to have to take it easy, okay? I'm not saying you have to go on bed rest, but you need to be careful. Can you do that?"

I nod, willing to do anything at this point.

"Is it still okay that I work? I'm a pharmacist, so I'm on my feet a lot."

"You can still work, but I don't want you on your feet the whole time. See if you can work something out with them."

"Okay, of course."

"And if there is even a slight issue, don't hesitate to call this office or if you think it's an emergency, you call the ambulance."

We spend the next hour getting everything sorted, and then Owen is finally able to hail a cab for us. I'm silent the entire process, quickly getting in next to him, his familiar scent providing me the only comfort to this tumultuous day.

I jolt when his ice-cold hands come to rest upon mine. My fingers briefly dig into the plastic-covered seat before loosening up. I wait a few more breaths, finally giving in to what I want, the one thing I always seem to want.

My body sags as my head tilts to the side, resting on Owen's broad shoulder. He's tense—I can tell from just being next to him, but feeling him is another thing. It takes him less than a second to relax as I lean on him, something I've become far too familiar with.

Neither of us speaks as the car begins to move, and I start to realize that today has been traumatizing not only for me, but also for Owen. I've dragged him into my mess and, in turn, given him emotional baggage I don't think he ever asked for.

But alas, we're here. And wanting to or not, we're feeling the weight of today's events epically. So we sit together in silence, hands clasped with my head on his shoulder, and for a small moment, we let ourselves feel it all.

Eleven

It took nearly an hour of convincing, but I eventually got Owen to go home. Despite his insistent questioning, I refused to let him stay, thinking it was best for each of us to have some time to process everything.

It's the next morning now and I sit on my couch, attempting to keep my pulse down. All this panic over the past twenty-four hours can't be good for me or the baby. Stana and Emilia sit in front of me, the fear on their faces clear.

I guess it's time to come clean.

"So obviously, I'm pregnant," I tell them. I try to laugh, keep things light, but it's a fail. They both just nod, waiting for me to continue. After a deep breath, I start from the beginning, taking them all the way back to July. All through Beck's cheating, my escape to London, then my realization about the baby. And then I get to Owen. About him being my rock for the past few months and how much he means to me.

They sit there, listening, Emilia continuously drinking tea because she is nervous while Stana is doe eyed, my pain prominent in her features.

Before I know it, I've explained the past six months in vivid detail, both of them with their jaws on the floor.

"I gotta go to the loo, gals. I'm about to wet myself. I'll give you two some time to decompress and digest it all. Lord knows I've had months, and you two have only had a few hours." I pat their hands, hoping to give them a touch of reassurance before I wander off. I hear them talking to one another after I've left the room, and despite my desire to listen in, I don't. I attend to my business and come back when I think they've had enough time.

Yet as soon as I see the two of them on the couch, I can't help but grin.

"I'm just happy I finally got to tell you gals," I say, their serious faces suddenly dissipating, Em jumping off the couch.

"Holy shit!" she says. "You're having a baby."

Stana begins to cry, both girls racing over to hug me, each being cautious of the special little girl growing inside of me.

We spend a few minutes crying with one another, celebrating that they will both be aunties, my soul feeling so much lighter now that they know.

"Do you know what you're having?"

"It's a little girl," I say, beaming.

"A little girl!" they both scream out, my eardrums ringing from it all.

Our little screaming fest continues, none of us able to contain our excitement, and despite already being privy to the information I've just shared with them, I somehow feel the joy all over again. Because sharing this with both of them, the two most important women in my life, finally makes it all real. And it's in this moment I know it will all be okay, because despite baby not having a daddy, I know she will have a mama who loves her more than life, and two aunties who will be the best role models she could ever ask for, and for me, that means everything.

Despite everything, it turned out letting the metaphorical cat out of the bag in regard to my pregnancy was just the thing I needed to relieve all the invisible stress I'd been feeling over the weeks leading up to January.

As predicted, Stana and Emilia couldn't help themselves, packages arriving at my flat daily for the baby. All were equally adorable, but I didn't have the heart to tell them she won't be able to wear six different pairs of overalls as a newborn before she grows out of everything.

The biggest surprise came my way when I spilled the beans to Joan at work as I had to cut down my hours. Apparently, she'd clued in a few months back. My mortification was strong since I thought I'd pulled the wool over her eyes. And despite my fear that she was angry with me for keeping the secret, her understanding extended to every aspect of work.

So, as the weeks of January passed by and my due date crept closer and closer, I finally felt free to experience pure elation and excitement. Not even the murky areas with Owen concerned me too much. I'd placed all my inappropriate feelings toward him in a small box and shoved it so far down in my soul, it would take an expedition team to find that shit.

Plus, it wasn't my love life that was the talk of our little group. Apparently—and not to my surprise, because let me just say, I CALLED IT!—Em and Reeve had secretly been seeing each other since October. Yep, nearly four whole months. I guess I wasn't the only one keeping secrets. And with Em's admission came the news that Reeve had swiftly ended things and left town to reconnect with his absent father, whom most of us didn't even know existed.

I felt like a side character in the romantic dramas Stana and Em always made me watch with everything going on. Unplanned pregnancies, secret relationships... Who knows what's coming next at this point?

It all led up to where I'm at right now, seven months pregnant and about to spill the beans to my parents. I already hear the silent judgment of many. How could I keep such a secret from them? What kind of horrible person am I?

But I know my mum. Despite no longer wanting to be in London, she'd drop everything and take care of me, and that's just not what I need.

So, as I stand here in the lobby of their hotel, waiting for them to come, I manage to inhale a few shaky breaths. My jacket and bag hide most of my small stomach and I'm thankful I haven't exploded yet, but it could still be coming.

"Darling!" I hear my mother across the lobby, her high heels ringing out against the marble floors as she rushes toward me. Her dark blonde hair is pinned atop her head, and she rocks a white skirt suit. My father is behind her, dressed in trousers and a button-down, his silver hair swept back while tortoiseshell glasses sit on the rim of his nose.

"Mum," I say as I meet her halfway, pulling her in for a hug. My father isn't far behind, his arms coming around the both of us.

"A little Lottie sandwich." He grins down at me and for the first time, I realize how much I've missed them. I think when you're away from someone for a long period of time, you can manage to convince yourself that their absence doesn't impact you. Yet the moment you're back together, you realize how untrue that is.

"I've really missed you guys," I tell them, the smell of my mother's familiar J'adore perfume filling my nose.

We pull away, my mum wiping under her eyes, which are now glassy.

"Should we go grab a bite to eat? Are you hungry?" Mum asks me.

Little does she know I'm always hungry.

"Actually," I begin, "there's something I'd like to talk to you both about before we go to lunch."

My mum's eyes widen, my dad taking a step forward. "Is everything okay, darling?"

I nod. "Yeah, it is. I'm okay. But there is something I need to get off my chest."

Literally.

"Should we go back up to the room?"

I look to my father and nod. Although I know my parents and am hoping this won't turn into a screaming match, you never know.

We walk toward the elevator, my dad slipping his large hand into mine. He gives it a tight squeeze, looking me over briefly.

The ride up is silent. I catch my parents looking at me a few times, but they cover up their worry with smiles.

It's not long until we're in the sitting area of their hotel room, both of them silent, waiting for me to start. And so I do. I recap everything that happened with Beck, all of which they already knew, and then my coming home to London and finally finding out I was pregnant in September.

Neither says a word as I continue, but I can see their gazes drifting toward my coat-covered stomach a few times. When I finish, my mum has tears in her eyes, but it's my father's silence that scares me the most.

"I know this is a lot to take in," I say, "but I want you to know I kept this from you for a reason. I got myself into this situation and it was important to me that I handle it. I needed these months to process what was happening and figure out how I felt about it. It was never a personal slight against you, but I know you, Mum. You would have dropped your whole life to come help me, and as much as I love you for that, it's not fair to you or me. I hope you can understand."

She nods, her big eyes filled with tears.

"I know this is a lot to just dump in your laps, and I don't expect you to have anything to say immediately. So I'm going to just step outside for a few minutes and give you both some time."

I stand, their silence scaring me a little more than I thought, and swiftly exit the room. My shaky feet carry me to a chair by the elevator, and I quickly sit down and call Stana.

"How did it go?" she asks immediately.

"Well, I told them."

"And?"

"They didn't say anything. Like nothing. Both just sat there in silence."

She pauses for a moment. "That isn't necessarily a bad thing. They probably are just processing."

I nod even though she can't see me. "I hope so."

"Lottie, it's Florence and Michael we're talking about. They would do anything for you and we both know it. Plus, they're probably the most understanding parents I know."

"That is true," I agree.

We speak for a few more minutes before I decide it's probably best to go back inside. I don't want them to think I've just left. I say my goodbyes to Stana and quickly message Owen before heading into the potential lion's den.

Both of them are still sitting on the couch, their bodies angled toward one another. They stop speaking when I walk back in, my mother shooting off the couch toward me. She wraps her arms around me for a hug I didn't know how much I needed.

After she pulls away, we walk back to my dad and settle in, Mum now seated next to me, our hands intertwined.

"I can't say I'm not shocked, Charlotte," my dad begins. "I think I can speak for both myself and your mother when I say you're our little girl and neither of us expected this day so soon."

I nod, biting down on my bottom lip. Even though I'm an adult, it's always scary when your father uses your first name.

"With that being said, we also can't begin to imagine what life has been like for you. And as much as we would have liked to have been by your side every step of the way, I think you're right—we would have come back to London instantly, and you clearly needed to do this alone."

"I did. I know it's hard to understand." My voice is low but holds strength.

"You've been on your own these past four years, Lottie. And it's your actions and the responsibilities you've taken on that have shown us enough to know you will be a great mother to this little girl. It would be a lie to say we don't worry, but you will soon learn that comes with the territory of being a parent."

"Are you really okay with this?" I ask my mum, who hasn't spoken much. I need to know the truth.

"I've never been that mother who dreams her whole life of her child getting married and having babies. My dreams for you were always that you would do what makes you happy. Have a career that fulfilled you, then if you wanted, meet someone to love and have a baby if you desired. And, well, you've been living your dream, pursuing your career for the past eight years. So really, you've been making me proud your entire life. I never wanted you to have to do this alone, Lottie. But I know if anyone can, it's you."

"Thank you for understanding," I whisper, tears blocking my vision as I tug her into a hug. She latches onto me, keeping me as close as possible before pulling back and looking at my stomach.

"Can I?"

I quickly remove off my coat, finally showing off my little bump for the first time. My mother gasps, her hands eagerly resting atop my stomach.

"Oh, Michael, you have to come feel this."

I laugh as the baby kicks, my mother's face the picture of pure joy. My dad comes over and kneels next to me. His eyes ask permission, so I grab his hand and place it beside my mother's. We sit like this for a few moments, all of us in awe of this small human moving around inside of me. My father wipes at his eyes before standing and taking a sip of water.

"Now, there are two things I need you to agree to in order for us to move forward."

My dad's stern voice catches me off guard, but I find myself nodding anyway.

"Next visit, I want to meet this Owen you've spoken about."

"Not this visit?" I ask.

"We only have a few days with you, and we intend to spend them all with *you*. Your mother has already gotten you a room next door. I think getting her to leave your side would be impossible at this point."

I laugh, my eyes clouding up. "Of course I'll stay," I tell them both. Mum's hand tightens around my own. "And what's the second thing?"

"I want the last known address of Beck. If that little shit thinks he can just fuck off, he has another think coming. A little visit from Uncle Carmine should set him straight."

"Dad!" I yell at the mention of Uncle Carmine. He isn't actually an uncle—he's an old friend of Dad's who isn't exactly on the up and up. Dad's never been one to involve himself in illegal activity, so his friendship with Uncle Carmine has always been just that, a friendship. Yet I'm not ignorant enough to not know what he would do. I look to Mum for assistance, but she merely shakes her head.

"Your dad is right, Lottie. He shouldn't get to walk away from this."

I pull my hand from hers. "All these emotions, this anger and rage you're feeling toward him—trust me, I've felt them too.

I felt them for the first two months of this pregnancy. It was humiliating that I gave over two years of my life to someone who not only cheated on me, but fucked off after I told him I was pregnant. But after that rage subsided, I began to feel acceptance, and with that came the understanding that we don't need Beck."

I pause, taking a breath. "You can't force someone to be a father, and trust me when I say he would only bring trouble into this baby's life. I need you both to promise me you won't attempt to contact him." I refuse to waver as I speak, my voice steady.

It takes my dad a few moments, but he eventually relents. "As much as I want to pay that dickhead a visit, I know you're old enough to make your own choices, and we respect that."

"Thank you."

We spend the next few hours filling one another in on what we've been doing over the past few months. My mother is desperate to only talk about the baby, but it's important to me to know what they've both been doing too. With every passing second my anxiety about today slips away a little more, my heart and soul grateful that I've got these two as my parents.

When Dad has to go take a work call, Mum manages to turn the conversation back around to the baby again. I happily let her. She needs this—she needs to catch up on what she feels she has missed.

"Have you thought about names?" Mum asks as she brings me over a hot cup of tea.

I shake my head. "I honestly can't pick one to save my life."

"That's okay! When you were born, you didn't have a name until you were five days old."

"What!" I laugh, unable to imagine not having a name by the time she is born.

My mum nods. "We wanted to use a family name, hence Charlotte, but as soon as you started to grow, we knew that it wasn't fully you. You will always be a Lottie."

I nod, thinking about how I never actually use my full name. Although I love it, it's just never fitted as well as Lottie does.

"I have a few ideas of some I like. Do you want to see?"

"Is the sky blue?"

I laugh, digging through my bag to find my phone and show her some options. And that is how my dad finds us an hour later, pages deep on baby websites with Mum throwing out the most ridiculous suggestions. Although I will never use any of them, I entertain each and every one, even when she starts suggesting fruits.

The next three days with them are everything I could have hoped for and more. I don't see anyone else except them, us attempting to make up for our all lost time over the past year. It's chaotic, loud, and full on, but it's also perfect.

Twelve

After the time spent with my parents, weeks continue to trickle by and soon enough, I'm only seven weeks away from my due date. My stomach gets bigger by the day, my closet no longer catering to my needs. The full brunt of my frustrations comes out when I'm scheduled to go to dinner with Owen and his brother.

"I'm sick of nothing fitting me!" I yell out, tossing my black skirt onto my bedroom floor, which is already littered with shit I can't be bothered to fold, let alone put away. I huff, sitting on the edge of my bed in nothing but my bra and undies.

I look in the mirror, my bleached hair now a mess with brown roots over three inches long bleeding into my blonde hair that rests way past my shoulders.

"Why don't you just wear a dress?" Stana's sweet voice infiltrates my ears, and I wish I could be calm like her. Too bad everything irritates me these days. I still have time to go, but I'm ready for this to be over.

"I don't want to wear a dress," I whine, knowing full well I sound like a petulant child. "I just wanted to wear that skirt." I eye the small black thing on the floor with deep disdain. My ever-changing body has finally hit the point of no return for many of my wardrobe items.

"I know, love, but the skirt doesn't fit right now." Stana's hand comes to rest upon my arm, getting my attention. "It will fit eventually once your little girl is born, but right now it doesn't, and that's perfectly okay. So why don't I pick something else out, something even better than that skirt, and then we can have a tea before Owen gets here."

I nod, feeling annoyed at myself that I'm irritated at a stupid fucking skirt.

"How about this one?"

Stana holds up a knee-length black velvet dress, tight on the top and loose on the bottom. I know it already fits because of the stretchy material, so it's worth putting on.

I reach for it, and Stana passes it my way, not even remotely fazed by my temper tantrum. After quickly pulling it over my head, I'm happily surprised with how it looks when I turn to the mirror. Most days I don't feel that great and it's impacting my niceness to people, niceness that was already weary to begin with. So it's a comfort to finally feel pretty for a night.

"See, Lottie, this looks beautiful." Stana hands me my hot-pink Dr. Martens to finish the outfit off.

"Ugh, you're right. This doesn't look bad," I tell her, now wanting to laugh at the ping-pong of emotions rocketing through me.

She nudges my side. "I know you're going through a lot, but you deserve to enjoy today."

"I know, I just think everything is catching up to me and I'm not really sure how to feel about it. I mean, this baby is coming so soon and although I'm excited, I'm also scared shitless. And I miss my parents even though I literally saw them last month. I think I'm just feeling it all."

"I think most people feel that way. Granted, you're definitely in different circumstances than some, but I have zero doubt in my mind you can do this."

I nod.

"But with that being said, you're allowed to have a bad day. You can have as many bad days as you want, but I'm going to be here to make sure when that happens, I can kick those pesky little thoughts straight out of your mind."

"What would I do without you, Stana?"

She helps me finally pull myself together before Owen messages me that he's out front.

"Okay, I need to go, but I'll message you later?"

"Sounds good."

We exit the flat and I meet Owen, not knowing this night isn't going to end as planned.

"Did you have a bad time tonight?"

Owen's voice catches me off guard as I throw my jacket onto my couch, not caring when it misses and hits the floor. I stare at it for a few moments before turning around, confronting him. Finally, time to face the music.

"No, Owen, I had a great time," I reply honestly, yet I know he hears the lingering hesitation in my voice.

"But?" He tilts his head to the side, his signature smile having disappeared on the drive home when he was met with my single-word replies and silence. Owen and I know each other well, in some respects too well for two people who are just friends. Hence how we've ended up at this impasse.

"I just," I begin before shaking my head, not wanting to hurt him in the process.

His face hardens slightly. "Say it, Lottie. Everyone always says how blunt and to the point you are, so be that person. Tell me what's bothering you and then we can fix it."

"But that's the point, Owen," I snap. "You can't fix it. *You* shouldn't be fixing it." Exasperated, I run a hand through my hair, looking anywhere except at him. I wait for him to reply, to say *anything*, but he stays silent.

"This isn't healthy, Owen. You've given up your entire social life to cater to the whims of a pregnant girl you didn't even know, and I let you."

"So, what, you're kicking me out of your life?" His voice is even, to the point of being unnerving.

"No," I say almost too quickly. "You're a huge part of my life, puppy, and I want it to stay that way, but I want you to be able to live your life too. I'm not kicking you out of anything at all. I just think we need to acknowledge the reality we've been living in."

"So, what, it's once-a-week visits, then what? Once she arrives I never see you again?"

My heart constricts at the thought. It's the last thing I want, but I can't be unfair to him. So, I do what I do best. I'm honest with him.

"I see the way our interactions have been changing. You're not the only one with the longing looks, but I can't act on them. For the sake of this baby I have to put her first, and lately it feels like we're in a relationship without any of the benefits going your way. I mean, how will you explain to the next girl you date that you need to run off to help a woman and her kid every few days? Because shit's going to happen in my life, stuff will get messy, and it's not fair that I drag you down with me."

His eyes shine as he stares at me, his presence digging deep into my soul and wrapping around it like a vice. I want to take everything back, beg him to be with me and the baby even though I know it's completely selfish. But I've come to the realization that I may be slightly in love with Owen Bower, and what's worse than my own agony from not being with him would be causing him any pain.

"Drag me down, is that what you really think?" he says, his voice low but holding a depth I've never heard from him. I nod.

Saying absolutely nothing, Owen turns around and walks out the door. My heart leaves with him.

I stare at the closed door, Owen's presence no longer occupying my flat. I used to joke about him being over the top, too much even, but now that he's gone, I can't think of anything I want back more.

I did this. I pushed him away because he's young and has so much more to do in life. The last thing he needs is to be shackled to a baby at twenty-eight. It wouldn't be right, and it wouldn't be fair. So, despite the fact my heart is aching, my mind weary from months of overthinking, I push it all down. Push all of it into a deep dark hole I never knew could exist inside of me. I push it down for *her*. Because she is too small, too unaffected by this life to be weighed down by her mother's dilemmas before she's even taken her first breath.

"It's just you and me, little one," I whisper to my overgrown bump, my hands moving up and down against the firm skin.

Exhausted from it all, I put my iPhone on shuffle as I walk over to my bed, needing just a few moments of being close to her.

Cat Power's "Sea of Love" drifts through my speakers. Perhaps it's the perfect song for this moment, for the love I feel for this little human I created. Or perhaps it's a dagger in my heart, a reminder that despite my denials, my feelings for Owen have only continued to grow. To bloom.

I pull back my frilled sheets, a gift from my late grandmother, something I've never been able to yet part with, and then I climb in, careful of my precious cargo as I turn to the side. The fresh scents of baby powder and faint gardenia cling to my nose as I breathe in the freshly made bed. My tidiness has only increased in recent months due to one person.

Owen pops into my mind yet again, but I push him out. Now isn't the time for selfishness. Isn't that what being a mother is all about? The ultimate act of selflessness, giving your everything, putting all your child's needs before your own?

I breathe in and out, trying to calm myself down. My protruding belly keeps me company as I drift my hands up and down, the two of us in our ultimate little safe haven.

"I promise to do everything I possibly can for you, little one, even when I can't." I whisper the words, as though maybe if I'm soft enough she will hear me. And as if on cue, her little arms move, or maybe it's her little legs, alerting me to the fact that I'm indeed not alone.

We stay like this together as the song plays, my mind feeling nostalgic, so I press the Repeat button, listening to it Lord knows how many times.

It's probably twenty minutes later when the front door opens, the song still playing in the background. I freeze, uncertain how to process the fact that Owen's come back.

Maybe he forgot his phone.

Or his jacket?

My question is answered when I hear the rustling of a shopping bag and the heavy footsteps of his boots. There is a pause outside my door before two soft *thumps*. I hold my breath, eyes staring straight at the wall in front of me, latching onto the stack of magazines I've had in that corner since I first moved in.

"You don't have to say anything, Lottie. But I'm not just walking away. This—" He pauses, voice strained. I stay still, saying absolutely nothing.

"I may not be your baby's blood, but she already means too much for me to walk away from her, from either of you. Despite your resistance, I'm invested. Even though you yell at me, like I know you like to do, I'm not just going to fuck off."

My stubborn nature doesn't let me look at him or give him the reassurance I can tell he also needs. Instead, I keep my frame rigid.

"I'm still living my life, Lottie. I'm just lucky enough to have one—well, nearly two—new people in it. You see it as a burden, but I see it as a blessing. If deep down you don't actually want me around, well, that's another thing and I'll have to respect your wishes, but you need to be honest about that."

"I do want you around," I whisper, face half-smushed into the pillow.

"Well, good, because I want to be around. And in case the message wasn't clear enough, I got you this." I hear the sound of a bag again, my interest piqued so I heave myself into a sitting position to finally give him my attention. In his hand is my favorite chocolate ice cream, and a smile I couldn't hide if I wanted to overtakes my face.

"But before you have it, there is another thing I need to say."

My insides clench; I'm not sure where he's going with this. I want to look away, but I respect him enough to give him my attention.

"Things have changed between us. God, maybe they were always different from the start when we met. There is something here, and I think it would do both of us a serious disservice to deny that."

I nod, unable to disagree. My mind is thankful for the honesty while also recoiling at what saying it aloud means.

"I think we're adult enough to admit how things might be different between us if there was no Beck or baby," I say. "And I want you to know, if there was none of this, no Beck, no baby, you would have been perfect for me, Owen. I would have gone there with you and reveled in every second of it."

His eyes close briefly as if he's pained by my words, my own throat tightening at the emotion behind it.

Instinctively my hands search out my stomach for comfort. "But all that's happened, and I would be lying if I said I'm unhappy with how things have turned out."

He places his hand on mine. "And I'd never want you to change it either. All these moments have led us right here and that's okay."

"Despite everything, I'm glad you're in my life," I whisper. "Most days it feels like I can't do this without you."

"That's where you're wrong, Lottie. If anyone can do this, it's you. I'm just happy I stumbled upon you in that hallway, so you don't have to."

Thirteen

I shove an abnormally large bit of croissant into my mouth, relaxing into Emilia's couch. My feet are red and swollen from ramming them into my boots when they clearly need Birkenstocks or nothing. Too bad I'll never be caught dead in a pair of those.

Emilia is taking care of me today, my emotions all over the place along with my hormones. Stana and Ali have opted for a few days away, while Reeve and Owen are up to something.

My mobile rings, a number I don't recognize flashing across the screen. I'm not usually one to answer these types of calls but for some reason, I do.

"Charlotte speaking," I answer.

"Hello, is this Ms. Knight?"

"Yes," I confirm.

"Ms. Knight, I was given your number by an Owen Bower. He's here at Royal London Hospital. It appears he and another passenger"—she pauses—"a Reeve Sawyer, were in a car accident earlier."

My mind goes blank at the words, panic etching its way into every inch of my body. The woman on the other line keeps talking, telling me where to go and how to see them but giving me zero updates on their condition.

"We'll be right there," I say quickly before grabbing my shoes and shoving my phone into my bag.

"Lottie? What's wrong? Where are we going?" Emilia asks, her voice filled with fear.

"Owen and Reeve have been in a car accident. We need to go."

I can tell she's confused as to why Owen would give the nurse my number instead of his own mother's, but I push those questions aside for later.

I finish getting my shoes on before I see Em still standing still. "Emilia!" I yell. "Em, I need you to snap out of it. I know this is scary, but I need you."

She seems to jolt into place at my words, and both of us hastily leave the apartment as I call an Uber.

"Did they say anything? On the phone, I mean, did they say if Reeve and Owen were okay?"

I shake my head as we walk outside to the corner.

"It's going to be okay, Lottie. I promise they are going to be okay."

"We don't know that, Em. For all we know they're dead and we have to identify their bodies," I reply, a sob slipping out.

Our ride arrives and we quickly get in.

"It's going to be okay," she says, but I can't accept her assurances.

"I'm scared, Em," I admit.

"I know you're scared, Lo. I'm scared too, but we can't think like that. I'm sure they're perfectly fine and this is all a huge misunderstanding."

We stay silent the rest of the ride to the hospital, my sobs only growing along with my hysterics. All I can think about is

Owen and his kind face and how I never got a chance to *really* tell him what he means to me. How he always only ever did things for me and I never gave him anything in return.

I'm a snotty, teary mess by the time we're at the information desk, Emilia having to ask all the questions. She grabs my hand and pulls me down the corridor to their room, neither of us knowing what we will find when we open that door.

"Let's just get this over with," I tell her, small hiccups bursting from me. Yet when the door opens and we find both Owen and Reeve sitting there, seemingly okay, I lose it.

"What the actual fuck!" I scream, rushing over to Owen and shoving him with my bag. "How the fuck are you alive!" It's a ridiculous question; of course I'm happy they're okay. But if they're as okay as they seem, why didn't *they* call?

"Huh?" His cluelessness only further infuriates me. On impulse I swing my bag at him again, but this time he grabs it out of my hands.

"Why didn't you call us? Some nurse said you were in a crash, and you were dead for all we knew! What the fuck!" I can't stop yelling. I've finally stopped crying, replacing it with chastising Owen for scaring the shit out of me. The pure panic I felt moments ago still lingers inside me.

"Fuck," Owen says, his face falling. He reaches for me, and I initially draw back before finally going to his side.

"I left my phone in his car and Reeve's died. I asked the nurse to call you guys for me while we were being checked out. I really thought she would have mentioned we were okay. Reeve's car is fucked up, but we don't have any serious injuries."

I stay silent, wanting to hear the full story, *needing* to.

"We got T-boned by some prick who ran a red light. It all happened so quickly. I smacked my head on the dash and the car's pretty fucked, but besides that everyone's okay."

I nod, unable to take my eyes off him for fear he will disappear before me.

"I promise, we're okay. I'm fucking sorry for scaring you like that." He looks me right in the eyes, but I can't seem to process it all, especially when Em and Reeve are having a moment of their own.

Owen motions his head toward the door, and I nod, both of us slipping out to give Em, who has been quiet the entire time, some space with Reeve. My money is on a reconciliation by the end of the hour.

Owen stays silent as we walk down the sterilized halls, my hand coming to rest upon my protruding stomach. In less than two months I'll be back here to have my little girl. The thought is sobering.

"Lottie," Owen says, but I shake my head, not wanting to lose it in these halls again.

"Are you okay to go home? Do you need to be discharged?" I ask, attempting to keep my voice even.

"The nurse came in before you arrived. We can leave."

I nod, walking toward the exit, making sure to keep a slow pace for him to follow. Once outside I get us a cab and tell the driver my address, Owen staying silent next to me. The drive isn't quick, but it feels brief, my mind racing over everything swirling inside of me.

I pay before Owen has a chance to, trying to have a quick exit, but my body isn't able to pop in and out like I used to. Taking our time, we get into my flat, some sort of switch flipping inside of me as soon as I know he's safe, we're both safe and here.

I bypass my couch, all my shit littered everywhere as I stand facing a wall, attempting to control myself.

"Lottie." His voice is soft as he says my name, pleading almost. I know my reaction is scaring him, but how do I even begin to express how much he scared me? How the mere thought of not having him in my life brought me to my knees. How his presence has revived me in my darkest hour.

Taking a deep breath, I turn to face him on the other side of the room. His eyes are like a torrid storm of blue and gray, practically pleading for me to say something.

"You scared me," I admit like a wounded child. "You scared me more than I've ever been scared in my entire life."

"I'm so sorry, Lottie."

He rushes forward, pulling me close to him. I sink into his embrace, letting myself relish in the moment before I pull away. I get myself together, a forced smile coming down like a mask.

We spend the rest of the night on opposite ends of the couch watching a movie, pretending that we don't want each other as much as we do.

A week later, I'm sitting in my favorite cake shop with Reeve and Owen, faking I don't know Stana and Em are setting up for a baby shower at my place.

"How long do I have to pretend to be getting my nails done?" I ask after finishing off a cupcake. It seems cravings for pure sugar hit at ten a.m. today. So, what baby wants, baby gets.

Reeve looks at me and lifts his shoulders.

"Well, you're no help," I tell him before turning to Owen. I could almost swear I catch a small grin on Reeve's face. Smug little bugger has been back with Emilia for the past week since the accident.

"Em wants it to be a surprise," Owen says, handing me my second cupcake of the bag. I scoffed the first one down in a few bites, and now it's sitting uncomfortably in my chest.

"I know, but it isn't. I already know they're throwing me a baby shower. We might as well sit in the comfort of my home rather than be out."

"Give them another thirty minutes?" he pleads. Of course, I concede.

"Not to be rude or anything, but why is Reeve here and Ali isn't?" I ask Owen before turning to Reeve. "No offense."

"None taken," he replies, features still showing the same cool indifference he's mastered so well. To be honest, I don't even think it's a façade. I think he just has resting bitch face.

"He was needed for something." Owen takes a bite of my cupcake and grins.

"Hey!" I snap, reaching for it back. I can't help but smile at him, his emotions contagious. His foot nudges mine under the table. I knock his back.

"So you two, huh?" Reeve's voice interrupts us and we both turn to him.

"What? No, we're just friends," I tell him.

"Yeah," Owen adds in. I kick him under the table. He bites down on his lips to hide his smile.

Reeve nods, clearly skeptical. He goes back to looking at his phone, genuinely seeming not to care. I narrow my eyes at Owen before finishing off the rest of the cupcake, smiling triumphantly when he eyes the crumbs with disdain.

We hang out for another hour before Em texts Reeve that we're allowed to come back to the flat. We walk up the main road, my bladder about to burst when I finally get inside.

"Surprise!" Stana and Em yell. I put on my best face of shock, pulling them each in for a hug when I see all the effort they've gone to. Thankfully they listened when I said I only wanted it to be our small group.

Pale pink and white balloons fill my living room, presents littered across the table while enough food to feed an army sits upon my dining room table.

"Wow," I say, clearly speechless.

"Did we go over the top?" Em laughs, but Stana lightly smacks her arm.

"Of course we didn't! Lottie's little girl deserves only the best." Stana beams, leading me over to the couch. I spot Ali in the corner, smiling. He's eyeing Stana with awe, clearly proud of his girl.

"This is all amazing," I tell them, giving each an extra-tight hug before eyeing the food and mentally deciding how I will eat all of it.

"Oh, wait, we have to show her the baby's room!" Stana squeals. My eyebrows draw together. This is a one-bedroom flat, so either the baby has taken over my room or I've misheard.

"What do you mean?"

Stana grabs my hand and leads me into my bedroom. I cringe when I think of the state it was in this morning when I left the house. Yet to my utter surprise, once the door is pulled open, it's unlike anything I've seen before. This room has always been big, but I've never been one to fully utilize it. I've got no time for decorating or folding laundry, so it's essentially just been one big messy closet for the past few years.

My bed has been pushed closer to the wall on the far right, perfectly made with my side table still there. But instead of all the dead space on the other side, there is a white cot, with yellow flowers painted on the wall behind it. Instantly I know Em did them. A far-too-familiar rocking chair sits in the corner. It's the same one my mother had from when I was a child.

I keep looking around, taking everything in. My old brown dresser has been refurbished, now a shabby-chic white with an assortment of teddies and baby essentials neatly placed atop it, also doubling as a change table. Photographs line the walls, keeping the room balanced between mine and the baby's.

"I don't even know what to say," I whisper.

"I take it we didn't destroy your bedroom for nothing?" Stana looks anxiously at me, and a laugh escapes my mouth at the fact that she could even imagine I might not like it.

"I love it. It's everything."

She places her hand over mine and gives it a squeeze.

"I'm guessing this is what you needed Ali's help for?" I ask.

"We needed him to help with building everything," Stana tells me. My gaze finds Ali across the room.

"Thank you," I tell him, throat thick.

Smiling, he nods. "Of course."

"How did you find the time to get all of this stuff? I mean, that rocking chair. All this furniture." I let my eyes scan the room again, trying to convince myself it's real.

"Well, we had help," Em says, motioning with her head toward Owen, who is acting way too casual.

Turning to him, I laugh. "Of course."

His cheeks redden lightly, a small smile tracing his lips. I try to hold back tears, knowing I will thank him later in my own way.

"Oh, and there is actually one more thing," Owen says. His lips purse together; he's clearly trying to hide something.

"Any more surprises and I think I'm going to faint," I reply.

"Well, we wouldn't want that," a voice says. I nearly do pass out when my mum buzzes into the room.

"Oh my God!" Stana yells out, seeing her aunt, my mother.

"You didn't think I'd miss today, did you, Lottie?" My mother's warm face smiles at me as she walks forward and encases me in a hug. I shudder in her arms, not having realized till this moment how much I missed her.

"It's okay, my darling girl, don't cry," she tells me, running her hand down my hair.

"I can't believe you're here. I mean, how?" I blink away the moisture, trying to pull myself together.

Her gaze darts to Owen. "Let's just say a little birdy told me this was not to be missed." His eyes meet mine across the room as I try to let him know how much this all means to me.

I lean into her again for a quick hug before pulling away, and Mum goes to greet Stana. After all the hugs and smiles, everyone exits the bedroom to dig into the food, but I stop Owen before he can leave.

"You did all this for me," I say to him, voice husky. My feet instinctively draw me closer to him, our toes touching.

"Of course," he responds instantly.

"You have no idea how much this means," I tell him, my breath warm against his skin. He tightens the hold as much as he can with a baby between us.

"I'd do it a million times over," he responds, only making my feelings for him grow even more.

"What about Evie?" I say suddenly.

"She'll be here in twenty minutes, had a client meeting. You think she'd miss this?"

I smile, happy to know she will be here. Plus, she can finally meet my mum.

"Imagine those two together." He laughs as we stroll back into the living room.

"Darling, you've got to try these pastries Stana got for you. They're simply heavenly."

I wave at Owen as Mum pulls me across the room, practically shoving an apricot Danish into my hand, not that I'm complaining.

That's how the rest of the day goes—people handing me things I don't need but definitely want, treating me like an absolute silkworm. It's a day filled with love and joy, and I couldn't be more grateful.

And it's when my mum tells me she's staying in London for the next two months, wanting to be here before the baby arrives and for the first few weeks after, that I finally feel at peace. I may not have known it, but I needed her here with me.

And it's even better when she tells me she's staying at an Airbnb down the street, my soul thankful for the reprieve we will each have from one another when the sun goes down. As much as I love my mother, us Knight women are a lot for anyone to handle. Someone probably should have warned Owen.

Fourteen

February soon blends into March, the leadup to my delivery creeping closer and closer. I've got less than a week left, yet I can't seem to slow down, wanting to have everything be perfect for her arrival.

Mum's been the biggest help imaginable, with Dad having flown in last week to help out too. They're currently at lunch with their friends while I endeavor to get some last-minute things finished.

I'm attempting to juggle my plethora of bags and navigate the hustle and bustle of Oxford Street when I hear my name being called. I pull over to the side street, away from all the people, when I see Maureen Johnson, an old uni mate of mine.

Before Stana and Em, I never really had a big group of close girlfriends. I was more the girl who was friends with everyone, plus Beck took up so much of my time. I don't regret it; despite what others may think, I'm happy with how everything has worked out.

"Lottie, I almost didn't recognize you!" Maureen shouts, her voice fighting for volume over the traffic.

I take a moment to look her over, it having been over a year since I've last seen her. Maureen used to be my go-to person for a night out on the town, but when I moved to Edinburgh last year we lost touch.

She still looks great, her deep red hair pin-straight and resting on her shoulders with her signature fringe bouncing as she walks to me. She rocks a tight pair of black jeans, a cropped sweater, and high-heeled black boots. How she isn't freezing her arse off, I don't know.

"Maureen," I finally reply as she halts in front of me. "It's been forever. How are you?"

She grins at me while going in for a hug, both of our bags disrupting it. Laughing, we pull back.

"I'm great! My fashion line I was working on got picked up. Next month you'll be able to buy the entire collection online, and we're opening up a boutique in Covent Garden."

Covent Garden is prime real estate, so she must be doing well.

"Wow," I respond. "That's incredible! Congratulations."

Her lips perk up at the sides. "Right! I couldn't believe it, honestly, but I guess the universe just had it all worked out for me. But enough of that, what about you? I thought you moved to Edinburgh. Are you back on holidays?"

I bite my tongue, wanting to tell her I've been back far longer than I was actually ever there for, but refraining. Maureen is good people, but she's also a terrible gossip. And as much as I'm one for a chat, it's only when I know keeping it in confidence is involved.

"Yeah, Edinburgh was good, but London is home. I've been back for a while now."

"I get that. I mean, how could anyone leave London? And Beck, is he back with you? You know, I heard from him the other day saying he was coming to London soon! Can we all hit the town? My job is so stressful I need something to decompress."

I can't ignore the tightening of my fist or the prickling of my skin at the mention of Beck and him reaching out to her. If he wasn't a piece of shit before, he sure is now.

"Um, Beck and I actually split last July," I tell her, my voice no longer holding the bubbly notes it used to. Instead venom has seeped in.

Her head turns slightly to the side, her dark lips pursing. "Oh wow, I heard he was still in Edinburgh, but I didn't know you split."

I nod, because I'm not exactly sure what else to say.

She begins to look around, as if she suddenly feels awkward about bringing him up. I don't blame her.

"It's honestly fine. He just wasn't a good fit."

Now it's her time to nod before she gives me her attention again, finally seeing my visibly rounded stomach. Despite being nine months pregnant I'm still relatively small, my shopping bags doing some of the work to hide my belly.

"Oh wow, Lottie, are you pregnant?"

I try to push out the panic I hear in her words, how she phrases it like an illness. I get it. We're young, and kids weren't really in the cards for us yet. I'm probably the least likely out of everyone we know to end up like this.

"Uh, yeah, I am." I stand proudly, my hand coming to rest on my stomach despite the shopping bags weighing it down.

"Holy shit," she says before catching herself. "Sorry, that was rude. I'm just surprised is all! I mean, I didn't even think you wanted kids."

Me neither.

"Sorry, who's the father?"

It's a rude question but one I'm asked frequently nonetheless. Just when I'm about to kindly go off on her, I spot Owen exiting the Apple store. Maureen's gaze follows mine, her eyes darkening.

"Well, isn't he a snack," she says, practically salivating at the sight of him. I retract my claws, not wanting to maul my old friend. Owen and I are in a murky area—we're not together, but neither of us are seeing other people.

"Yep, he's my snack," I let out. "A whole ten-course meal." I have no idea why I say it. Well, I kinda do. I feel the need to piss all over him and if I weren't pregnant, I know I'd do the same thing, maybe even more. What can I say? I'm slightly territorial. It's bad and I know it—Owen isn't mine. Hell, I'm pushing him to other women at every chance, but I won't let her have him. Call me a bitch.

Owen finally reaches us, a smile broadcasted across his face as he looks me over, then my bump, something I've noticed him doing more frequently. He doesn't even seem to notice Maureen with me, his concern focused on me and the baby.

"Hey," he says, his hand coming out to take all my bags without me asking.

"Hey," I whisper back, fucking ecstatic to see him.

"Wow, so you must be Dad?" Maureen interrupts our moment, and Owen stiffens as he turns to her. He plasters on a smile, not wanting to be rude, yet I know it isn't genuine.

"Owen," he says, reaching out to shake her hand. She looks to me quickly and winks in approval.

"I'm Maureen, an old friend of Lottie's." She pauses, blatantly eyeing him. "Well, Lottie, putting two and two together, I can see why you left Beck."

It's clear how she views it. I left or cheated on Beck with Owen and got knocked up. It pisses me off, but I say nothing. The last thing I need is to air my dirty laundry to someone who will call ten people. I've made my bed with Beck; I don't plan on lying in it again and catching fleas.

Owen stiffens beside me, and I risk looking up at him, seeing the smile fall off his lips.

When neither Owen nor I say anything, Maureen takes that as her cue to continue talking, her hands animatedly in the air.

"So how did Beck take the whole thing?" She signals to my stomach, and I feel my eyebrows rise. "Was he heartbroken? When he reached out he didn't mention anything had happened between the two of you, so I just assumed you were still together."

"Beck is a sorry piece of shit who wouldn't know the word 'heartbreak' if it bit him on the arse. He probably didn't mention Lottie because he's too much of a coward to admit the hell he put her through. She doesn't need him in her life; she's got all she will ever need."

I'm taken aback, and from the way Maureen's jaw has hit the pavement, it appears she is too. It's an outburst I've yet to see from Owen, but one I wouldn't hate to see again. Sure, I'm a strong, independent woman, but holy hell, it wouldn't be terrible seeing him defend my honor. Screw airing dirty laundry—I'll lay it all on the pavement for Owen.

"Um," Maureen says, her manicured hands coming up to scratch her neck. "Wow, Lottie, I really didn't know."

I want to laugh. It's probably the tenth time Maureen has said "wow" this conversation, but she clearly means well, so I hold it in.

"It's okay," I tell her. "Beck and I didn't end on great terms, but he's in my past now, so it's just not something I bring up because he honestly doesn't matter to me."

"Of course," she says all too quickly, her head nodding up and down like a little bobblehead. "Well, I hate to cut things short—we really do need to catch up, Lottie—but I've got a hair appointment." She looks at her watch. "Well, five minutes ago! But text me and we can get a drink. Uh, shit, no, I mean a coffee!"

She leans in for a quick hug before waving at Owen and disappearing through the crowd.

Owen and I stand there for a few more moments before I turn to him, noticing his eyes staring off into the distance.

"Hey," I say, nudging his arm. He blinks a few times, his tall frame finally turning to me.

"You okay?" I ask.

"I'm sorry I let her think I was the dad." The words spill out of him, and I see remorse, but I also don't fully see regret.

"You're fine. She assumed," I reply casually, beginning to stroll down Oxford Street, knowing Owen will stay by my side.

"But I didn't correct her."

"Who cares? I doubt I'll see her again anyway." To be honest, I couldn't care less if people think Owen is my little girl's dad. Lord knows any dad is better than Beck.

Owen stops behind me, people shouting as he blocks the path.

"I promise, it's not a big deal."

We walk through the busy crowds, my feet thankful when Owen hails a cab. I quickly get in and sit next to him. "I was thinking," I tell him. "Once she's old enough, I should take her out to visit my parents in France. I mean, it's probably too soon to make all these plans, but I want to have things to look forward to."

"I'm sure she would love that, your parents too."

"I thought if you wanted, you could come. I mean, I'll ask everyone else to come too, but I definitely want you there."

He grins. "I'd love that, Lottie."

I'm still smiling like an idiot when a strange sensation like I've just peed my pants hits me. I look down, mouth agape when I see water covering my pants and the seat below me.

"Oh shit," I whisper.

"What?" he asks, before his eyes widen when they land on my legs.

"Driver, can you get us to Royal London please?" he instructs, quickly going into takeover mode. I see the driver's eyes glance into the rearview mirror before widening and going back to the road.

"It's too early," I say, knowing a week early is okay, but the reality of what is happening crashing down on me. I'm about to have a fucking baby!

"Hey." He cups my face, our gazes locking. "You can do this. You're ready. There is nothing more to prepare for, okay? You don't have to be scared, Lottie. I'm here."

I nod, trying to keep my breathing even as we drive. Owen calls my mum for me and texts the group to keep everyone updated. I know some people don't want to tell anyone until the baby has come, but I'm not that girl. I need my people with me.

We make it to the hospital in quick time, Owen wasting not a second to get me checked in. I'm in a gown and into a bed and before I know it, the contractions begin, my labor coming along faster than expected. My friends and family still aren't here when it's time to push, my face sweaty and hair sticking to it.

"You can do this, love," the nurse says next to me, attempting to calm me down.

"Okay, Lottie, start pushing," the doctor says, preparing for the arrival of my baby girl. I shake my head, suddenly petrified that I indeed cannot do this.

"I don't want to do this alone." I begin to cry to Owen. Thankfully, he lets me hold his hand in a death grip. I try inhaling deep breaths like they taught at the one Lamaze class I went to, but fuck that shit. Who has time to focus on their breathing in these types of moments?

"I'm here. You're not alone. Neither of you will ever be alone, you hear me?"

I nod, but another wave of pain takes over and I scream out. Fuck, no one ever told me it's this bad.

"Okay, love, you need to start pushing. Give us a big push," the nurse with the Cockney accent says.

And boy do I push, using all my strength again and again until I hear it. The loudest little cry wails from the end of my bed, the doctor holding her up for me to see.

A sob catches in my throat at the sight of her, all pink, covered in white shit. She's fucking perfect. And all mine.

"Does Dad want to cut the cord?" Her question is directed at Owen, whose face has gone a whiter shade of pale.

"Uh..." His hold on my hand begins to loosen, as if he somehow doesn't belong, but I tighten my grip. His gaze snaps to mine as I nod, motioning my head toward the baby and nurse.

The nervous Owen from months ago when he first burst into my life reappears as he walks over and grips the scissors. I can't look away from him as he does it. He's been here through everything. If anyone should be doing this, it's him.

"Perfectly healthy baby girl," the nurse tells me, placing my daughter's crying red body on top of my own. I quickly put my hands on her to keep her supported, her wails calming.

Owen walks back over to me, a sheen of liquid coating his eyes.

"She's perfect, Lottie. Absolutely perfect," he whispers from next to me, awe overtaking his voice. I just nod in agreement. Stroking her skin, I try to comprehend how I managed to create such an important, beautiful little life. How I got so lucky.

Eventually they have to clean her and wrap her for me. My soul already misses her presence.

"So, Mummy, do you have a name?" the nurse asks as she brings her back to me, my arms impatient to hold her again. She's all wrapped up like a little burrito as I take hold of her again, something deep inside of me settling.

I nod. "Rosie. Her name is Rosie Knight."

Fifteen

Rosie's scream wakes me up exactly three hours after I put to her bed. It's been like clockwork—every three hours she needs to be fed, changed, and cuddled.

I groan as I look at the clock, which is telling me it's only three a.m. Ever since we got home from the hospital last week, I've been attempting to get used to my new routine, yet I mainly feel like a zombie. Like all the bloody time.

I pull myself out of bed and go to her, each cry a little louder than the one before.

"Shhh, shhh, Rosie, Mummy's here," I say as I pick her up. Her face is bright pink while her mouth trembles with each wail.

I situate myself on the rocking chair before she begins to feed, latching on without any issues and quieting instantly. Her tiny little hand rests atop of me while I run my free hand over her blonde hair. I never knew a baby could have as much hair as Rosie. With big blue eyes and the mop of hair, she's a little replica of me as a child, says Mum, only she's cuter. I don't disagree. I was blonde as a little girl before my hair started to darken. Clearly I liked being a blonde more, hence the bleach.

We sit together rocking back and forth until she's full, her eyes drifting shut again. I right her on my shoulder, then burp her until I know it's okay to put her down again. As soon as she's back in her cot I want to pick her up again and nuzzle my face into her soft, warm neck. But I could never wake her, so I drag my over-exhausted body to bed and let sleep take hold. Well, at least for another few hours anyway.

"Darling, why don't you go take a nap and I'll watch Rosie?" My mother's voice infiltrates my fuzzy mind as Rosie sleeps upon my chest. She sits next to me, knitting in hand. It's a rare sight, but one I don't mind.

"No, it's okay, Mum. I need to stay awake anyway."

"What time are the girls coming over?"

I scratch my head. "Uh, I think five? They're going to stop by before the guys' show tonight."

"You know if you wanted to go, I'd be more than happy to look after her."

"I know, Mum. I think it's just a little soon for me to be leaving her."

She nods. "I was like that with you. It took your father practically forcing me out of the house alone one day when you were six months for me to finally understand mums need time too."

"I'm sure I'll get there, just not yet."

She pats my hand before going back to her knitting. "So, I was talking to Evie this morning and we were thinking of going to dinner tomorrow night, but I wanted to make sure you didn't need me."

Since my mum and Evie meeting at my baby shower, the two have become fast friends, going as far as to plan upcoming FaceTimes for when Mum's back in France.

"I think that's great. You deserve a break. Lord knows you've been doting on me for weeks."

She dismisses me with a wave. "I'd never have it any other way, Lottie. You're my little girl and you will be until you're my age. I'd never want to miss these moments."

Smiling at her, I mentally thank the universe for her being here over the past month. Despite me having Owen and the girls, they've all got jobs they need to go to during the day, and since I can no longer go to mine, well, let's just say I've been bored and overwhelmed.

The next three weeks fly by, with Mum staying a little longer to help out. It was the biggest help I could imagine because despite reading every baby book and watching all the documentaries, I still wasn't prepared for what motherhood entailed.

Before I know it, Rosie is one month old, her personality growing daily. We've managed to get into a slight routine, but she's still so small that it holds little ground. Everyone comes over when they have the chance, but the reality is they all have full-time jobs and commitments, not able to drop everything and come see me when I'm feeling lonely.

I see Owen the most, despite still pushing him to date. I know it pisses him off, but luckily he says nothing, just entertains me. I don't know if he's actually gone on any dates, but I like to hope he has. As much as it does something to my insides, like twisted-up wet laundry *something*, I can't hold him back. I know if he had it his way we'd be together, but I've just had a baby. It's less than practical.

So instead we accept one another's friendship, both of us pushing away any other thoughts to the best of our abilities. Because our friendship means more than anything, his relationship with Rosie means more. She needs all the strong male figures in her life that she can get.

So, when he comes over later that night, with my favorite takeaway, I know I've done the right thing by pushing him away. It's better to keep this type of relationship than attempt a romantic one.

An hour after eating, with me sprawled across the couch while Owen sits on the floor with his back against it, I scroll through his dating profile I made him set up.

Call me crazy—maybe I'm even a glutton for punishment—but in order to be okay with how much time he spends with me and Rosie, I need to make sure he is still living life.

"What about this girl?" I hold up her profile in his face. She's a brunette, big smile, big boobs, and she loves music and a drink at the pub.

I tell him she seems great but he says nothing, his eyes looking away from my own.

"Oh, come on, Owen, you need to give these people a shot or you will never meet anyone."

"Lottie," he says, voice suddenly serious. He turns his head from the TV, his attention suddenly on me.

"What?"

He huffs. "Why are you being so aloof about this? Glazing over everything that's happened between us? Pushing me on other people?"

"Owen, we've been over this. I can't give you what you want. I'm in zero position to be in a relationship and honestly, I don't have it in me to try," I lie. Lie, lie, lie. It's always a lie with him these days, because in truth, it's only him I want, but I'm too much of a little bitch to admit my feelings. Plus, I have a one-month-old.

"Baggage" is an understatement.

He nods for a second, his gaze drifting off. "Sure, she looks fine," he says.

"Great! She wants to meet for coffee tomorrow." I waggle my eyebrows at him, trying to show off my best moves and he smiles back, but it's forced.

Maybe it is fucked up I'm doing this to him, but I can't bring myself to stop.

I continue to arrange a date for the man I want with a girl I already irrationally hate. Yet I do it anyway because I'm a sick sadist apparently.

When he leaves later that night, I feel a strange shift in the air between us, but I ignore it. I've become good at that recently. I just hope these actions don't backfire.

I lean forward, dotting little kisses all across Rosie's face. She's still so small that I don't get a huge reaction, but I love it anyway. Her big blue eyes stare up at me, her mind probably wondering why some crazy lady is looming over her. Little does she know she's so cute she's stuck with me for life.

My phone vibrates in my pocket, Evie's name flashing upon the screen.

"I was wondering when you'd call," I say, answering the FaceTime. Since Rosie's birth, Evie calls me at least three times a week, always around her lunch break, while Mum's calls come every single day. Apparently the two keep one another updated when I fall behind. Which these days happens a bit.

"I just needed a little Rosie pick-me-up before I went into court this afternoon. Remind me to tell Owen never to get a divorce. In fact, Lottie, I'm telling you too. Be sure you marry someone good because these arseholes can play dirty."

I laugh, knowing marriage is an extremely far off idea for me, if one at all.

"Noted," I tell her, making sure the screen is showing Rosie and not my messy self.

"Hello, my darling girl, your Evie misses you very much. Are you going to come see me soon?"

"I was thinking we could come visit for lunch one day. There's only so much time a girl can spend inside before she loses her mind."

Evie's wistful laugh drifts through the phone. "Oh, I remember those days. Luckily with Hugo I had Owen to keep me on my toes."

I smile, thinking of a small Owen helping his mum out. If he was anything like he is now, I know she was a lucky woman.

"But yes, Lottie, please come visit. I can get my secretary to book us somewhere delicious."

"I'd love that," I tell her, my mind drifting to all the terrible food I've eaten since Rosie was born. I either go all day, forgetting to have something, or I pick up the nearest packet of crisps and before I know it I've inhaled the whole thing. My only solace is when Owen comes by with food.

Evie and I speak for twenty more minutes, both of us catching up while I tell her all about Rosie's daily habits, which aren't exactly a lot, but she wants every single detail. Eventually I have to go because Rosie's hungry and in desperate need of a nap.

We make plans to get lunch the following week and say our goodbyes. I quickly get to work on Rosie, putting her down for a nap before I myself need to take one too.

"Lottie, I swear she is the most perfect thing I've ever seen." Stana rocks Rosie back and forth in her arms, her gaze attached to my little girl. We sit in Saint Street, appreciating the fact that the place isn't packed for once, Ali keeping it closed during the day. Cue us girls using it as a quiet hangout when our flats just feel too small.

I eye all the presents they've brought, sprawled across the table.

"You know you didn't have to bring all of this stuff. I will love you even if you come empty handed." Although Rosie's already a month old, every time they see her, the girls squeal as if it's their first encounter.

"I want to hold her," Em whines. I turn to her.

"Wake her up, and you die," I say, to which she playfully rolls her eyes at me.

"I mean it, Emilia Ronan. This is the first hour I've gotten to myself in over a month."

"Fine," she sulks, taking a sip of her drink.

"Onto other news, I heard you're pushing Owen to date?" Stana's voice is soft so she doesn't disturb Rosie, but I hear the question in it.

I nod. "It's not normal for him to dedicate all his time to me and the baby. I've been saying it for months—he needs to date, find a nice girl." I look away from them, reaching for my cold drink. The bubbles feel rough against my throat, but I welcome them.

"Cut the crap," Em says, taking on my old role. "Tell us your true feelings, Lottie. It's us."

I sigh, knowing I wouldn't have gotten the lies past them anyway. "Yeah, I'm pushing him to date, going as far as making him a profile on the apps, and yeah, it hurts me because I want him, but I can't have him. And I figured the only way I can have him around as much as he is in good conscience would be to help him out in his romantic life."

"But we all know it's you he wants," Em says. Stana quickly nods.

"So? That doesn't matter. I'm not available and he will get over it quickly. Trust me, I've seen the women out there. They're young, hot, and have no children waiting at home."

"Do you hear yourself right now?" Stana says, eyes wide as if she doesn't know me.

"Of course I do."

"No, Lottie, I don't think you do." She sighs. "You sound bloody mental. You want Owen but you're setting him up on dates despite the fact that he wants you too. It's only going to end in hurt for everyone involved, trust me."

"I know how it seems. Even I think it's ridiculous, but it's the only way. I have a newborn—I can't date right now. Even having this conversation feels utterly ridiculous. Owen's a twenty-eight-year-old stunner who plays in a band. I'm sure he's never waited too long to find someone, and I won't make him wait for me. Because that's all he would be doing, waiting."

Both girls shake their heads, clearly disagreeing, but they say nothing. I know deep down what I'm doing isn't normal. But look at the situation I'm in. None of this shit is normal. I'm just trying to make the best out of it.

An hour later I'm walking out of Saint Street when I call Owen, hoping I'm catching him on a break. Rosie is fast asleep in her pram, so I decide to circle the block a few times, not eager to wake her.

"Hey," he answers.

"Hey, you. Is this an okay time?"

"Yeah, it is actually. Just finished up in a meeting."

"Awesome, well, I just wanted to see if you were keen to come to dinner tonight. I'm thinking of finally cooking something. Be warned there is a chance you could get food poisoning."

He chuckles through the line and I can't help but smile. Something about the husky laugh warms my insides.

"So, is that a yes?"

"Uh…" He pauses, suddenly reluctant. "I can't come tonight—I've got plans—but what about tomorrow?"

"Ooh, hot date?" I tease as I walk by the cupcake shop, my feet forcing me to keep moving.

"Well, actually I'm getting drinks with Zoey, the girl from the app you set me up on." His voice is hesitant and I can practically imagine how his face looks. Probably how mine does. Despite the digging feeling in my chest, I try to be happy for him.

"Lottie?" he asks, getting my attention.

"That's amazing! I'm glad you're taking my advice and putting yourself out there," I lie with false cheer. My hands dig into the material on the pram.

"It's not that big of a deal. You know I'd rather hang with you and Rosie. Why don't I just cancel and we can hang out?"

And there it is. The reason why he *needs* to do this. I can't give him a relationship right now; I honestly can't give him much in general. It would be all too easy and selfish to get him to cancel the date, like I'm sure he's canceled many in the past because of me. But I need to take a leaf out of Owen's book and put others before myself.

"No way, you're going on this date. And anyway, I'll probably be too tired to cook tonight. We both know I'm ordering." I try to lighten the mood with the rest of our conversation, but there's an unspoken feeling between us I can't shake.

I know if I sat down I would be able to see what that feeling is in a second, but the little bitch inside of me refuses to dissect things. For the first time in my life, I'm willing to live in ignorance.

I can't sleep that night. I try pinning it on the glass of wine I had after I put Rosie down, but these days that knocks me out faster than anything. I know it's because I'm stressing over Owen's date. Wondering if she's amazing, what she loves to do for fun. I'm sure she's spontaneous and can drop everything in a second to go out.

I used to be that girl.

But as much as I want to feel sorry for myself, I just can't. Rosie is my world now and I wouldn't change it for a thing. I won't even let myself be pitied.

It isn't until he calls me the next morning that I find out his date was a bust. Apparently she only cared about his band and nothing else. But instead of doing a mini dance, I push him to keep dating. Exploring all options.

And so he does. Once every few weeks for the next three months until we hit July, Owen occasionally goes out, always coming home saying it didn't work out.

Until one day in July everything changes.

Sixteen

July

Rosie is nearing four months old. Every day she gets bigger, more curious and engaging. And every day I grow to love her a little more than before. Life isn't perfect, but it is surprisingly easier than the first few months.

She has found a sleeping schedule, now only waking up once or twice in the night for milk. The lack of a full sleep no longer bothers me, my body adjusting to her schedule. I still manage to see everyone, not as much as before, but still quite frequently, Rosie being such a good little girl that she will go almost anywhere, not making a sound of complaint. The fear and anxiety I've had over her first year of life has proven to be slightly irrational. Sure, we've had hard times, but for the most part it's amazing. My life didn't stop when she was born like I thought it might; in fact, it's better than ever.

So when Owen comes over one afternoon, telling me he's met someone, suddenly all the fear I'd had about wanting to be with him just vanishes. In its place, the feeling of pure loss hits me.

"So tell me about her," I say, pouring my tea. For the past three months Owen has gone on a handful of dates, none of them panning out to anything, but today it was different.

Grinning ear to ear, he graciously takes the cup from me. His gaze latches onto mine as he speaks. I try to steady my shaking hand, not wanting to spill the hot liquid everywhere. Despite it being warm in the flat, I grab the nearest blanket and cover my bottom half as I turn to him.

My fingers weave in and out of the knit material as he talks, his face lighting up with each word.

"Well, she's in her mid-twenties, highly intelligent, absolutely stunning." He pauses, pointing to the plate of biscuits. I nod for him to have one, not able to speak for the knife that's been shoved into my chest. Through all his words, I remember I did this.

"Anyway, yeah, she's great. Good banter, we get along like a house on fire, plus she's got a great group of friends."

"Wow, she sounds amazing," I manage to whisper, my voice sounding foreign to my own ears.

He takes a bite out of the biscuit, nodding, his eyes not leaving mine. "You've got no idea," he confirms.

I swallow a few times before biting the side of my cheek, attempting not to cry in front of him. This whole thing is so ridiculous, I've pushed him to this and now I'm going to have a meltdown because he finally did what I've been telling him to do for months. What a fucking psycho I am.

"You okay?" he asks casually before sipping his tea. I just nod and give him a tight smile.

"So, how long ago did you meet?" I croak out. From what he's saying it already seems serious.

"It's actually just come up on a year."

A year? And he never mentioned her to me.

Despite what I'm sure is a look of astonishment on my face, Owen keeps talking, his voice animated.

"I could tell she was hesitant at first, and she's got some baggage, but I've just come to realize none of that matters. You see, I can read her like a book and have managed to know when she's bullshitting me. So, I decided to just take charge."

"Yeah," I respond, not sure if I'm even listening anymore. He's known this girl a year and never mentioned her. The need to cry hits me all over again.

"Plus, did I mention she has the best little girl in the entire world? Cutest kid, I swear."

He's dating someone with a kid! I stop my mind mid-thought, my head snapping up. A cheeky smile flashes across his face.

The asshole is talking about me. He's fucking talking about me!

"Catching on yet?" he asks, leaning forward, taking my hands in his own. I try to blink away the tears, but he catches one that falls.

"I can't keep letting you push me towards other people when we both know the only one each of us wants is right here. Rosie doesn't take away from you, Lottie. She only adds to everything that makes you incredible."

I can't help but hiccup, my mind catching up to the carnage that was my chest only moments ago. The fucking fear of thinking I'd lost him without fully giving him a chance.

"You scared me," I whisper.

"I'm sorry," he says, running his hand across my own.

"No, Owen, you don't get it," I whisper, surprised he can still hear me. "It's because you mean *everything* to me."

He inhales quickly, appearing to have an internal battle with himself before he clearly says fuck it and rushes toward me. I accept it this time, meeting him halfway as his strong arms lock around me. I inhale his scent, needing that extra reminder that he's still here, that he's okay.

"You mean everything to me too, Lottie. You both do."

His breath is warm against my shoulder, comfort overtaking me as I nuzzle closer to him. We stand like this for a few minutes, both seemingly needing the closeness of one another. Owen finally pulls back, looking down at me.

"Lottie, I know we said if things were different we would give us a shot, but I don't want them to be different. I don't want to miss another moment with you because we're scared of the unknown."

"What are you saying, Owen?"

He shakes his head, smiling. "I'm saying I'm sick of pretending I don't want more with you. I've never met someone more outspoken, honest, and caring than you, and you set my mind on fire constantly. I know it isn't traditional to start something when you've got a newborn, but nothing about us is conventional. I want us to be more, if you're willing." He looks me in the eyes, a slight dash of panic on his face, as if he fears I'll reject him. And who knows, if today had never happened I might not have had the courage to give this a go, but it did.

"I know this situation isn't something anyone would sign up for, and I can't give you everything you deserve," I begin.

It's his turn to hold up his hand, silencing me. "I wouldn't change this for the world, Lottie. I want to be here; no one is forcing me. I want to be here for you and your daughter, and nothing would make me happier."

My throat tightens, tears prickling at my eyes. "You have no idea how much that means to me, Owen. She'll be lucky to know someone as honorable and strong as you. I'm lucky to know you."

"So, is that a yes?"

I shudder before nodding. My heart clenches at the words, wanting nothing more than to accept him into my life fully, but I know I'm not there yet. He isn't her dad despite how much I want him to be. Maybe, who knows down the line that could change, but for now I still have to be cautious, not for myself, but for her.

"My life is a whirlwind of mess and even more clutter than before, but I'm excited for it. And stepping into a relationship is probably the worst idea ever right now, but I can't seem to say no. So, if you're sure you can handle it, then I'm willing. But I need you to promise me, if it is ever too much, you tell me. You're allowed to walk away."

"I don't want to—"

"I *need* you to promise me, Owen."

He nods. "I promise if it's too much I'll walk away."

Although the words hurt, they're what I need to seal the deal. Without thinking of how terrible this idea probably is and that it will probably end in tears before bedtime, I lean forward on my tippy toes, my hands going to Owen's shoulders. He clues in, wrapping his arms around my waist as I connect my lips to his. It's every bit as explosive as I expected, every bit as magical. My heart races as I link my fingers through his hair and we invade one another's senses.

As if we've done it a million times, warmth floods my system as he pulls me closer, deepening the kiss. A cry breaks out from the monitor, alerting us to Rosie's presence. We break away, laughing, only able to see the hilarity in this weird-ass situation.

"I guess we'd better get used to that." He smiles, his hands coming down to rest upon my hips. In that exact moment she begins crying.

"Shall we?" he asks, pulling me up from the couch with him. I nod, following him into Rosie's room. She beams at the sight of him.

"I think she might be obsessed with you," I whisper as he goes to get her.

If possible, the smile eating up his face only grows. "The feeling is mutual," he whispers to her. My chest feels heavy as Owen speaks with such love and care for her.

Not having to say anything else, he pulls me into him, my head resting upon his shoulder while he cuddles Rosie on his other side. We stand together until Rosie begins to squirm, clearly wanting to have some mat time. Owen leads us over to the floor as we've done a million times. Only this time, it's different. *We* are different.

Over the next few days, things between Owen and me just fall into place. Nothing has really changed, our day-to-day routine and interactions still the same, except now there is hand-holding and kissing. Stealing little moments together when Rosie is asleep.

If the past week has confirmed anything at all, it's that Owen and I were living the life of two people in a relationship without the benefits.

I come clean to the girls about Owen and me the day after we get together, not wanting to keep secrets anymore. They understand, telling me they're surprised it didn't happen sooner.

A few days later, while Owen's at work, I'm waiting for the girls to drop by. Around five on the dot Em and Stana buzz in, their arms filled with presents and food. My eyes instantly lock onto the box of Maltesers and I'm happy. Chocolate will win my heart over any day.

They each give me a quick hug before rushing over to Rosie, her fist in her mouth as she eyes them both.

"Look at those rosy cheeks," Em coos.

"And that head of hair. What baby is born with blonde hair all over!" Stana throws in.

"She really is perfect, Lottie," Stana says as I rip open the chocolate container and shove some Maltesers in my gob.

"She's pretty special," I try to say over all the munching. I think they get the gist due to their grins before they go back to fawning over her.

"You know," Em begins, "I was going to say I'm sorry you can't come see the guys perform tonight, but I think you win for plans. I'd way rather be with this little angel."

The guys have a show at Saint Street tonight, and despite Evie offering to babysit, I just didn't have the energy to leave her.

"I can't disagree," I joke. I walk back into the kitchen and place the Maltesers down. "Gals, do you want a drink?"

"No, I'm okay, thanks," Stana says.

"Are the lads keen for the show tonight?" I ask, filling up my own glass before joining them on the couch.

"I think so," Stana says, her attention still on Rosie. "I know Owen is bummed you can't be there, but it's Owen so of course he understands."

"Speaking of Owen," Em cuts in, "can we get some more clarity on that specific situation?"

I playfully roll my eyes. "It's complicated, that's for sure, but at the same time it's so easy with him. I mean, does that even make any sense?"

"Kinda?" Stana says, not looking entirely sure.

"I guess what I mean is, look at the situation we're in. I've just had a baby; I've birthed a literal child and should be in absolutely zero position to be dating, yet I am. Like the situation itself has potential to be extremely messy, but somehow it isn't."

"So, you're officially a couple now or are you still taking it slow?"

I look to Em. "Honestly, we're taking it day by day. Not a whole lot has changed since we first met, except now I guess we are affectionate with one another. I'm so busy with Rosie that I don't have time to overthink things. The great thing about Owen is he just gets it. Never puts pressure on or anything."

"But doesn't that tell you everything?" Stana grins. "The fact that not a lot has changed since you started your friendship, doesn't that show you it was more than a friendship to begin with?"

"She's not wrong," Stana says.

I nod. "I know you're right. Owen has always given me that emotional support I've needed, even when we weren't together. Plus he's amazing with Rosie. You really should see him." I rub my lips together as I think about the trip we took to Hyde Park yesterday. He's a natural.

"Oh, trust us," Em says, "we've seen the two of them together. Give Rosie a few years and she and Owen are going to cause you some trouble, Lottie."

"Oh God." I laugh. "I just worry I'm putting too much on him too quickly. Like he's not Rosie's dad and I would never want him to be giving up everything he loves just to take care of us." Ugh. I shake my head. "I'm getting ahead of myself. This is still so new."

Stan's hand comes to rest upon my own. "We know Owen, and we know he would never commit to something he wasn't ready for. My advice, don't overthink it. Keep doing what works for the two of you. It's no one else's place to judge that."

I smile, knowing she is right. In this moment what Owen and I have works, and if that ever starts to change, well, we'll cross that bridge when we get to it.

"God, you should have seen him the other day. He came over here telling me all about this amazing girl he was into, going on and on about her, and despite the fact that I pushed him to be dating, I nearly broke right there!" I shake my head at the memory. "I swear he is going to be the death of me."

"I've got to admit," Stana says, "it was kind of brilliant. I mean, would you have given him a shot if he hadn't gone on and on about this girl?"

I bite my cheek. "Honestly? I don't know. It's Owen— he's easy on the eyes, in a band, and successful. I doubt it would be hard for him to find someone. So who knows, but I won't say I'm mad he gave me the little push."

Em grins. "I just love it, the two of you together. I mean, what friend group has the entire group paired off with one another?"

"Uh, like every cheesy teen romance movie or TV show?" I offer, knowing that our situation is not the norm.

"Whatever." Em waves her hand, dismissing me. "Anyway, I think it's romantic."

"Me too," Stana gushes.

"You two." I playfully roll my eyes but don't hide my smile, knowing deep down I feel the same way.

Seventeen

Despite a peaceful four months since Rosie's birth, I knew there was bound to be a bad day in our future. I just didn't realize it would be today. She's absolutely hysterical for no reason, red faced and angry. I'm near tears when Owen buzzes on my door after the day we've had.

I pat Rosie on her back as I walk to the door, hopeful it will get her to stop crying. She's been fed and had a fresh nappy, so I have no idea why she won't settle.

"Jesus, Lottie, are you okay?" He eyes me, then Rosie.

"I can't get her to stop crying." I hiccup as he reaches forward and takes her out of my arms. She still cries but begins to calm down.

"What the hell?" I say. "I've been doing exactly what you're doing for over an hour." I wipe my sleeve across my snotty nose, recoiling at the thought of how I must look right now.

"Babe," Owen says, placing his free hand on my shoulder, "why don't you go take a shower? I'll do my best to soothe her."

"But what if she needs me?" I ask, worried about even leaving the room.

"I promise if she needs you, I will bring her in right away, okay?"

I nod, my chest still shakily moving up and down.

"Is someone giving their mum a hard time?" I hear Owen whisper to Rosie as I walk into the bathroom. I can't help but laugh at his baby voice toward her. She has him wrapped around her little finger.

I don't waste any time throwing off my stained clothes and getting under the spray of the hot water, relishing in every single moment. Yet, not wanting to leave them alone for too long, I quickly wash my hair and hop out. The cold bathroom tiles jolt me back as I wrap the towel around myself to dry off before dressing.

"Sorry that took so long," I say as I exit the bathroom, rubbing the towel through my locks. I quickly look around the room, finding Owen making tea in the kitchen, Rosie nowhere to be seen.

"Where is she?" I asked, my voice slightly panicked.

Owen walks over with a steaming hot cup of tea and takes my hand with his free one.

"She's asleep. I promise she's okay."

"She slept for you?" I can't keep the shock out of my voice. I'm her mum and I tried for hours, and she went down for him within minutes?

"Lottie, I can guarantee it wasn't me. She was so exhausted, I think she honestly didn't have a choice."

I look around the room, still not believing she's asleep.

"But why didn't she sleep for me?" My lip can't help but wobble at the question.

Owen's eyes soften when I snuggle into his side. "Because you're her mum and she probably wanted to stay up with you. She loves you the most in this world, you know that."

I sniffle a few times, knowing he's just being nice. I probably smelled and Rosie could sense my own hysterics coming on.

"Do you want something to eat?" he asks.

Shaking my head, I cuddle into the couch.

"Why don't I turn on a show and we can just relax? I'll keep an eye out for Rosie, okay?"

I nod, feeling my eyes already closing as I lean into him. Next thing I know, it's lights out.

I wake up with a jolt, my body jumping off the couch, the apartment now dark. That tells me I've been asleep for some time. Owen is no longer on the couch, but a pillow is under my head, along with a blanket on top of me.

I doubt he would leave without telling me, so I walk out of the living room and push open the slightly ajar door to my bedroom.

The sight before me nearly brings me to tears. Owen is asleep in the rocking chair, Rosie protectively held against his shoulder as she too is out like a light. An empty bottle sits next to him, my mind thankful I don't need to go over her feeding schedule with him. Owen being Owen, I said it once and he didn't forget.

As if sensing my presence, Owen stirs, his eyes opening while a sleepy smile lines his lips. "Hey," he whispers, voice husky.

"Hi," I mouth, unable to move from the spot I'm in. It's these small moments when I see him with her that I wish it. I wish he were hers. And that brings me back to the fact she has a dad, one who refuses to be here. The thought alone crushes me, because how could any father not want this beautiful girl? How could anyone abandon her?

I motion my head toward the bed, somewhere Owen and I have yet to share. But it's late, and there is no way I'm making him leave now. He seems to understand, slowly standing with Rosie in his arms. I hold my breath while he places her back into her cot, still sound asleep.

I don't hesitate to get under the covers and extend my hand to him. He looks at me for a moment, seeming to ask if I'm sure, but I quickly nod. So he removes his shoes and jacket, then climbs in with me as quietly as possible.

We turn to one another, my hand reaching up to trace his handsome face before he takes it in his own and kisses my knuckles. And that's how we both fall asleep. Embracing one another, me feeling a comfort I have never felt in this life before. Safe, happy, and warm. With Owen.

After that first night that Owen stays over, it's rare that he goes back to his house to sleep. He doesn't care when Rosie screams three times a night for milk or a nappy change. He still occasionally tries to get up, but I draw the line there. Rosie is my responsibility, especially during the night, and it feels like accepting too much to let him.

So, as the days continue on, Rosie keeps getting bigger and bolder. Life is still as crazy as ever, my flat feeling smaller by the day, the mess always piling up, but I wouldn't trade it for anything.

She is everything I didn't know I wanted or needed. My little girl.

"So, I hate to ask, but I'm going to," my mum says through the line as I check the baby monitor. Rosie's been sleeping for the past hour, and I'm hoping I get another hour out of her before she wakes so I can get some laundry done.

"What is it, Mum?" I ask, not having the time to beat around the bush.

"Have you heard from Beck?"

Annoyance prickles my skin at the mention of his name. But my heart doesn't drop, and I don't want to sink into the couch, so I take that as a good thing. I'm long past my heartbreak from him, it now having been over a year since I sold his shit and hightailed it out of Edinburgh.

"No, Mum," I respond. "He didn't reply when I told him about her birth, and that was the final nail in the coffin. I refuse to waste any more time on that asshole."

"Good," she says, making me laugh. "He's a right tosser and doesn't deserve to know your beautiful baby girl."

I grin, despite her not being able to see it, and go to grab some of Rosie's baby singlets. They fold in one turn, and I manage to move through them quickly, wanting to have the house looking semi-decent before Owen gets here later.

Mum and I talk for a little longer before the baby monitor goes off and I have to say my goodbyes. I throw the rest of the clothes back into the basket, where they will probably stay for the next week, and hurry to my room.

What I'm not prepared for is the smell that wreaks havoc on my senses when I open the door. I nearly gag as I turn on the light and go toward Rosie, already knowing the carnage I'm about to find.

Looking down, I see my giggly little girl, her big blue eyes shining up at me as she sucks on her fingers. Yet that isn't what gives me pause. It's the big brown stain seeping out of her nappy.

Every mum I spoke to told me this day would come. They called it a poonami because it is a literal wave of shit. I didn't get it then, but I sure as hell do now.

"You're pretty pleased with yourself, aren't you?" I ask as I stare down at her, her small face looking up at me.

"You're really making Mummy work for it today, aren't you?"

Reaching over, I hold my breath, knowing I'm going to have to change her bottom sheet and probably clean the mattress. *Gross.*

She continues to smile, not a care in the world as I attempt to get her outfit off before tossing it into a pile across the room. Putting on the nappy and wiping the mess without her wriggling is the hard part.

She continues to think everything is hilarious, and despite literally being covered in shit, I can't help it. I smile.

After a fresh nappy and a long walk through Hyde Park, Rosie and I are exhausted, anxiously awaiting Owen to get home. To say she's infatuated with him would be an understatement; she's obsessed.

At six p.m. sharp the front door buzzes, Rosie's eyes widening at the sound. I make sure she is secure in her little seat and go open it. Owen's handsome face is focused on his phone as I pull the door open. He doesn't hesitate to put it away and pull me into his arms.

Our lips connect all too briefly before Rosie begins cooing, Owen's face lighting up at the sound.

"Someone has been waiting for you," I tell him.

"Have you been waiting for me?" he asks in a soft voice as he beelines to the kitchen, always washing his hands.

Rosie reaches out her small grabby hand, practically begging for Owen to pick her up. He carefully undoes her straps then pulls her out, immediately kissing her head.

"You should have seen the mess she did in her crib earlier," I say as I hand him a beer. He takes it and I throw myself down on the couch.

He sits on the floor, his back against the couch so he can lean Rosie against his bent legs, facing him.

He laughs. "Oh God, was it traumatic?"

"Yes! It took me nearly an hour to get the smell out. She, on the other hand, thought the entire thing was hilarious. I mean, how does something that small create a mess so big? It's not like she eats anything other than breast milk and formula!"

"Wait till she starts solids next month."

I cringe at the thought.

"Did you make a mess for Mummy today?" he asks her, pinching her chubby little cheeks.

"It's okay, Rosie. Mummy forgives you."

She beams, looking at Owen as he plays with her, the two of them like a little duo.

"So, I spoke to Evie today. She wants everyone over for Sunday dinner this weekend."

Owen laughs. "I feel like you and Mum speak more than she and I do."

I casually lift a shoulder. "What can I say? We're basically best friends."

"Oh, trust me, I know."

He turns, facing those deep ocean blue eyes at me. I poke my tongue out before rolling off the couch to sit next to him with Rosie. I have to shove all her toys and stuff out of the way as I go.

"Ugh, this flat never felt small before, but now it feels like I can't do anything without stepping on toys or my leg smashing into the side of a table. Plus Rosie's nearly four months, and all the books say she should be sleeping alone at six months. Where am I supposed to put her? The closet?" It's a joke, but Jesus Lord, where else can she go?

Owen's eyebrows draw together. "So are you thinking about moving?"

"I don't know. I mean, I really should have given it more thought before she was born. What was I thinking—she and I would share a room forever?"

He places his free hand over mine. "If you want to move, I can help you look into that."

I nod. "It's just, this place has been home for so long. It was Mum and Dad's and then it became mine. I would literally have to sell it to even entertain moving, and it's been home for so long."

Rosie starts to coo, getting back our attention. "So, what, you don't want to sell? This is a great space. I'm sure you wouldn't have a hard time."

"I've been approached a few times to sell, but it just never felt right, and now having Rosie, I don't know if being directly in London is the right choice for us in the long term. I mean, right now it's fine, but when she's five and wants to run around, I want her to have a home."

"What about leasing then? If you're not ready to sell this place, why not lease it out and you can find another place with Rosie, something bigger?"

I nod. "That's a good point. I don't know why I didn't think of that."

"You've still got time, Lottie. Rosie isn't turning six months for another two months."

"Oh God, even the thought of decluttering all this shit gives me anxiety." I turn to Owen, face serious. "It may surprise you, Owen Bower, but I have a lot of junk."

He bursts out laughing. "I'd never know," he says, sarcasm dripping from every word. I playfully roll my eyes before turning back to my little girl, who is now fast asleep in his arms.

"Looks like someone was tired," he says, motioning to her.

"That makes two of us."

"Good thing I ordered Chinese food on the way over. It should be here in twenty, which means you can be in bed by seven thirty."

I want to cry with joy. "You are a godsend!"

He just winks before standing up and taking Rosie into my bedroom. I silently follow him in and watch as he puts her into her baby sleeping bag with perfect care, not once stirring her from her sleep.

After he exits the bedroom, he pulls me into his arms.

"How about a proper hello?" I ask.

"Who could say no to that?" He grins before ducking his head and connecting his lips with my own. My hands go straight to his hair and pull him closer.

His tongue explores my mouth as I open for him, my teeth nipping at his lips. We stand there, getting overexcited for a few minutes before the buzzer goes off and Owen has to pull away.

"I'll get it," I tell him, trying to hide my laugh as I walk to the door.

Now that's how you say hello.

Eighteen

"I can't believe how much she's growing up!" Evie smooshes the sides of Rosie's cheeks, my little girl turning everyone around her into mush.

"I know, right? It seems like only yesterday I was pregnant."

Evie pulls out another new toy she's bought Rosie and shows it to her, her chubby fingers trying to grab the toy giraffe.

"I feel like I never see her enough. I really do need to reinstate this Sunday dinner to every Sunday."

"I wouldn't complain about that," I joke, the smell of roasted potatoes and chicken filling the air. I got here early so Evie could have some one-on-one time with Rosie; I know once the other two girls get here, all bets are off.

"God, I can't imagine how much your mum must miss her. We were speaking the other day, and I'm thinking of taking a little time off and visiting them in a few months."

I can't help but smile. "Mum would absolutely die if you came to visit her. I think she can get lonely at times in France; that's probably why she travels so much."

Before we can continue, the doorbell rings, signaling the first round of humans. Stana and Ali enter, and as predicted, Stana goes straight to Rosie and picks her up off the mat. Her frilly pink dress is bunched up around her thighs, but Stana is quick to fix it.

"I've missed you, Rosie," Stana says in a baby voice, rubbing her nose against Rosie's.

"What am I, chopped liver?" I tease, knowing I would have skipped over anyone for Rosie any day too.

"Sorry," she replies, but her attention is still on the baby.

"Hey, Lottie," Ali says, leaning in for a hug.

"Ali, how's it going? Still keeping Saint Street running like a well-oiled machine?"

He chuckles. "Doing the best I can. Looking forward to the gig tonight."

I beam, excited to finally have a night out of the house. Evie is going to look after Rosie for a few hours so I can go watch Owen and the band perform. Lord know it feels like years since I've gone anywhere that doesn't involve a trip to the store to buy nappies or formula.

"Stana mentioned you're gonna come?" he asks.

I nod. "First night of freedom and I'm spending it watching you guys. You better not disappoint," I tease.

"We'll do our best." At that the door rings, and Owen barrels through with Em and Reeve behind him.

"Hey, you," Owen says, pulling me into his arms. I give him a brief kiss, not one for PDA, especially in front of his mum.

"Hey," I say as I pull away from him.

"You excited for tonight?" he asks and I nod, not able to contain my excitement.

"Rosie is obsessed with your mum, so I doubt she will even know I'm gone. I'm more worried about myself than her."

"I'll take care of you." He winks at me before Rosie starts calling out, clearly noticing he's in the room.

'How's my number one?" he asks, bending down to pick her up.

"I thought I was your number one?" I tease. He just gives me that pretty-boy smile over his shoulder.

"Hey, lovely," Em says, and I realize I've yet to say hi to her and Reeve.

"Sorry, this fella"—she motions to Reeve—"took all my attention. How are you guys?"

"Busy. Work is kicking my arse right now, but I guess that's better than being bored?" Owen replies, still infatuated with Rosie.

"Mine is overall the same. Tonight's my first night out in months, so I'm pretty keen for a wine and to watch the boys. They better not disappoint."

Owen lifts his head to look at me while Ali and Reeve laugh. "I promise we will do our best!" he says, and I just grin.

Everyone spends a few more minutes catching up before Evie calls for dinner. Her mood is extra chipper now that she knows Owen and I are together. She tried to play it cool when we told her, but I heard her go into the kitchen and squeal when she thought we weren't listening.

"So, Owen, do you have any birthday plans?" Evie asks while I serve myself a heaping pile of potatoes, thankful Rosie is napping.

"It's what, a week away?" Stana asks from across the table. Ali hands her the salt without her asking for it, her gentle smile towards him adorable. I swear those two are headed to the altar sooner rather than later.

Owen nods and I mentally pray that the gift I got him goes over well. Despite my pure panic at leaving Rosie for the night, the girls have agreed to look after her while I get a hotel for Owen and myself. Well, I also got them a room on our floor because let's be real, neither myself nor Owen will be able to stay away from her for a full night.

But either way, it's a surprise for the day of his birthday, both girls sworn to secrecy.

"I think maybe a night in with everyone," Owen says from next to me, answering his mother. His hand finds mine under the table and gives it a squeeze. I bite into my food to hide my smile. I've got something else planned for him; he just doesn't know it yet.

"Well, you know I wouldn't want to miss my boy's birthday. How about we all do a picnic to celebrate in the coming weeks?"

"Sure, I bet Rosie would like that too," he replies, looking to me for confirmation.

"She would. She's obsessed with ducks, even though I'm not sure she actually knows what they are."

"Perfect!" Evie beams. "I'll organize it. Maybe you want to help me, Lottie?"

I nod. "Definitely. Lord knows I need some other things to occupy my time. Don't get me wrong, I love my girl, but sometimes I need a little bit of human interaction that isn't from a four-month-old."

"Oh, love, tell me about it. I used to think I would go stir crazy."

"Do you think you'll go back to work soon, Lottie?" Steve asks me before taking a sip of wine.

"I've spoken to my old boss and we've decided I'm going to go back in two months when Rosie's six months. It won't be full time, probably only two or three days, but it's a start."

"You need things for yourself," Evie confirms.

"Will Rosie go into daycare?" Em asks.

"I'm not sure. To be fully honest, I'm still trying to figure it out. I don't want to leave her with a bunch of strangers, but at the same time I know ultimately I will have to."

"Understandable," Em replies.

Conversation eventually shifts to other things, banter easy with my close friends. It's not long before I'm checking on Rosie with Evie right behind me.

"You know, Lottie, I work part-time now," Evie says from next to me while we exit the room after seeing a fast-asleep Rosie.

I turn to her, not fully sure what she's implying.

"I didn't know," I respond. "But you've been working your arse off for years, Evie. You deserve a break."

She raises a shoulder. "I'm still young, Lottie. I was younger than you when I had Owen. Fifty is nothing these days."

I wink. "You don't look a day over twenty."

"I know you're a strong girl. Stubborn too," she says, eyeing me. "I see a lot of myself in you, especially when I'd first had Owen. I was desperate to get back to work but at the same time panicked to leave him or miss even a second of his life."

"I know the feeling," I say.

"I bet you do. That's why I'm going to make you an offer. You don't have to say anything right now, okay? But I need you to promise to think about it. Can you do that for me, Charlotte?"

I nod, knowing I could never deny Evie, especially after all she's done for me.

"I promise."

"I want you to consider letting me look after Rosie for the days you go back to work. I know your initial instinct will be to say no, but I need you to think about it, okay? I wouldn't offer if I didn't want to. But the reality is, I adore your little girl more than anything, and I like to think I'm looking out for you while your mum can't, so will you please consider it?"

My throat feels tight, the love and support pouring off of Evie too much for me to handle. So I just nod, letting her pull me into a hug, offering more comfort than I thought I needed.

"So, are you having fun on your night off?" Em asks, shoving a fresh glass of wine in front of me. The lads are all together having a drink at the bar before they go on in five. Saint Street is packed with the hustle and bustle of locals, something I've slightly forgotten as it's been so long since I've been here at night—nearly five months, to be exact.

"Em, I don't think it's considered a night off, but yes, I'm having a great time." I laugh, looking at my first glass that is still very full. "But I've still got to be a mum in the morning and from what I've heard, having a baby with a hangover is hell."

"Oh God." Stana grimaces. "Sounds like it."

I nod. "You'll both understand soon enough."

Stana tries to hide it, but I see her smile.

"You thinking about babies, Augustana Prescott?" I dare ask. Her face goes beet red at my question.

"No, uh," she sputters, reaching for her drink. "I don't know."

I laugh. "You've got a man who adores you, a place together. A ring and a baby are the next steps for you two. Am I wrong, Em?"

Em shakes her head, her bun full of curls dancing as she moves. "She is not wrong," she chimes in.

"I guess so. I mean, I'm so young—I'm only just about to be twenty-four—but yeah, I would be lying if I said it hasn't been on my mind," Stana admits.

"Wanting those things doesn't mean it has to happen now," I reassure her. "But it's good to know it's Ali who you want them with."

She smiles at his name. "It's definitely Ali I want them with."

I wink. "Thought so." Turning to Em, I give her a look. "What about you, Ronan? Babies in the future?"

"I think Reeve and I would have to move in together before babies and marriage come up, but sure, in a few years it's definitely something we want. But for now, I think we're just happy being us two."

"We're all young. We don't need marriage and babies now." I pause. "Well, I mean, I'm clearly not following the latter, but no marriage for Lottie anytime soon."

They both burst into laughter right as some cheers ring out, the guys heading to the stage. Owen takes his place behind

213

the drums while Ali picks up the guitar and Reeve stands up front.

All three of us lean forward as Reeve starts to sing, probably looking like some lovesick puppies, but we don't give a shit. Those are our lads up there, and I'm going to enjoy every single second of it.

And enjoy every second I did. I got to stare at Owen in his element for thirty minutes before we socialized with all our mates for another two hours after that. By the time we were finished it was ten p.m., my body thankful I'd stopped at two drinks.

Everyone wanted to kick on, so Owen and I slipped out as Saint Street was really heating up. Despite their set usually being around nine, I know they played early for me, which honestly means the world.

Through all of the past few months, this group of humans has only continued to solidify the fact that they're my makeshift family, being there for me through everything.

It's late when we finally get to Evie's, Owen and I sneaking upstairs like a couple of kids and tiptoeing into Owen's old bedroom while Rosie sleeps peacefully in the corner.

I can't help it, so I hover over her crib, her body wrapped up tight in her sleeping bag while her curls glisten in the moonlight that peeks through the window.

I feel Owen come up beside me, his hands going around my waist.

"She really is perfect," he whispers ever so quietly in my ear.

"She really is," I confirm.

Eventually my fatigue gets the best of me, so Owen takes my hand and leads me into his double bed. It's definitely smaller than my queen that we're used to, but it does fine.

I snuggle into his warm chest, trying not to laugh at the situation. Owen is nearly twenty-nine and I'm twenty-six, both of us sleeping in his mum's house with my little girl next to me. Yet despite it all, I manage to drift off into a deep sleep, thankful to have Owen's arms wrapped around me.

Nineteen

"Are you sure you're okay leaving her for the night?" Owen asks me, panic on his face. I'm starting to think he's the one who isn't ready. I've just told him about his birthday surprise and he's hesitant, to say the least.

"Owen, we're literally one room down from her. This doesn't even count as leaving for the night. Stana and Em are in the hotel room next to us. I promise it's okay."

He nods, but I see his uncertainty. To be completely honest, it scares the shit out of me not having her sleep next to me, but it's been nonstop since she was born, and Owen and I deserve a break. No mum guilt allowed today. Okay, maybe a little, but I'm trying to ignore it.

"So, are you going to tell me the plan for this afternoon?" he asks, his hand laced in mine while we walk down the hotel corridor.

"The plan is to have a movie marathon with room service and a comfy hotel bed."

He perks up. "Really?"

"I know it's nothing crazy, but I figured it might be better to just spend time together and relax. Work's been busy for you lately, and it's hard to get that one-on-one time with Rosie always at my side. Don't get me wrong, she's my entire world, but sometimes I feel like you and I need some time together."

He gives my hand a squeeze. "Honestly, Lottie, that plan sounds fantastic. As much as I love our outings, there's nothing I want more than to lock myself in a room with you for twenty-four hours."

I beam, happy I'm going to make his birthday special. Lord knows he deserves it.

"You know what I was thinking about yesterday?"

"What?"

"It's been a year since I moved back, since we met."

He shakes his head thoughtfully as we reach the door. "Look how much has changed in a year."

"A lot."

"You know the first time I saw you, there was just something about you. It struck a chord within me right away."

I tilt my head. "It did?"

He nods before pushing open the door. "It's like a switch flipped inside of me. I was so drawn to you, and when you shut me down, I knew if it couldn't be romantic between us, I'd need you as a friend."

We walk into the room, Owen tossing our bags onto the floor.

"Despite everything that happened to me before coming back to London, I can't lie that the night we met you intrigued me," I admit. "But I wasn't ready then; it would have complicated things." I pause. "Well, I don't know if we could have gotten ourselves into a more complicated situation, if I'm being honest." I can't help but laugh at how it all turned out.

"I wouldn't change it for the world," he says, pulling me into him. My body warms instantly at his touch. Due to us only recently getting together and Rosie being attached to my hip, we haven't exactly had time to be intimate, but I'm hoping this weekend changes that for us.

I lean forward, connecting my lips to his, Owen catching on pretty quickly about what I want. It's an unspoken understanding that we have one whole year of sexual tension to live up to.

Not having it in me to waste time, I quickly latch my grabby hands onto the hem of his shirt and pull it over his head with his help.

Jesus Christ.

Sure, I've seen him shirtless a lot, but it has never been the time, until now. I let myself explore him, running my hands up and down his toned golden chest. My hands are cold against his warm skin as I get my fill.

Owen wastes no time pulling my top off, somehow managing to pin me under him in the process.

"You use these moves with all the ladies?" I joke as we remove the rest of our clothing. It's rushed, crazy and frantic. It's us.

Owen laughs as he runs his hands through my hair. "Only the special ones." He even throws in a wink.

I roll my eyes before crashing our lips together again, each of us fighting for dominance. I decide to let him have it, just this once anyway.

His hands roam my body, exploring every single inch of me, mapping out a path from top to bottom. I lie on my back, no complaints coming his way. He takes his time, worshipping me like a treasure he doesn't deserve. I feel the same.

Every touch, every kiss feels different with Owen. It screams love and devotion, two things I didn't know how much I needed to feel until now.

Eventually there are no more barriers between us, Owen and I connected in the most intimate of ways. My breath hitches and I bite down on my lip.

"I've wanted this for so long," he whispers from above me, no longer playing around. My hands find his as I pull him closer, our bodies flush against one another.

"Me too," I whisper. "But I'm glad we waited."

He nods, so close to me I can feel the warmth of his breath. "Me too, Lottie. Me too."

We move together as one, my heart and soul never having felt as full as they do right now.

It's an hour later as we're lying in bed, Owen having fallen asleep sometime in the past twenty minutes, that I realize—in all the time we were together, not once did I feel insecure or self-conscious about myself or my body. Sure, I'm a confident girl, always have been, but pregnancy changes your body and I'd be a liar to say otherwise.

Yet despite it all, Owen made me as comfortable as I ever could be, and I relished in his presence rather than squirming.

I feel him stir next to me, my face resting on his chest. I turn my head up, then look at him with a grin.

"Sorry, I must have dozed off," he says, pulling me up to kiss him.

"You're fine. I know work's been crazy."

He looks around, rubbing his sleepy eyes with his free hand. "What time is it anyway?"

"It's a little after three. You hungry again?" I lean away from him, keeping the sheet to my chest while I grab a room service menu from the nightstand.

"Starving," he responds, but I don't think he's talking about food. I playfully roll my eyes before shoving the menu at him.

"Pick something and I'll order."

He takes his time, my stomach practically speaking by the time he's decided on a burger. I get one too and order it hastily.

Then we settle into one another, Owen picking the stupidest comedy he can for us to watch, but I don't mind. It's one of the things I like most about him. Although he's a huge goofball, he's extremely caring and sensitive.

He's my guy.

We spend the rest of the afternoon in bed, doing all sorts of things, but as six p.m. rolls by, that nagging feeling hits me.

I miss Rosie.

"You know, she's right down the hall," Owen says casually as he strokes my hair. My eyes meet his, and I know he wants to see her as much as I do.

"We've had enough time just us two. We should get her."

I turn, looking at him. "Are you sure?"

"Positive. The only thing that could make this day any better is ending it with my two girls."

He doesn't need to tell me twice. I lean up and kiss him passionately before jumping off him and quickly getting my clothes. He follows suit, and both of us are at Stana and Em's door before we know it.

It swings open, a grinning Stana looking at me, Rosie's bag already packed in the corner.

"You knew?" I say.

Stana pushes her dark hair over her shoulder, eyes latched onto my own. "Honestly, we thought you two would have been here a lot earlier. I'm impressed."

I laugh, pulling her in for a hug before entering the room, finding Em playing with my little girl on the floor.

"Hi, my baby, did you miss me?" I coo as I sit down, then give Em a quick hug before picking up Rosie, giving each of her squishy cheeks a big kiss.

I feel Owen crouch down next to me, her little hands reaching out for him.

"Ugh, gals, I'm sorry for wasting your night," I say, turning to them both. Neither seems upset, both wearing matching smiles.

"Are you kidding? We got a whole day with Rosie to ourselves, plus now we can have a girl's night in a hotel room. We should be thanking you," Em says, to which Stana nods.

"Can't complain over that quality one-on-one time," Stana adds in.

"Thank you," I say, standing to collect Rosie's bag and mat.

"Ready?" Owen asks me, Rosie happily holding onto him. I lace our hands as we exit, repeating my thanks and goodbyes one more time as we go.

When we're back in the room, Rosie sits between us as Owen puts on *Paddington Bear*. Rosie giggles like she always does, her curls bouncing up and down with her excitement.

"Really is the perfect ending to the day," Owen whispers to me, his hand on my shoulder rubbing up and down.

The perfect day it was.

Twenty

September

After Owen's birthday, the days blurred into months. I'd just started back at work, Evie looking after Rosie two days a week. It still didn't sit right with me that her only days off she was dedicating to my little girl, but Evie wouldn't hear a word about it. So, every day for the past two weeks Evie's at my place at nine a.m., ready and waiting to take Rosie for the day.

I worried at first Evie wouldn't get anything done during her day, but I quickly learned that Evie and Rosie are a little dynamic duo. Turns out Rosie loves Evie as much as she loves Evie's son.

As the days went by, soon Rosie was reaching six months old and it was clear my flat wasn't going to cut it anymore. So began the search for a new place.

Despite Owen and I never being closer and him sleeping over most nights, I still wasn't ready for him to take the lunge and move in. Yet of course, Owen being Owen, he took me to every flat viewing, leading us to where we are today.

"This feels hopeless." I groan as we leave the fifth flat of the day, nothing matching what Rosie and I need.

Owen's hands come to rest upon my shoulders. "I know it's frustrating, but we will find a place."

"Am I making a mistake? Is this the wrong time to be moving? I mean, Rosie is still so little and who knows if all this change is good for her."

Owen stops rubbing my shoulders and turns me around on the spot to face him.

"Babe, Rosie's a baby. She won't notice the change. *You*, on the other hand, will. You're in a one-bedroom flat and Rosie is growing by the day. It won't work like that forever; eventually you're going to need your own space."

I nod, knowing he's right. All the baby books say by six months she can be in her own room, and we're past that, so if not now, when?

"I think I'm just stressing. With going back to work and leaving her, it just feels like a lot of change." I lean into him, nuzzling his neck.

"I know, but you're not alone in this. We're all here to help you. I'm here to help you."

"I know," I whisper, sometimes wishing we could stay in this little bubble together forever.

"Let's make this new showing our last one, then get home to little Rosie, okay?"

"Okay," I agree. We hop into the car and head back to Notting Hill, hoping this final flat we view might actually be the one.

The trip back to Notting Hill takes forever, traffic an absolute nightmare, and I wish we'd taken the Tube. Just another reminder I don't want to leave our little bubble. Owen interlocks our fingers as we walk up to the last showing of the day, one other couple standing out front together, clearly interested.

A woman in a tight black suit comes out, her stilettos drumming the ground with every step.

"Everyone ready to go in?" she asks.

After a few nods we follow her inside, my heart melting on the spot. A white kitchen sits off to the side with an open floor plan, looking into the living room on the right. Big windows line the back wall, flooding the room with light, something I've missed having for the past four years.

The woman is showing us around, but my feet take off on their own expedition, finding two bedrooms down a small hallway, one to the right and one to the left. The master isn't huge, but what do I expect. It's got built-ins and two windows while the other bedroom is slightly smaller, no closet space, but still good lighting. It would be perfect for Rosie.

The one bathroom sits off to the left of the master bedroom, a shower-bath combination and white tile, and even the lack of windows can't bring me down.

"So, what do you think?"

I yelp, startled at Owen's voice behind me.

I turn, then walk over to wrap my arms around him. "Honestly, it's perfect. It reminds me of my place now, just a shit-ton lighter and with an extra bedroom. Sure, the flat isn't massive, but if I'm going to be picky by staying near work and Notting Hill, I don't think I've got the choice, and this place definitely wouldn't be settling."

He grins down at me. "As soon as we walked in, I knew you'd like it."

I nod, my heart feeling a bit lighter from all of this. "I really love it, Owen. I want to put in an application."

His arm leaves my waist and he pulls out a business card. "I had a feeling you'd like it, so I got the real estate woman's card."

I beam. "You know me so well."

His dark blond eyelashes fan out as he looks down before pulling me in for a kiss. As soon as his lips meet my own I melt into him, wanting to stay in this spot forever. I deepen the kiss, an embarrassing moan coming out of my mouth.

"We should probably stop the PDA if we want you to have any shot at this place," Owen says into my mouth. I pull away, laughing before checking the room. Thankfully we are alone.

"Agreed," I respond, grabbing his hand and dragging him to look at the kitchen.

After we get home, with Rosie fast asleep in her bedroom, I submit an application for the apartment—in my name alone. Does guilt gnaw away at me from the knowledge that I probably should have asked Owen to come with us? Yes. But I still go ahead alone, lingering fears of abandonment telling me this is the best way.

I could see it in his eyes that despite telling me how excited he is for me and Rosie, he wants to be a part of it too. And that only crushes me a little more inside knowing I'm hurting him. How much longer can I go down this path, pulling him along beside me without ever fully letting him inside?

"So, you got the flat?" Stana carries over a plate of treats while Em rocks a sleepy-eyed Rosie back and forth on her shoulder. I should really take her to bed, but the connection she has with these two is so strong, she'd probably wail her head off at me for taking her away.

"I got it!" I confirm, then take a huge bite of croissant. *Ugh, so good.*

"When's the big move?" Em asks, her voice at a slight whisper. I look over at my daughter, both of her eyes fully closed as her doughy hands cling to her auntie's overalls.

"Next week. I just can't believe how quickly it's all gone by. I mean, I thought it would take months for us to find the right spot, but who knew it was literally down the road the whole time."

"Us?" Stana asks with a grin.

"I mean I," I quickly correct.

"You sure you're not thinking about a certain blond-haired, blue-eyed drummer?" Em throws in.

"Well, of course I'm thinking about him. I mean, have you seen the guy? He's a ten-course meal."

They both laugh, Em clearly trying not to wake Rosie.

"But?" Stana asks.

I hug my arms to my chest. "Honestly? I don't know. Owen and I have been together for a while now and he practically lives with me, but I've got some mental block from letting him fully in."

"I hate to break it to you, Lottie, but I've seen the guy. He's head over heels for you."

"I know he is, and I am for him too. I've never met someone so caring, funny, thoughtful, and loving as him. So, what's wrong with me that I can't let him in all the way?"

"Is it that you don't want to? Or are you afraid to?"

My Stana, always asking the right questions. I guess that's why she's on track to get a degree in psychology.

"I want to, I really do, but I'm scared," I admit. "I think there is still a part of me that's worried he's gonna leave, and it won't just be me who is hurt this time. I've got a child to think about."

I look over at my little girl, sleeping so peacefully, unaware of her mother's conflict.

"Is it because of Beck?" Em asks. "Do you worry he'll try and come back into her life?"

"Beck didn't just break my heart. What he broke the most was my trust. And Owen rebuilt that, when he really didn't have to. He stayed through it all. He's more a dad to Rosie than Beck ever was, ever will be."

I pause, running my gaze over my chipped nails. "I know Beck, and because of that, I know he will never want to be a part of her life. As far as he's concerned, she doesn't exist. And it's horrible and unfair, and one day I'm going to have to tell her all about why he didn't want to be around, and I know it will crush her. But at the same time, I've got this amazing guy here, clearly wanting to be around, yet I can't seem to find the balls to ask him to fully stay. I mean, what does that say about me?"

"That you're human?" Stana says. "It's okay to be scared, Lottie. If this isn't the right time for Owen to move in, you don't need to push it. He's not going anywhere, and he wouldn't want you to be feeling like this."

I nod, but despite their words of wisdom, I can't fully let it go. Can't move past why I'm so stuck when I have such a great guy in front of me. As if Owen's ears are burning, not five seconds later the front door opens, and he, Ali, and Reeve all walk in after their practice.

Like magnets, the three of them disperse around the room. Ali pulls Stana into his side while Reeve cautiously sits next to Em, who's holding a passed-out Rosie. Reeve eyes her for a few moments, his features softening at the two of them.

"Miss me?" Owen whispers into my ear as he perches himself on the arm of the couch, directly behind me. I lean into him, taking comfort in his presence.

"I think she might have missed you a little more." I nod toward Rosie, who cried for twenty minutes after Owen left this morning. If that doesn't eat away at your heart, I don't know what will.

"My girls," he says with a smile, his hands coming up to rub my shoulders.

"She really is something," Ali says to me, his vision latched onto Rosie. Em runs her hands through Rosie's golden curls as everyone glances over.

"What can I say? I lucked out."

"I want one," Stana says in a dreamy voice.

"Me too," Em replies, and I try not to laugh. Reeve looks slightly panicked, but I know from personal conversations with Em it's definitely on the table, just not yet.

"You think you'll have any more, Lottie?" Ali asks.

I shrug. "Down the line, I'd like for her to have a little brother or sister, but for now I'm happy. I mean, I never imagined I'd have her at twenty-six, but now she's here, I can't imagine being without her."

"What was life like before Rosie?" Em whispers. "Sometimes I can't even remember."

"It definitely wasn't as good," Stana throws in, sending a wink my way.

"I second that," Owen says from behind me. His warm hands stroke up and down my arms. As if Rosie doesn't want to miss out on all the action, her big eyes shoot open, immediately spotting Owen.

"Looks like someone is happy you're back," I tell him as Rosie begins to pull away from Em, her hand reaching out to Owen. He's quick to jump up and reach for her.

"Hey, little girl," he coos, taking her in his arms. She grabs his cheeks, and both of them stare into one another's eyes.

"You've got some competition, Lottie." Em laughs as she watches them.

"Oh, there is no competition," I say. "This little girl has everyone wrapped around her finger."

Owen brings her over to me, then sits down on the spare spot by my side. Her back faces his front as she begins to play with her toes.

"Hello, my darling girl, did you have a good sleep?" I ask her, leaning down to rub her little cheek. She gives me a small smile before her attention is redirected to her toes.

"So, when's the big move?" Reeve asks from next to Em, who is now situated in his arms.

"Next week," I confirm before looking around the room. "Still a shit-ton to do, but it will be worth it to get out of this miniature flat and give Rosie her own space."

"That's so exciting, Lottie!" Em says, her lips melding together right afterward. "Well, I've also got some news of my own. Well, Reeve and I do." Em places her hand over Reeve's, and I swear Ali's eyes nearly pop out of his head. What the hell is their news? Stana turns her head to the side, clearly also unaware.

"Reeve and I are moving in together!" She grins as Reeve laces their hands together, a small smile playing on his face. They deserve this; they didn't get an easy go to begin with, but they well made it.

I hear Ali exhale, clearly his mind along the same lines as mine. Pregnancy. Em wants to be a mum for sure, but she still has so much to do before she's ready. Her words, not mine.

"Congratulations, guys, that's so exciting." I smile before turning to Owen. "I'm assuming you already knew?"

He nods. "Reeve told me this morning."

Owen and Reeve have lived together for a few years now, and my mind instantly veers to where the hell Owen is going to live. Or is he keeping their two-bedroom flat?

My hand instinctively rests on Owen's leg and gives it a squeeze. I guess now more than ever it's time to reconsider what our plan is moving forward.

"Do you know when it will be?" I ask, trying to suss out the situation.

"Our lease goes for another month and a half, plus Em's roommate, Cora, is already planning on moving next month, so I'd say some time in November," Reeve answers.

So, I have a month to get my shit together enough to ask him to move in.

Fuck.

Twenty-One

"Jesus Christ, Lottie, who let you hoard this much stuff?" Em says as she pulls out another pair of leather pants. *Shit, maybe I do have too much stuff.* It's the day after moving day, and Rosie is with Evie. The boys are handling building the new furniture, although I don't know if that's going so well, and I've recruited the girls to help me organize my room. Apparently I have too much stuff.

"Seriously," Stana says, shaking her head, "I didn't know one girl could own this many sequined dresses."

I laugh, thinking that I should to pull those out again. Despite Rosie being my world, I still need to have "me time," and expressing myself through fashion has always been an outlet. Now I just have to do something about my overgrown bleach-blonde hair. That's next on the list after we get all this shit unpacked.

"Did you really need all these tights?" Stana says, holding up a hot-pink pair. Okay, maybe I can get rid of those.

"You think she has a lot of tights," Em cuts in, holding up a pair of my lace-up heeled combat boots. "You have six pairs of black shoes that look like this. I mean, I know I have a lot of clothes, but Charlotte!"

I hold up my hands in surrender. "Guys, it's no secret I have a shopping problem. Plus, those boots are all different. See, this pair has zippers and these don't." I grab the shoes from Em's hand and shove them into the back of my new closet.

"Oh, they have zips. Did you hear that, Stana?" Em says sarcastically. I playfully shove her side before going back to the chest of drawers I'm attempting to organize. "Attempting" being the key word as I've got no idea how to be tidy.

"How are you girls doing?" Owen peeks his head into the room. "Need help?"

I burst out laughing. "Have you already failed at building the bookshelf, puppy?"

He looks around sheepishly. "I may or may not have drilled the shelf to the outer part, and I still don't know what that means, but in layman's terms I've been kicked out of the room."

I hear Stana and Em laughing before I nod, knowing he will need to provide us with entertainment if he's in here.

"How about a song?" I ask them all. Owen nods, clueless as to what I'm about to do, as I pull out my iPhone.

"Ooh, can you play Lady Gaga's new one?" Em asks, but I shake my head.

"I've actually got a song just for Owen here. I reckon he's gonna like it." His head bolts up as if he's heard the mischief in my voice, his eyes narrowing. A cheeky smirk overtakes my mouth.

I press Play.

"Fancy" starts blasting through the Bluetooth speaker I have, and Stana and Em both look at me with curious expressions before getting into the song, moving and shaking while still unpacking my shit for me.

Owen gives me a challenging look before he stands.

"Isn't this your part?" I ask him as Iggy begins to rap. I don't think he'll do it in front of the girls, but boy, I shouldn't underestimate him because it seems like all this boy does is surprise me.

He opens his mouth and starts spitting the rap, giving me the pleasure of seeing him dance too. I hear the girls laughing behind him but don't turn to see; I'm too engrossed in him.

Eventually I give up and go to him, showing off my best, worst moves. The four of us are a laughing mess when the chorus comes on, screaming it at the top of our lungs.

When the song is finally over, we find Ali and Reeve in the doorway.

"Uh, are you guys okay?" Reeve asks, which earns him a chuckle from Ali.

Owen pulls me into him, still grinning like a Cheshire cat. "Never been better, mate."

A week later Owen and I are relaxing after a long week of work. These days it feels as if all he does is work late, but despite my wanting to spend time with him, I understand.

After only getting home ten minutes before Rosie's bedtime, he offered to put her down. He was grinning when he went in yet when he returns, the smile on his face is no longer prominent.

"What's wrong?" I ask as I grab his hand and lead him to the couch. I hand him a beer before taking a sip of my wine.

"There's something I've been wanting to talk to you about, but I don't want you to get upset." He leans forward, placing the cold drink on my coffee table. I cross my legs and face him.

"What is it?"

He lets out a breath. "It's about Beck."

I can't help but roll my eyes. I'm over the phase of hatred and anger. It's just pure annoyance that we even have to bring him up anymore.

"Okay?" I say, attempting to keep my voice neutral.

"I've been thinking a lot lately. I know you haven't heard from him at all, and I know it's been nearly a year. But what is there to stop him from trying to come back into the picture and potentially trying to get custody?"

My hand tightens on my glass, the chill from it sending a shiver down my spine. The thought has always lingered at the back of my mind. Despite thinking Beck wouldn't do it, I also have to acknowledge I clearly don't know him as well as I thought I did.

"Hey," he says, reaching forward and linking his hand with my own. "I'm not saying this to hurt you or upset you, but it's crossed my mind a few times."

"No, it's fine. I'm not upset. To be totally honest, it has crossed my mind a few times too. I don't know for sure if he would want to be a part of Rosie's life, but I feel pretty confident that he won't. Either way, it wouldn't hurt to talk to a lawyer, make sure he signs his rights away."

Owen places his hand on my arm. "Can I ask something?"

"Yeah."

"Is it seeing him you're dreading? Because we can serve him with papers and you never have to deal with him again."

Owen always seems to know what I don't say aloud. Doesn't that tell me everything?

"I don't want to see him," I admit. "But it's not because I'm still holding onto old feelings and can't let go. It simply comes down to the fact that I'd probably lose my shit and punch him. And he's not worth spending a night in jail for."

Owen chuckles lightly. "I feel like I might do the same thing."

It's so strange to me, Stana being the only one to have met Beck despite him being such a huge part of my life for years, being Rosie's dad. But is he really her dad if he doesn't show up? Doesn't that make him more of a sperm donor?

"It's weird," I start. "I gave that guy everything and he just fucked me over royally. I'm sure you think I've got terrible taste in men." I quickly look at him. "Besides you, of course," I say, grinning.

He smiles. "I think Beck deceived you. I'm sure your entire relationship wasn't a lie, but when you needed him, he let you down in the worst way possible. It's okay to hurt over it, Lottie. I don't want you to ever feel like just because we're together, you can't talk about him."

"Honestly, Owen, I've had over a year to get over it. Sure, it fucking hurt and I was angry for a really long time, depressed even, but that was more about the fact he made me feel like a fool and I was angry for Rosie. The fact that she might grow up wondering why she wasn't enough. That's what hurts the most." I sniff a little, my throat tighter than it was a moment ago.

"Hey," Owen says, voice firm. "Look at me."

I do, but it's through foggy eyes.

"Rosie has the best mother in the whole universe, plus a shit-ton of uncles and aunts who would do anything for her. She will never feel alone, you hear me?"

I nod, squeezing his hand. "I thank the universe every day that you found me throwing up in that toilet, Owen Bower."

He laughs, running his thumb up and down the top of my hand. "Me too, Lottie. Me too."

I lean in to give him a quick kiss before pulling back.

"And if you're worried about legal advice, you could talk to my mum about it," he says.

"I'll call her tomorrow," I say. "Thank you for caring about me and my baby as much as you do, Owen."

He takes the opportunity to pull me into him, our bodies perfectly aligned. I bring my lips to his, thankful for our little moments alone. I know from experience that the beginning stages of a relationship usually mean more time with one another, but we've never had a typical relationship to begin with.

So, while we have this time together, we take full advantage of it. Both our clothes end up in a pile on the floor. Neither of us stop the exploration of one another until we're exhausted, a heaped mess, tangled together.

"I have to say, I was a little surprised you called." Reeve stares at Rosie sleeping in her pram while he sips his piccolo. That's Reeve for you, dark coffee to match that dark exterior.

We're at the café where Stana used to work, a small coffee shop in my neck of the woods. After my talk with Owen, I figured it might do me some good to get the perspective of someone who's been in a position similar to Rosie's. Reeve's dad abandoned him before he was even born—well, that's what he was told, anyway. The reality of the situation was much more complicated than anyone could have known.

"I figure I should have reached out months ago, but with everything that went on with you and Em, it probably wasn't the right time."

His face pinches at the memory of the turmoil he had with Em at the start of the year.

I wrap my hand around my warm drink while the other rocks Rosie so she'll stay asleep.

"You need to do these things on your own time."

I nod. "Well, either way, I appreciate you meeting me on your lunch break. I know how busy you are."

"It's really no problem, Lottie. I'm assuming you want to know about my childhood?" He leans back in his chair. "Ask away."

"Uh, okay," I say, suddenly unsure how to begin. "I guess what I really want to know is how you felt growing up without a dad. I know Owen didn't have his around either, but different set of circumstances. I guess I just wanted to get a perspective from someone who really knows what it's like to be—"

"Abandoned?" he cuts in, no malice behind his words.

I nod. "Yeah, I guess to put it bluntly." That's the thing about Reeve—he doesn't beat around the bush and waste time.

"Honestly?"

"Don't sugarcoat shit for me. I want the truth."

He chuckles. "I don't think anyone has ever accused me of sugarcoating a situation, Lottie."

My lips pull slightly at the sides. "So?"

"In short? It felt like shit and gave me a plethora of long-term issues that then spread into my relationship with Emilia and nearly cost me the most important thing in my life."

My mouth drops open, a spot of coffee spilling out.

"But," he says, leaning forward, his arms resting upon his long legs, "it wasn't as simple as Dad leaving did all that to me. I think the biggest part of my issues stemmed from how it was handled by my mum. She's not a bad person, but she refused to tell me anything about him, wouldn't speak of him, had an excess of husbands over the years, and I didn't handle it well."

I nod, knowing the home situations of Rosie and Reeve are quite different.

"The root of my anger with it all was that I felt lied to. I never had another father figure. Hell, I struggled to feel like I had a mum most days. But Lottie, hear me when I say this. Not having a dad around isn't a recipe for disaster."

"Okay?"

"I know Emilia filled you in on everything that happened with my dad last year."

I nod, thinking back to the fact it came out that his father didn't know he existed, his mother keeping the secret from them both his entire life. But as a mother myself, I feel the need to think she must have had her reasons.

"I thought my entire life if I just had a dad, everything would have been okay. But over the past year I've come to realize that sure, Mum handled it terribly, but she did it because she loved me. My dad was in no state to be a father; I still question if he is. I don't think it would have done me any favors to have him in my life. Sometimes them not being there is better. And sometimes they just can't be there, even if you want them to."

I nod, knowing that as much as I wish Beck had stepped up, if he was only planning to disappoint her, that wasn't the type of role model she needed in life.

"Plus, I think we both know Rosie isn't lacking a father figure in her life. I have zero worry for you and her. I had a different situation than her, but I get it and if down the line when she's older she has questions, she can come to me."

I'm speechless. In the year I've known Reeve, I've never known him to say so much. I could swear this is more than I've ever heard him talk combined.

"You know, Reeve Sawyer, I might have to guess you're a big softy under that hard exterior."

"I wouldn't go that far," he says, suddenly out of words.

I chuckle, clearly making him a little uncomfortable. I think I've just uncovered another layer to the mysterious Reeve Sawyer.

"So how did it go with Reeve?" Owen asks, exiting Rosie's room. His favorite thing is putting her to bed and since I get to do it most nights, I let him tonight.

"Surprisingly well. He made me feel a lot better about the whole situation. He's very insightful."

Owen grins. "For the people he lets into his circle, he's a great friend. I'm glad you two spoke."

"Me too. It gave me a perspective on everything that I never even thought of. I sort of assume sometimes it's black and white, like Beck letting me down just automatically meant bad things forever for Rosie, but I know it isn't like that now. I mean, sure, I know his absence will have some impact on her life— how could it not? But I no longer feel like it's this black cloud."

He comes to sit next to me, the couch dipping with his weight. "I'm glad you sought him out. Despite none of the lads, myself included, having alive or present fathers, I had a feeling he could help you in a way Ali and I couldn't."

I think about Owen and his father, a man he never even had the opportunity to meet. A man we never really talk about.

"Do you miss him?" I ask. "Your dad, I mean?"

Owen lifts a shoulder, his blue eyes connecting with my own.

"Sure," he says. "I mean, I have no memories of him since he died when I was a baby, so my life never had some drastic change I was cognizant of. Mum spoke about him plenty growing up, answered any and all questions I had in order for me to get to know him, but it just isn't the same. It was a hurt I dealt with as it came along, and I'm at peace with it now. Sure, it's unfair I never got a shot with him, but I had Evie."

I reach out and wrap my hand around his wrist, attempting to offer any ounce of comfort I can.

He smiles at me. Kind of a "what can you do about it?" smile.

"That's why I wanted you to talk to Reeve. Although we both grew up without fathers, our situations were different. There was never a reality in which my dad could come back. I was able to accept that he was gone and would always be gone. But with Reeve there was always that lingering thought. My dad didn't leave willingly, but Reeve's did."

Just like Rosie's.

"I think that's why I waited so long," I say in a whisper, surprised I can even get the words out.

"Waited?"

"God, it sounds so bad, but Owen, I was embarrassed. I think that's a part of why I kept my pregnancy a secret. I mean, it's not exactly normal to keep a pregnancy to yourself for six months without telling your friends."

"You were embarrassed of being pregnant at twenty-five?" His words don't hold judgment, only a desire to understand.

"No, not that. Twenty-five isn't that young. I don't find any shame in the fact I was pregnant; it all stemmed from Beck. I mean, after what he did to me, not only did I sleep with him, but I got pregnant." Even thinking back to that final night with him gnaws away at my insides.

"Lottie, look at me. Beck is the embarrassment, not you. So what, you had a slight error in judgment. Beck was an important person in your life for a long time. It's natural in times of hurt to retreat back to a comfort zone, even if that comfort zone was the one who hurt you."

I nod. "I know. I see that now. It's just hard to get over it. So much has happened in the past year, and if I think about it for too long, it gets so overwhelming."

Owen takes my hand that's covering his wrist and maneuvers us until I'm draped over him. His fingers move up and down my back in soothing motions, my body instantly calming at his proximity.

"It's been a huge year; anyone would be overwhelmed. But remember when you feel that way, you've got a huge support system just waiting for you to lean on them."

I nod into his chest but say nothing. His words only confirm my fears. He shouldn't have to be waiting for me to need him. He should be living his life to the fullest, not always be catering to my needs. That voice in the back of my mind rears its ugly head, but I try to push it down, opting to snuggle into Owen rather than face my fears.

A few hours and a couple of glasses of wine later, I'm checking Instagram when I notice Saint Street's Instagram featuring Reeve and Ali performing.

Why are they playing without Owen?

The comments below are people asking where the blond drummer is. A bartender who works there called Stella has replied, saying Owen had plans and couldn't make it.

My heart sinks at the comment.

Owen does nothing for himself except be in this band, playing once every week or two if the guys are lucky due to their busy schedules. I know for a fact the only thing Owen had on tonight was seeing me and Rosie. He missed his gig just to see us. And instead of feeling giddy that he put me first, like I know many girls would, I feel pure guilt. My initial fear about starting a relationship comes back—that by committing to me, he's going to miss out.

"Why didn't you tell me you had a gig tonight?" I ask, trying to push down my internal panic alarms that are blaring. The ones telling me he is giving up his life to be with me. Giving up his passions and dreams.

He slowly puts down the remote, his bare chest still on display as the blanket covers him. I see him pause for a few moments before turning to me.

"It wasn't a big deal," he tries to soothe, but I pull out of his reach.

"Why didn't you go?" I can't keep the panic out of my words, and I know he hears it. He's silent for a few moments, so I decide to keep going.

"You missed your own band performing because you were worried about me? Why didn't you just tell me you had a performance, Owen? I want you to go to those things. It's important you keep living your life!" My voice continues to rise as I speak, I'm unable to keep it down.

"It was more important for me to be here with you," he shoots back, not giving in.

"You're with me every day, Owen!" I yell. I'm probably being irrational, but I don't give a shit. This is how I feel.

"Lottie, why is this bothering you so much? It was one gig. There will be a hundred more in the future, and it's not like I've missed out on this big thing." He looks me in the eye, and I can imagine the wide-eyed mess he sees staring back at him.

"One gig now, one there, then eventually you won't even go," I whisper, my gaze locked on the carpet.

"What's that supposed to mean?"

"I just don't want you to resent me down the line, the fact that at twenty-nine you basically abandoned your life for some stranger and her daughter. I mean, what the hell are we doing?"

He rears back as if I've slapped him. "When have I once made you feel guilty about being with me? When have I once complained about the life you've breathed into my lungs? About the joy I get every single time I think about being with you and Rosie?"

He huffs, running a hand through his hair, his relaxed demeanor no more. "Jesus, Lottie. I get you were hesitant initially—no one wants to jump into a relationship when they're pregnant—but I thought we had moved past that. How are we back here?"

"I'm not taking us back anywhere, Owen. But I think it's reasonable for me to be concerned that you had a gig tonight with our friends and not only didn't you go, but you didn't mention it." I try not to yell; the last thing either of us needs is to wake Rosie.

He rubs his eyes before nodding slowly. "I don't want to fight with you, Lottie. I should have mentioned the gig, but to be honest work is kicking my arse and the last thing I felt like doing was socializing. I just wanted to be here with my girls, so I'm sorry. Okay? Can we just move past this and enjoy the rest of our night?"

Despite my mind telling me to remember this, the fight slowly leaves my body. I nod at Owen. "Yeah," I whisper.

He approaches me with caution, clearly unsure if I'm going to go apeshit at him again. When he senses it's all clear, he moves forward, pulling me into him. I relax into him, but that little voice inside my head won't stop whispering one thing.

You're holding him back.

Twenty-Two

Over the next few weeks Owen continues to be swamped by work, Rosie and I spending most of our time together or with Evie. I'm finally back in the swing of things with work, contemplating upping to three days a week when Rosie turns one and I'll be comfortable with her going to daycare.

After the fight between Owen and me, it seemed as if I was finding anything to sabotage our relationship. I just didn't know how far my mind would have traveled by the end of the week.

After two missed dinners due to work, my mind starts to panic and run with the situation. What if there is someone else? What if he's finally realized I'm not enough?

I'm sitting on the floor, playing with Rosie when my phone rings. Owen should have been home ten minutes ago, so I'm not surprised to see him calling.

"Hey," I answer, eyes still on my girl, who's probably wondering where her favorite guy has gone.

"Hey, babe, I'm not gonna be home for dinner tonight, I'm sorry. Work's so busy, and I've just got a few things I need to get done. I will probably be another two hours."

My heart sinks, the dreaded feeling that's been pulling at my skin all week awakening. He doesn't outright seem like he's lying, but I can tell something is off from his voice.

"No problem. I'll go ahead and put Rosie to sleep, then." My voice is calm, even to my own ears. I'm surprised I've managed to keep myself contained. Sure, I don't know if he's cheating, but why else is he suddenly working late all of a sudden and taking secret phone calls?

"I'll see you later, Owen," I say before we hang up. My fingers are quick to message Stana and Em that I need them to come over.

I'm sick of waiting, not knowing. Sure, it might be deceptive as hell and make me look like a right psycho, but I have to know.

I pick my little girl up from next to me, then take her into her room to change her nappy. Reminders of Owen are everywhere here. Little things he's made not only me but her. Despite me not wanting to admit it, we've created a life together.

"No matter what happens you and I are going to be okay, you know that, right?" I ask her, despite knowing I won't be getting a response.

After a fresh nappy and a full tummy, I tuck Rosie into her bed, making sure to give her an extra-long hug, my shaken heart needing it.

It's not ten minutes later when Stana and Em arrive. I tell them my absolutely bonkers plan, and skepticism is written all over their faces.

The plan is for Em to come with me and Stana to watch Rosie. We're just going to check to see if he's actually working and if not, well, I guess I'll just have to go from there.

I look back at both of them, the panic in their hearts evident. I push it out, only able to handle my roller coaster of emotions right now.

"She shouldn't wake up until I'm back," I tell Stana, grabbing my jacket from the couch and sliding it on. "But if she does, I have formula over there. It's four scoops for two hundred mils—the directions are on the back of the container. She's only been asleep for thirty minutes, so I really doubt she'll stir."

Stana is quiet, her big eyes uncertain as she looks me over, yet she says nothing. Her fingers knot together as she nods, giving me some indication she heard what I said.

"Lottie, are you sure you want to do this?" Em says, voice uncertain, her small frame sitting on the end of the couch. I don't have time for uncertainties; I've been living with them for the past two weeks. I snap my head her way, not wanting to hear her worries.

"If you can't do this, then it's fine, Em, but I'm going." My voice is firm, sounding a bit like how I used to before Beck, before Rosie. "You can stay here with Stana if you need to. I won't take it personally."

She sighs, her big green eyes showing her disappointment in the situation. "I'll go get the car," she relents, getting up and exiting the flat. I take a deep breath, quickly checking the monitor one more time. Rosie's face is right up against the side of the cot, her eyes shut peacefully as she dreams of things I can only imagine are better than how I feel.

"I won't be long," I tell Stana.

"Lottie…" She finally speaks, her voice harder than usual.

250

I turn to her.

"I know you think he's hiding something from you, but wouldn't it be better if you just asked him? I mean, this is Owen we're talking about. Owen, who followed you around like a lost puppy all those months ago. Owen, who raises your daughter like his own."

I flinch at her words, them hitting their intended target. "It's because of that I need to know, Stana. I never thought Beck would do it, but look at me now."

Her face hardens. "We both know he isn't Beck."

I nod, understanding she doesn't want to think poorly of her friend, but I have a daughter now and protecting her comes first, at all costs.

"I know what I'm doing, Stana. Okay?"

"If you're sure." She doesn't bother to smile or hug me as I leave the flat, and I don't expect her to. I'm accusing one of her friends, her and Emilia's boyfriends' best friend, of being a cheater. I don't expect them to understand; they've never gone through the pain of trusting someone so deeply and then having them shove a hot knife into your side when you're not looking.

I spot Em out front in Reeve's idling car.

"So where to?" she asks.

"To his work," I announce, my eyes latching onto the darkness outside my window. I wonder if it crept its way into my heart recently. Accusing Owen of this would be the highest form of offense to him if he found out. Worse than that, it would hurt him.

We drive into the night, eventually stopping outside his work building. Em finds a spot across the street, one covered in shadows.

"So now what?"

"Now we wait," I tell her.

And wait we do. Twenty minutes later Owen walks out of the building, a woman in a tight pencil skirt and blouse by his side. I can't see her up close, but it's enough to know she's beautiful. Tall, skinny, a luscious wave of dark hair.

"Lottie," Em whispers from next to me, her voice laced with shock.

I put my hand up to silence her, my eyes still trained on the wreck I'm seeing in front of me. I've been in this position before. Only how come it hurts so much more with Owen?

I dig my nails into my flesh as I watch them approach a car. She leans in, hugging him tightly before pulling away and handing him something. The grin on his face when he looks at it could only be described as one he directs at me. At Rosie.

I flinch when Em's warm hand comes down on my own, a stray teardrop betraying me and slipping from my face onto her hand.

"There has to be more to the story. I mean, they probably just work together."

I shake my head, eyes still latched onto them as they talk. "I've been to his office with Rosie before. I know she doesn't work there. Plus, he said he was the last one in the office tonight, wouldn't be home for another two hours." I sniff. "So tell me, Em, where could they be going for another two hours?"

She turns her head back to the car crash I'm watching, a small gasp leaving her lips as Owen gets into the passenger side of the woman's car.

"Follow them," I command before I swallow a few times to keep away the bile that wants to push its way out of my stomach.

Thankfully she says nothing, pulling the car onto the street and following the black Audi. We drive for ten minutes, the path they're taking looking more and more familiar as we go. They stop at Owen's apartment, where Em manages to find a spot across the street. We wait a few minutes before Owen gets out, his gray suit clinging to his body. The woman doesn't appear, Owen waiting in the same place until she puts on her indicator and pulls out of the space.

Why didn't she go in with him?

I briefly look away until Em's voice cuts through my mind.

"Oh shit," she says, and my attention snaps back to the window, beyond which a stern-faced Owen strides across the road. Right up to our car. He stops at my window before tapping on the glass.

"This isn't good," she whispers to me.

I tell myself to keep a strong, brave face, that perhaps he was going to do something with her and just got spooked out by seeing us. I mean, he did lie to me.

I latch onto that bit of information while I press the button to roll down the window and turn to him.

He leans down, his head coming into view, and I want to run. Instead of him being angry like I would be, raging in fact, hurt encompasses every aspect of his face.

"Do either of you want to tell me what the hell is going on?" he asks. His voice is abnormally low, and I know he's attempting to keep his emotions in check.

"I think I should call a cab," Em says from next to me.

"Don't bother," I snap, instantly feeling bad it was directed at her. "This is Reeve's car—you need to take it home. I'll call an Uber."

I don't give her a second to question it, throwing open the door, just missing Owen. "I'm sorry, Em. I'll call you tomorrow."

She nods in understanding before turning on the engine. Owen steps aside quickly as I get out and beeline across the road. He follows me as I go.

"What the fuck is going on, Lottie?" Owen catches up to me as I stop and turn to face him. I guess it's really now or never.

"Who is she?" I ask, looking him directly in the eyes. He visibly flinches at my question before realization dawns on him.

"Are you serious right now?"

I stand my ground. "You said you were working late, working *alone*."

"And you thought I was lying? So, what, you followed me?"

"You were lying!" I yell at him. "I caught you with her and you got into her car, Owen!"

He shakes his head, as if he can't fully believe what's happening.

"Lottie, I know a lot has been going on lately and I've been busy with work, but I'm telling you it's not what you think. I would never cheat on you. I'm asking you to take my word on this."

My head and heart meet one another in battle, crashing together at his words. I desperately want to believe him, to take his word, but my past refuses to let me do that.

"Who was she, Owen?" I ask again, his face falling at my refusal.

"She's a lawyer, Lottie. She's married to Amanda, my coworker. You met her, remember?" His voice is flat and filled with disappointment as I remember the blonde in his office who mentioned a wife named Sarah.

"I don't understand," I admit, feeling far too confused about this whole situation.

"I didn't have a car, so she offered to give me a ride home. Offered to have me over for dinner with Amanda too, but I wanted to grab some stuff from my place so I could get to you sooner."

Okay, shit, here comes the guilt.

"Did you really think I'd cheat on you? Me of all people?" I have to look away from him, unable to take the pain I've caused.

"I—" Clearly unable to form a coherent sentence, I stare at the ground.

"And instead of coming to me, you followed me with Em? I mean, who is with Rosie right now?"

I snap my head up at her name. "She's with Stana, and I'm allowed to go out. She's *my* daughter. I would never put her at risk."

"I wasn't insinuating that." He lets out a shaky breath. "God." His mouth pinches together as he nods. "I think a part of you is so desperate to sabotage this that you were hoping I was cheating, just so you don't get hurt again."

"That's ridiculous," I retort.

"But is it?"

I don't have the heart to agree he might be correct. That my initial fears are keeping him away from a life he deserves and I don't know how much longer I can keep them at bay.

Before I can respond, my phone buzzes, Stana texting to say Rosie's woken up.

"Fuck," I mutter. "It's Rosie. I need to go." It's a bullshit excuse; we both know Stana is perfectly capable of handling things. But something about having this fight in the street feels wrong.

"I'll call an Uber," Owen says, his tone still filled with animosity.

We stand on the corner, waiting for the car, only the sound of the wind to keep us company. When the car arrives, Owen goes straight to the front seat, something he's never done before, and I know things are bad.

A heavy silence, thick like fog, swarms the car. My eyes lock onto my hands so I have something to focus on, so I don't cry.

Once we arrive home, Stana is already on her feet, clearly having been pacing. Her eyes widen when she spots the both of us.

"I put her back to sleep with her bottle. She's out like a light."

I give her a tight smile, feeling a world of guilt about how I've treated her and Em tonight. "Thanks, babe. I'll call you in the morning?"

She nods, grabbing her jacket and slipping out, but not before giving Owen a sad smile.

I turn to Owen, the hurt from tonight the only thing I can hold onto. Sure, I was wrong, but who knows if I will be in the future. I can't continue to live with these feelings of uncertainty. I know I'm being irrational, but right now all reasonable thought has flown out the window.

"I think it would be better if we had some space." As soon as the words slip out of my mouth, I know I'll eventually regret them. But right now, I don't have the ability to manage my wild emotions and look after my daughter. Lately it feels as though all I've been consumed with is fear. Fear of fucking up as a mum. Of Owen cheating on me, *leaving* me.

"Are you serious right now?" Disbelief encompasses his words; he probably expected a fight before we made up, not this curveball I've decided to chuck his way.

"Jesus Christ, Owen, don't you get it? We've been playing house together, big happy family, but it isn't real. At the end of the day, it's just me and her. We are the ones who will always be here. You've got a life you need to get back to living. You need to meet someone, fall in love, start your own family."

He rears back as if I'm a stranger. "I thought I'd already done all that," he whispers. It's his stare that guts me. Like he doesn't even know me at all.

When I say nothing, he shakes his head, clearly disappointed. "Are you even hearing yourself right now, Lottie? What the actual fuck. I'm not just some placeholder who's been filling in all these months. You're not listening to what I'm saying."

I shake my head, not willing to listen. I've already made up my mind. I won't condemn him to a life he thinks he wants right now, when five years down the line he will understand what he's lost out on. "No, you're not listening, Owen! I can't do this. I don't want to do this. I have to put her first. And lately my mind has been running off with all sorts of scenarios and I'm not giving her the attention she needs."

"So it's my fault you followed me tonight?" His eyes are wide, clearly panic stricken.

"No, Owen. None of this is anyone's fault. We got ourselves into a weird situation and neither of us wanted to let go, but I have to be an adult now, so I'm setting you free from all this."

"Setting me free? We've been together for months, Charlotte. Fucking months and now out of the blue you decide to end it? I'm the one who wants a permanent spot in your life, Lottie. It's you who is pushing me away."

Before I can reply, Rosie's cries break through the baby monitor.

"Shit, I've got to get this," I tell him before he cuts me off.

"I'll get it," he says, moving toward her bedroom.

"Owen." My voice is firm, hard almost, something I've never had to use with Owen before. "I'll get her."

He rears back, understanding the hidden meaning behind my words. *She's not yours.* I'm being cruel, and I know it. Yet I can't seem to stop.

"It's time I start standing on my own two feet." I pause, knowing my next words will be the final nail in the coffin, but he doesn't deserve to be shackled down by this life.

"I think you should go," I tell him, my tone foreign. I practically see the moment his heart begins to break, but I stay strong, knowing this is all better for him in the long run, no matter how much it hurts now.

"Lottie…" He says my name on a whisper. "Please."

I shake my head, unable to look at him. "I'd like you to leave, Owen. I won't ask again."

And as I stand here, watching the man I so desperately love walk out the door, I realize something. Words. You can't take them back. No matter how many *I'm sorry*s and *I didn't mean it*s, the words came from your lips. They were said, whether you meant them or not. And they have an impact.

It didn't take me long to realize what a gigantic, epic mistake I had made with Owen. The one person who has been there for me through everything, I kicked him out because of my fears. They whispered in my ear that I've ruined his life and dragged him down, despite him telling me numerous times how wrong I am. How much he adores not only me, but also *our* little girl.

And that's the thing, isn't it? She's never just been mine. She's been Owen's since he was right next to me for the very first breath she took upon entering this crazy world. He's the one who rocked her to sleep when I was dying from exhaustion. He's the one who looked after her in the morning when I had to start back at work and he wanted me to sleep in, when the both of us got sick. And through it all I put up every hoop and barrier, thinking that he would eventually have some moment of clarity and run.

Run just like Beck did.

But as much as I tried to shove him down into that category of asshole men, waiting for him to slip up like Beck and countless others, all he did was step up. And I threw it all in his face due to a moment of utter panic. Panic because he's come to mean the absolute world to me and my little girl. I see it in her eyes when he walks into the room—those little blue orbs absolutely light up when they connect with his, her chubby little arms reaching out for him to take her.

So as I sit here the next morning, with all my calls going straight to his voicemail, I realize I've deeply stuffed things up, and it just might have been one time too many. I hurt him, not just surface hurt, but a deep wound. I pulled out every cruel thing I could imagine, because it's what I've grown up knowing how to do.

I don't get in physical fights, never have even though I look as if I might be scrappy. No, I've always known the most power is held within your words. And last night I wielded mine like a weapon, cutting Owen where I knew it would hurt the most.

The insinuation that it's just Rosie and me. That she's solely mine.

But now I reflect on it, perhaps I've been hurting him longer than I realize. I never offered for him to move in with me, despite it being the perfect time and him already staying every night. I shied away from saying "I love you," just because I was scared he would say it back but not really mean it.

To put it simply, I've been stubborn, not selfish like I thought.

I've been so set in my old ways of thinking, that I don't need a man, that I overlooked the one right in front of me. And usually I think being a little selfish is okay; sometimes we need to be, especially after having a baby. I needed to be selfish for her and myself, but I'm starting to realize I wasn't even looking out for my best interests.

If I were really being selfish like I feared, I would have been with Owen the first night we met, then let him in with open arms the first few times I saw him trying to get in.

But instead I waited a year, and he stayed. Despite it all, he stayed.

The girls have been messaging me all morning, but still no sign from Owen. He's not answering any of my messages and this time, it really feels as if my fuckup is final.

I spend the day in a zombie state, going through the motions and thankful I have work off this week so I don't have to face Evie. The girls want to come over, but the truth is I just can't see anyone. I've never been one to cower, to hide, but this time I have to own that I'm ashamed of my own actions.

By nighttime without a word from him, I've officially accepted things between Owen and me are over. And to put it plainly, I'm heartbroken. I've never loved anyone besides Rosie like I love Owen and instead of telling him, I used every excuse I could think of to ruin it.

It's seven p.m. and Rosie has finally fallen asleep. It took an hour longer than usual, her little eyes looking around every once in a while as she wondered where Owen is. Eventually she tired herself out and went to bed, unable to keep waiting.

An hour after that I'm sipping wine, contemplating all the ways I can convince Owen to give me a second chance when the front door opens.

I nearly shit myself at the sight of him walking through the door. My heart jumps forward at his presence, and the only thing I want to do is jump into his arms. But I don't. I wait for him to make the first move.

Getting up from the couch, I place my wineglass down on the coffee table, and then I slowly walk toward him, mentally scolding myself for being in an oversized pajama top and having my hair in a bun.

"Hey," I whisper, my eyes greedily taking him in. Denim jeans, white T-shirt and all.

"Hey," he says back.

My chest heaves up and down as I look at him, wondering which of us will speak first. Finally I break, stepping forward. "I didn't mean it," I blurt out.

He closes his eyes and breathes out, "I know."

I can't stop the tears leaking out of my eyes at his words. I step forward, hoping he doesn't recoil, and I take another step when he stays in the same spot. Eventually I'm in front of him, toe to toe.

"You were right," I say. "I was looking for any excuse to sabotage us, but I'm done with that now. I don't want to be that person. I'm so lucky to have this life, with you, with Rosie. I don't want to run from it anymore, Owen. So I'm asking, can you forgive me for my epic fuckup last night? I can't promise I won't be an asshole again, but I can promise I'm going to give this my everything." I pause, taking a deep breath, ready to tell him what's been in my heart for a year now.

"I'm ready because I love you, Owen. And the ache I've been feeling since you left is worse than any I've ever felt before. So I'm asking—hell, I'll even beg—for a second chance."

He closes his eyes and they momentarily tighten as his chest continues to rise and fall. I bite the inside of my lip, waiting, internally pleading he takes me back. That he feels the same way.

"Say something," I whisper, selfishly no longer able to take his silence.

His eyes open and that deep ocean blue I'm familiar with latches onto mine. "It's never been a question for me if I loved you, Lottie," he begins. "Not once. I've always known that I was gone from the first moment I saw you. So yes, I can easily say I love you too. I love you and I love your little girl."

A whoosh of air leaves me and I lean forward, a deep sense of relief rushing through me at his words. I feel his hands come to rest on my arms, steadying me.

"And I want to explain where I've been the past few days."

My stomach sinks but I stay silent, wanting him to explain it all.

"I understand your reservations and hesitance—you've been burned before—but I'd be lying if I said your actions the other night didn't gut me. I needed time to process everything and I knew if I answered your calls, it would just pull me back in before I was ready."

"Okay," I say, understanding where he's coming from.

"But there was more than that. After I'd processed it all, I just wanted to come back here and try to fix things. But I did something else, something you might be angry at."

Oh God.

"Were you with someone else?" My voice cracks mid-sentence.

Panic flares behind his eyes. "God no. I, uh, I found Beck."

I involuntarily rear back. "What?"

"I didn't go and see him or anything—I'd never disrespect you like that—but I found out where he's been living. I know you said you were scared he might try to take Rosie from you down the line, so I wanted to make sure we knew where he was, and I've found him."

"Where?" I risk asking, knowing he long ago vacated the old address we shared.

"He's in Glasgow."

"Glasgow," I repeat. I've never really liked it there; guess I have a solid reason to dislike it now.

"I don't want to push anything on you, but if you wanted to get him to sign the papers, I just wanted you to have a way to find him."

"Thank you," I whisper back, thankful Owen had the balls to do what I'd be dreading.

"But I want to make something so perfectly clear that you never question it. So that when your doubts creep into your mind, you can reference this exact moment for peace and clarity. Okay?"

I look at him, nodding.

"There is zero doubt in my mind, heart, and soul that you are what I want. Rosie is what I want. My entire life I've been looking for something worth sticking around for, and last July when I met you, it felt like I'd finally found that. And every day since then, nothing has changed. I'm giving up nothing by being with you, but gaining everything. Do you understand me, Lottie?"

His voice is firm, full of conviction and passion. Full of love.

"I finally fucking understand. I'm so sorry I was so cruel," I tell him through shaky sobs, hoping he puts me out of my misery soon.

Finally, a small smile drifts across his face. "It's in the past. We're only moving forward."

He pulls me into him, his mouth crashing against mine. His tongue explores every inch of my own, my hand automatically grabbing his hair for support. He bends down and his hands slide under my legs, then lift me so I can wrap them around his waist.

"I want you to move in," I say before going in for another kiss.

"I'll pack my shit tomorrow," he says, then bites my bottom lip.

"Good."

I continue to ravage him as he walks us down the hall to my room.

Correction.

Our room.

Twenty-Three

"Are you okay?" Owen asks as we exit the train, our fingers locked together. My bag sits heavily on my shoulders, the legal papers Owen got from Sarah, his coworker Amanda's wife, inside.

Yep, that Sarah whom I followed him with. Turns out she was looking into getting Beck to sign his rights away for me.

"I am," I confirm quickly as we exit the station into the cobbled streets of Glasgow. It's been years since I've been here and hopefully this will be the last time.

After much discussion and speaking with Evie, I decided it was best to go see Beck myself. He'd ignored all my attempts at contact, and I was over waiting.

We head to the pub I know he's currently working at, the smell of beer and cigarettes lingering in the stale air. It's no Saint Street, I will say that much.

It's not hard to spot Beck. His tight leather jacket, probably a size too tight now that I think about it, is his dead giveaway. I look down at my own attire, my bleach-blonde hair back to its normal self. It's not hard to see why so many people used to call us Sid and Nancy.

Now that I'm older, the names don't seem so exciting.

"That him?" Owen asks, clearly seeing where my gaze has landed. I nod, unsure of what he's probably thinking. Beck's fit for sure, his sandy-colored hair and charming smile a draw. But next to Owen? Nah, he doesn't stand a chance.

"Let's get this over with," I say, beginning the walk to my ex.

A girl with raven hair sits next to him, both of them having a few beers. She notices me first, shoving Beck with her arm before he turns around.

From the sight of him you'd think I was a ghost. I guess I am in some respects.

"Jesus Christ, Lottie?" His face pinches together as though he can't believe it.

I pull out the envelope and a pen, then place them on the only spare space on the table.

"Let's skip the pleasantries, shall we, Beck?"

A soft chuckle comes from Owen and I grin on the inside.

"You need to sign over your parental rights and you need to do it now."

"You've got a kid?" the girl screeches.

I look at him expectantly, his face fifty shades of red.

"I don't have all day, Beck." I tap my foot for added measure.

"So, what, I sign this and what happens?"

"You relinquish all legal rights to my little girl. I don't want you having a come-to-Jesus moment years down the line and trying to take her from me. You had a chance—hell, you've had over a year—and you didn't care then, so why care now?"

"What, are you gonna take me to court?"

"Sign the papers and we don't need to. But I'm warning you, Beck, you don't, and I'll come for child support and you're not going to like how much that is."

I'm bluffing. I don't want shit from him, but he doesn't need to know that. Beck is cheap, always has been.

"Fine, fine, that's good then," he says as he grabs the pen and hastily signs all areas. "If you promise you won't try to come after me, that's fine."

The girl next to him scoffs before grabbing her purse and walking away. Yep, he's not such a prize after all, sweetheart.

I want to reach out and strangle him. Not once has he asked about her, only worried I might make him pay, literally. Piece of shit.

I want to go back in time and kick the younger Lottie who only cared about being in love and having fun with him. But then I wouldn't have Rosie, so I guess some bad things happen for a reason.

"I don't want anything from you ever again, Beck. In fact, I hope this is the last time I ever have to set eyes on you." I snatch the papers off the table, careful to not let them get ruined by the little wet spots from his beer.

"We had some great times together, Lottie. It's a shame it had to go bad," he says, his gaze doing a once-over on my body.

I snort. "If by good times you mean cheating on me for a year and leaving me knocked up and alone, then yeah, they were great."

I shake my head and mumble "wanker" under my breath.

"Who's that?" he says, motioning his head to Owen but not addressing him.

"I'm the lad who's gonna make sure *her* little girl doesn't grow up wondering why she wasn't enough for some deadbeat. I'm the one who's gonna love her, love them both."

I try to hide my smile, but I know parts of it peek through. Since the moment Owen found out about Rosie, he's never left my side.

Beck lets out a humorless laugh but says nothing. I can tell seeing me move on pisses him off, but it's because he's territorial, no other reason.

Owen stiffens next to me, so I grab his hand and link our fingers in hopes he will calm.

"I'm sorry it turned out this way, Lo."

I turn to him, my fingers still laced with Owen's. "I'm not."

With that I squeeze Owen's hand, both of us ready to take the next train back to London and leave this all behind us.

If someday my little girl wants to know about him, I'll tell her the truth and let her make the choice. As for Beck, I already know he's not going to come knocking.

Twenty-Four

One Year Later — Christmas 2020

"Are you sure you want to do presents before we go see everyone?" Owen asks as Rosie bolts around the room. Owen and I have been living together for a little over a year, and things between us have never been better. It's safe to say after getting Beck to sign those papers a year ago, I've finally felt as if I can move on.

"It's just a little something I want you to have before we're with everyone," I say. I smooth my hands over my red velvet dress, my attempt to add some holiday cheer into the wardrobe. Also, the three of us have on ridiculous reindeer ears. To say we look like a silly Christmas card family would be an understatement.

Rosie rushes toward the tree, her red tartan dress with a white collar swaying as she runs toward us. Big golden curls sit atop her head, pinned together with a bow, while her blue eyes shine at the row of presents surrounding her.

"Okay, sit down," I instruct Owen, my insides about to burst with excitement. Also fear. And anxiety. But mostly excitement.

"Down, down!" Rosie yells at Owen. Of course he does it instantly. She's got him wrapped around her little finger.

I no longer have the fear of Beck taking Rosie, and in the past year conversations of Owen's permanent presence in Rosie's life have come up. I know she sees him as her dad. Hell, I see him as her dad too.

We've never talked of anything official, but I know Owen. I know how badly he wants official longevity in her life.

"Rosie, come here, baby," I call to her. She comes running at the sound of my voice but goes straight to Owen, who is sitting on the couch. He doesn't hesitate to scoop her up, then plop her down next to him. Her frilly white socks occupy her while I turn back to him. With shaking hands, I hand him the envelope. His eyes are curious as he rips open the top.

Rosie, being Rosie, wants in on the action, her little paws attempting to grab the paper from him. He just laughs, picking her up and placing her on his lap. She beams, wiggling on top of him.

"Hurry," I tease, my anticipation getting the better of me.

Finally, Owen pulls out the set of papers that could possibly change everything for us. For the past two years, Owen has been by her side since before she was even born. Every appointment, every milestone, we've shared it with him. Plus, numerous conversations over the past two months have indeed let me know this is something he wants. Something I want too.

Slowly he looks over the paper, his mouth forming a small O shape. He continues to read it and from his sharp inhale, I know he understands what I'm asking.

"I know it's soon, but I wouldn't ask you unless I was one hundred percent sure. You've been a dad to Rosie since the moment we went to that first ultrasound appointment together. She adores you as much as I do, and to be honest, I'm pretty sure she already thinks you're her dad. So, Owen, I wanted to make it official and ask. Would you like to adopt her?"

I pause, waiting for his response. He shudders out a breath, and his eyes latch onto my own. They're slightly damp, something I've yet to see from Owen.

"I'm not sure what I did in this life to deserve the two of you, but God, Lottie, you've just given me the greatest gift."

My lips turn up slightly at the sides as my eyes close briefly. Bringing my palms flat against my chest, I try to let him know how much that means to me. "Thank you," I mouth, not only for this, but for everything.

I don't know when my feet move on their own, but the next second I'm on the couch, next to my little family. Owen has his arms around me, his lips pressed against my head. We sit like that, Rosie slumping against Owen, her round eyes looking up at us in awe. I don't know how much her ever-forming mind understands, but it's clear to me in this moment, she notices the shift.

"You hear that, Rosie?" Owen whispers to her. "I'm officially your dad."

"My dadda," she says, her squeaky little voice repeating his words.

And her dadda he is.

Two hours later we're at Evie's for Christmas dinner. My mum and dad have flown in, Mum attempting to help with dinner, but truthfully she seems to be making Evie more frazzled. Dad and Steve have seemed to form a friendship, their love of historic literature keeping them occupied.

Then there are my humans.

Stana and Ali snuggle close to one another, their three-year anniversary of meeting right around the corner. Owen may or may not have let it slip Ali has a big plan for them. A sparkly kind of plan.

Reeve sits on the edge of the couch while Em is on the floor between his legs, her attention solely focused on Rosie and trying to get her to say "Em."

She's only just started saying "Mama," but I don't want to crush Em's dreams, so I stay silent.

Owen's arms are wrapped around my waist while he holds me tight against him, the news of his impending adoption of Rosie the highlight of the night as soon as we walked in. Owen has been absolutely beaming ever since. I'm not sure what it would take to wipe the grin off his face, not that I want to.

Hugo and Louis, Owen and Reeve's brothers, are chatting about their respective unis, but I suspect their interest lies more in the girl I heard Hugo mention earlier. An American girl he met at a pub a few months ago, reminding me of another couple I know.

"Okay, everyone, dinner in five! Take your seats," Evie calls.

Everyone starts moving to the table, Rosie bolting away from Em and shakily walking to a few books tilting out of the shelf.

"I got her," I tell Em so she and Reeve can sit down.

She takes his hand and leads him into the dining room with the others, leaving us to get Rosie.

Owen links his fingers with my own and we walk over to our girl. She doesn't hesitate to come running toward him, her grabby hands reaching out. "Dadda!"

The moment catapults me back to when Rosie first said that magical word to him.

Owen and I are lounging on the grass at Hyde Park, enjoying an afternoon in the sun with Rosie, when it happens. "Dadadadada," she babbles, her gaze set on Owen.

"Holy shit," I whisper as Owen's eyes widen.

"Did you hear that?" He turns to me, a look of awe splashed across his face.

I nod, mouth open.

He doesn't hesitate, scooping her up in his arms and cradling her to his body.

"I am your dada, Rosie."

Her hands cup his face, her round head tilting to the side as she looks him over, pinching parts of his skin. He just takes it, completely mesmerized by her.

I blink a few times, attempting to rid myself of the tears coating my eyes. If I ever had any doubts of Owen's permanence in my life, that one word from Rosie squashed them in an instant.

I snap back into the present, my body warm from the memories of that day. My sight sets upon the two people whom my days end and begin for.

"It still doesn't feel real," he whispers without looking at me.

I come up to his side, leaning my head against his shoulder as my hand rises to play with her curls.

"Sometimes I wake up and wonder if this is all just a really good dream," I admit. I never thought being a mum would be in the cards for me, especially this early in life. Yet now that it's happened, I find it impossible to imagine any other scenario.

"I know the feeling."

"You changed everything for me, Owen. You revived me."

His grip on me tightens. "No, Lottie, you revived me first. You gave me the family I've always wanted, and I can't thank you enough for that."

"I don't need thanks, puppy. I just need you."

He bends down, connecting his lips with my own. I don't hesitate to reach up and link my free hand through his hair before a small hand grabs my face.

We pull apart, laughing as Rosie eyes us both, clearly upset to be left out.

"I love you, Charlotte Knight."

"Not more than I love you, Owen Bower."

Epilogue

Years Later

Owen

"Daddy, you can't catch me!" Rosie screams as she runs past me, the wind seizing her blonde ringlets with each step. The hem of her red tartan dress is covered in mud from our backyard antics all afternoon and we've no doubt left footprints on the kitchen tile, but neither of us seems to mind.

"Be careful!" Lottie calls out from the steps of the garden, Leo on her hip. He eyes his sister, clearly jealous of her ability to run around when his eight-month-old legs have yet to master it. Unlike Rosie, who was blessed with an abundance of curls from birth, he only has a patch of brown fur on his bald little head, but his eyes are a duplicate of hers.

"I'm okay, Mumma!" Rosie calls back. "I promise!" Grabbing onto the ladder of her tree house that Steve built her last Christmas, she begins her ascent to the top.

It was only a matter of time for Lottie and me to realize the apartment life wasn't great for our little girl. After her third birthday we got a place a little outside central London. Although the commute is longer and we don't see everyone as much as before, it's worth it because it means we get to have this house, this home. Plus, Stana and Ali seem to be looking for a place around here, their growing family needing more room than their two-bedroom flat can provide.

"Hey, puppy," Lottie calls to me. The old nickname occasionally makes a reappearance. It brings me back to where it all started with her. Who would have thought Saint Street would bring so many people together?

I look to Lottie and raise my shoulder. She rolls her eyes, but I see the grin peeking out. I walk over to her and take Leo from her arms, giving him a big wet kiss on the cheek.

"How's my little lad doing today?" I ask. He replies by taking my cheeks in his hands and smushing them together, something Rosie used to do.

"Everything okay at work?" I ask.

Lottie lifts a shoulder. "As okay as it can be without me there. But I'm sure Liz can handle it."

Around two years ago Lottie bought a local pharmacy ten minutes from our home. It was no small purchase, and a risk for sure, but so far it's been paying off. She's never been happier, and I've never been prouder.

Since then, I've become a stay-at-home dad, still doing my graphic design, but now it's more of a side hobby. Life has never been better.

Lottie snakes her arm around my free side, her body leaning into me.

"Everyone is going to be here in less than thirty minutes and Rosie looks like she's been swept up in a hurricane."

"At least she'll be the cutest girl here," I say, to which Lottie nudges me in the ribs.

"Don't let Reeve hear you say that. He might scoop your eyes out with a spoon. As far as he and Em are concerned, that spot goes to Penelope and Mirabelle."

"As any parent would think, that spot goes to their child."

I laugh, thinking about Reeve with his twin daughters. For a guy who didn't know if he wanted kids, he sure came around quickly. When those two were born two and a half years ago, you would have sworn he thought the world started and ended with them. As it should be.

"Are Stana and Ali bringing Billy?"

Lottie looks over my shoulder and her eyes light up. "Speak of the devil."

Lottie

I slip out of Owen's embrace and bolt over to my cousin. She looks stunning in her flowing maxi dress with her newly cut dark hair sitting just past her shoulders. Her small belly is slightly rounded, my new niece set to arrive in less than four months.

Three-year-old Billy bolts from his father's side, searching for Rosie. Despite their three-year age gap, they're attached at the hip.

"It looks like America treated you well," I say, pulling her in for a hug. I haven't seen her in nearly two months due to her and Ali galivanting through the States together.

"I've missed you, Lottie," she says into my hair, and a calmness settles over me at having her back.

"How's the baby?" I ask, my hands going to her stomach.

"Honestly, amazing. Nothing like with Billy where I was sick for what felt like forever."

"God, I remember how it was with Rosie and Leo, bloody hell." I pause, looking around. "Now where did that handsome husband of yours go?" I scan the garden, only to spot him holding Leo while Owen grabs Ali a beer. I suspect it will only be a matter of hours till those two, plus Reeve, pull out the instruments and attempt to relive their time at Saint Street.

Despite Ali still owning it, their playing has drastically decreased. After we all started having babies, their weekly performances began to slow. Now they're lucky if they get to play every other month, but that's life. Growing up is giving up some of the things you enjoy in order to gain the fulfillment of others.

"Have you heard from Em?" I ask, leading Stana over to put her bag down.

"Knowing her, she's gonna be late."

"Oh God, I can already imagine Reeve being all ready to go on time and Em still putting on her makeup."

Stana's mouth turns up. "I swear she and Reeve are polar opposites. I see that in Mirabelle and Penelope too."

I think of their two raven-haired twins. Mirabelle is her father's spitting image physically and personality-wise. She's got a kept-together seriousness about her for her young age, always appearing to be watching while Penelope is an outgoing and outrageous tornado. They give their parents a run for their money, that's for sure.

"Can you imagine when they're teenagers? The trouble those two are going to be…"

Stana's shoulders shake, her mind clearly thinking about the future. "I can't. I'm sure Reeve will have a heart attack the first time one of them brings home a boyfriend. Although they're only two and a half, I sometimes see him glaring at the small boys on the playground when they get too close."

"Lord help us."

Giggles are heard around the corner before Em and Reeve round the side of the house, each with a twin on their hip. Em's strawberry locks are piled atop her head, and Penelope twists in her hold, clearly attempting an escape.

Mirabelle, on the other hand, rests her head on her daddy's shoulder, while his other arm is piled with bags.

"Someone is early," Stana calls out, walking over to her sister-in-law, myself in tow.

"It was no easy feat," Reeve replies, dropping the bags to the grass, Mirabelle still glued to his side. Pen is already on the ground, running to find Billy and Rosie. Bless her, at less than three years old, she thinks she's already one of the big kids.

"You want to go play with the others?" Emilia asks her daughter. Mirabelle snuggles into her dad's side, shaking her head. My heart melts a little with each action.

"I'll take her over," Reeve says, quickly giving Stana and me a kiss on the cheek each before heading to the others.

"Now that I'm child free, give me a hug, you two!" Em tries to hug us at the same time, a sort of squished sandwich of an embrace.

"God, it feels like forever since we've all been together," Em says, pulling away.

"Only two months," Stana adds.

"It feels like longer," I reply. Life without all of them in it just doesn't feel like life at all.

"It's weird, you know. I'm so used to being around you ladies all the time for the past eight years, it felt so strange leaving for two months. It was even weirder being in America for that long."

Since Stana moved to London eight years ago, sure, she's had the occasional trip back to LA, but never for more than a few weeks. I think with Billy being older and them about to have another, it was the perfect time to show Ali and Billy where Stana was from.

"Are Steve and Evie coming?" Stana asks.

"Yeah, they've been away for the weekend with Mum and Dad. I think all four of them should arrive this afternoon. Plus Hugo and his girlfriend are coming too."

"Wait, *the* girlfriend?" Em asks, her body jolting forward.

I nod. "Yep, that one."

"Ah, I can't wait to meet her," says Stana. "Is Louis coming?"

I look toward Em.

"From what Reeve said, I think he's coming with Hugo."

"The gang's all here." I smile.

"Man, it's so good to be home," Stana says.

"It's good to have you home," I tell her, linking our hands together. "It's good to have everyone home."

Em's eyes crease at the sides. "It just isn't home unless we're all here."

I nod, feeling my throat tighten slightly, my emotions running high. I don't know if it's all that's changed for us over the years—coming together, creating these new families with one another—or just the fact we're getting older, but I've never been more at peace with my life. With where I'm at.

We head over to the lads, and Owen pulls me into his side as I watch the children play, Leo rolling around on his mat on the floor as Mirabelle looks upon him with a watchful gaze. Billy chases Rosie around while Penelope does a good job of catching up, never being one to be left out of the action.

It's this peace right here that means everything to me. All the bullshit we've overcome—the ups and downs, fights and tears, breakups and makeups... It's all led up to this moment.

To us being right here together as a family.

Being home.

The End

Thank you for reading Late Love. Start Ali and Stana's story in SAINT STREET, out now!

Acknowledgements

Thank you to everyone who helped Late Love come together. To Nikki, my beta reader and editor, my story would be incomplete without you. My beta reader Emily, thank you for taking your time to give me invaluable feedback. Thank you to Sarah Hansen for a beautiful cover. To Brenda, for a beautiful interior as always! My PA Aurora Hale, thank you for everything you do for me. To all the bloggers and ARC readers who read and promoted Late Love, thank you! And my incredible readers, thank you for continuing to read. The biggest thanks to my team at The Next Step PR, you all guide me every step of the way, I'd be lost without you. A huge thank you to Kiki, who is not only a colleague but also a friend, I don't know what I was doing before we met! And finally, to my friends and family, thank you for always supporting me.

About the Author

Scarlett Hopper was born in Sydney, Australia and moved to Los Angeles when she was 10 years old. She currently lives back in Sydney with her family and their two pugs. When she isn't writing or reading, she spends her time traveling and searching for the best record stores while eating at 24-hour diners. Eventually, Scarlett hopes to begin a new adventure in Edinburgh, and then Seattle.

Scarlett Hopper

Other Titles by Scarlett Hopper

SAINT STREET
NEVER NOW

THE ENCOUNTERS SERIES:
BRIEF ENCOUNTERS
CHANCE ENCOUNTERS
MISSED ENCOUNTERS

CPSIA information can be obtained
at www.ICGtesting.com
Printed in the USA
BVHW081555050321
601818BV00002B/418